Beyond The Road To Key West

Mayan Gold Book VI

Michael Reisig

BEYOND THE ROAD TO KEY WEST

ISBN: 978-0-9863801-7-4

Cover design by Powell Graphics

Published by Clear Creek Press
P.O. Box 1081, Mena, AR 71953
1-479-394-4992

This book is dedicated to my lady, Bonnie Lee,
who has always been my island in
tumultuous seas of life…

Author's note:

This novel has somewhat of a long prologue, but I can promise it won't bore you. Just sit back and enjoy it. Soon enough you'll find yourself in the company of those daring rascals, Kansas and Will, and you'll find the tendrils of the past entwining with those of the present.

Writing is a solitary profession, often fraught with doubt and insecurity. Even when you finally type "The End," you're still not sure if the ship is going to sail. That's where my editors and beta readers come in—those people who make me appear better than I actually am.

Once again my longtime friend, Bob Simpson, has offered "first eyes" on this novel, laying the groundwork for quality wording and shaping the pile of clay at the beginning. (bobsimpson1947@yahoo.com)

Then there is my incredibly talented final editor and dear friend, Cris Wanzer. She takes what has been collected and sculpts it into a professional, accurate medium for publishing. Frankly, I don't know what I would do without her. (www.ManuscriptsToGo.com)

I would be remiss to not mention my buddy, Dale Powell, whose artistic talent has provided me with such wonderful book covers, and this time I also owe a special thanks to Barbara Martin, for her insights, editing, and suggestions.

Finally, there are my beta readers (Virginia Williams, Kenneth Morris, Steve Kittner, and Tim Slauter), who get the final draft and offer thoughts on how I can improve the book prior to publishing.

I can honestly say I owe the lion's share of my success to these people, and I am so grateful…

—Michael Reisig

OTHER TITLES BY MICHAEL REISIG

The Road To Key West

Back On The Road To Key West

Along The Road To Key West

Somewhere On The Road To Key West

Down The Road To Key West

• • •

Caribbean Gold Book I—*The Treasure of Tortuga*

Caribbean Gold Book II—*The Treasure of Time*

Caribbean Gold Book III—*The Treasure of Margarita*

• • •

The Golden Persuader

The New Madrid Run

The Hawks of Kamalon

PROLOGUE

The Heart of the Mayan Empire – 1516 A.D.

The jaguar issued a deep, choleric cough. Every creature in the jungle knew that sound. It bore trepidation and fear—and death. The cough morphed into a throaty growl and the big cat's cold, yellow eyes glittered with anger. But it was also uneasy. The animal's flanks rolled with a tremble, and its claws bit into the hard wood as the creature crouched on the limb of a large mahogany tree, lowering its center of gravity and becoming one with the leaves and branches. Only the jaguar's tail still dangled from the collage of green and brown, drooping down, inadvertently lashing, the neglected appendage of the species and a savior for more than one intended victim.

It had settled quietly on the limb—tense, still as death, its eyes searching the dark-green surroundings cleft by trellises of early morning sunlight. The creature could smell them and hear them, moving in around him. He coughed angrily again.

Ata Aalam had led the contingency of Itza Maya warriors from the city of Chetumal. He had earned this right with blood and courage, but today was different. Today he was to challenge the jaguar alone. His companions were there to witness the hunt, but they could not assist or interfere, even if it meant their commander's life. Aalam had to take the creature's spirit by himself. It was an age-old rite of position and power, both an honor and the ultimate test. Less than a quarter of the men who set out on this quest returned with a pelt; less than half returned at all. Once the jaguar realized it was being pursued, it became the hunter—savvy, vicious, and vengeful. But Aalam welcomed the opportunity. He had attained this privilege through what had been a long, remarkable path.

Ata Aalam's darkly tanned skin was different from the reddish complexion of his companions, and his wary gray eyes stood him apart from the hunters now well behind him, all of whom bore dark-brown eyes. Most remarkably, his hair—worn in a single, long, side lock like his compatriots—was a sun-lightened chestnut, and he spoke their language with a distinct Spanish accent. That was a story in itself.

He hefted his long, obsidian-bladed spear and moved forward.

The jaguar crouched on the limb of the huge tree, watching one of the two-legged, reddish creatures move cautiously forward, carrying a stick with a shiny black point. He knew those "sticks" well. The scar on his shoulder reminded him often. The others had silently fallen away. He could smell smoke on the one that approached. There was the foul odor of charred flesh on its breath, and the creature reeked of sweat. A deep, angry hiss emanated from the cat's heavy chest, and involuntarily its tail swished again.

The movement was not lost on Aalam. He scanned the foliage above the tail, and there were the eyes—golden and soulless, and full of the desperate violence that only a cornered creature could possess. He had heard the stories of the jaguar's killing techniques and incredible speed. As with many big cats, it was the "grasp and disembowelment" technique that was most difficult to release from the mind's eye. Aalam had witnessed it once, and that was enough—the cat grasping its prey with its front claws and its jaws, then bringing up its rear pads, with razor-sharp, extraordinarily long talons, and burying them in the belly of its victim, then ripping downward in one lightning-quick motion.

An old-timer in Aalam's company told the story of having watched a jaguar attack a troop of Hooter monkeys. He said the blinding speed was simply beyond belief. The big cat grabbed and ripped the intestines out of three monkeys, splattering the ground with blood and bowels before the rest of the troop was fully aware of what had happened.

It was that involuntary swish of the tail that gave Aalam a chance—a small chance. The cat came out of the tree like death on claws, its speed astonishing. Fluid and powerful, it touched the ground for a split second, then leaped at the man in front of it, no longer quiet, but roaring with hatred and anger, front paws out wide, razor claws extended. Aalam was a brave man. He had fought storms at sea, and starvation when shipwrecked. He had killed the howling Indians of Hispaniola and strangled men with his bare hands in the Mayan arena, but he had never felt such gut-wrenching terror as when that roaring, fanged monster screamed and threw itself at him, its cold eyes alight with a single intent.

Every inch of Aalam's body wanted nothing more than to break and run. It wasn't courage that held him firm, it was the sure knowledge that the moment he turned, he would feel those claws in his back and the saber-like teeth at his neck. As the huge cat leapt, Aalam forced down the scream in his throat and brought up his spear. Kneeling slightly for a lower center of gravity, he jammed the butt of the spear shaft into the dark, volcanic soil of the jungle floor and aimed the razor-sharp obsidian spear point at the chest of the snarling cat. It was one of those defining, unforgettable moments in Aalam's life. Suddenly, the strangest thing happened. The fear, the palsy of terror, was gone. His eyes were sharp and clear, his nostrils flared. He could smell the jungle, and the jaguar. He could feel the warmth from a beam of sunlight that had found him through the boughs. The hammering of his heart was forgotten as he was enveloped in a primitive, captivating silence. In just those few seconds, the trappings of civilization had fallen from him like autumn's last leaf, leaving him at the nexus of the beast that is man. Aalam cried out in defiance as the cat fell on him, its inertia snapping the heavy shaft of the spear as it slashed at him with its talons, trying to reach him with its fangs. But Aalam's spear had been true, driving deep into the cat's chest cavity and slicing an artery to its heart.

The man, now on both knees, held tightly to the remainder of the spear shaft, keeping the screaming animal away from him as best he could, but he was paying for it. The blood from their mutual wounds dampened the jungle floor. The jaguar was losing strength, but it was working its way inexorably down the shaft, pushing the obsidian blade through its body as it tried to reach the man with its wide, bloodied jaws. Finally, with the fangs of the snarling cat barely two feet from his face, and its claws buried in his shoulders, Aalam tried one final, desperate gambit. He reached out and grabbed the snarling cat by the fur of its throat. Pushing up its head, he pulled a razor-sharp, flint knife from his waistband. With the last of his strength, Aalam drove the blade up, under the throat, and into the brain of the writhing animal.

The cat's eyes went wide with shock, and in the next second, life disappeared from them. The creature sagged onto its adversary and a moment later gurgled out a death rattle. Instantly, Aalam's soldiers were at his side, cautiously but quickly ripping away the cat and attending to their leader. Trogo Catan, Aalam's captain (a large man by Mayan standards, with dark eyes and long, black hair bound in a topknot), was already staunching his *nacom's* wounds with cloth specially soaked in natural antiseptics. Another of his soldiers offered him a jug of *pulque*, to numb his mind and his wounds. By some miracle, no arteries had been cut, which could have meant amputation. After binding the worst wounds, they put Aalam on a litter they had brought, meant to bring back their *nacom*...or his body. They needed to get him to the medicine men of Chetumal as quickly as possible, to fight infection.

Although Aalam was barely conscious from his wounds and loss of blood, he couldn't help but notice the slight change in the nature of his men. While they had always carried respect for him, there was a reverence now, in their words and actions, and a distinct pride that they were "his men." By fulfilling this ritual, Ata Aalam had not only crossed over into a position garnering new respect for his prowess, but there was a spiritual attribution that this carried—that the gods had allowed this. He was no longer just a soldier or a leader, he was now a *"jaguar nacom,"* and the story that was his life had added another legend.

And by the flattened forehead of King Nachán Can, it was a tale from the lips of the gods…

Half a decade ago, in 1510 A.D., Aalam had been a young Spaniard from Castile, looking for excitement and wealth. He joined a troop of adventurers headed for Havana in the Caribbean. He hadn't been disappointed regarding the excitement, but the wealth had eluded him. A year later, in 1511, he had taken sail aboard the Spanish caravel *Santa Maria de la Barca*, traveling from Panama to Santo Domingo, when they were shipwrecked by a vicious storm. Before the caravel went down, 20 of the crew managed to board the ship's lifeboat. They drifted for two weeks, until the currents carried them ashore in what would eventually become known as the southeastern coast of the Yucatan Peninsula.

What was left of the crew (nearly half had died on the brutal voyage in the lifeboat) had little time to celebrate the fortune of solid ground. They had barely set foot on land when a well-armed Mayan hunting party materialized from the jungle and surrounded them. Communication with the reddish-colored, heavily tattooed natives was nearly impossible, but that failed to inhibit the arrogant Spanish captain, who boldly approached the Mayan *nacom* (military commander).

Although gaunt from lack of food and water, with his clothes bleached and worn from the sun and the saltwater, he rose up and faced the heathens with a tad more arrogance than he should have. The captain offered the universal sign of friendship used by natives in Hispaniola, then spoke. "I come on behalf of His Majesty, Ferdinand the Second of Aragon, King of Spain." He brought his hands up, using some simple sign language. "We would require sustenance immediately, and we would be taken to your superior so that we might—"

That was as far as he got. The *nacom*, who was attired in the battle gear of an Itza Kingdom warrior, including heavy leather sandals, quilted cotton armor, and a jaguar cape, brandished his *macana*—a wooden sword with razor-sharp obsidian embedded along the edges. He barked a short burst of words at the Spaniards.

The captain, a veteran of the relatively manageable Hispaniola campaign, shook his finger at the exotically tattooed savage in front of him, placing his other hand on the pommel of the sword at his side. "You will take us to—"

At that moment, the Mayan leader brought up his *macana,* and in a lightning swift move, split the captain's head like a soft papaya. Shaking the man's brains from the obsidian teeth of his weapon, the *nacom* shouted a series of commands. The terrified Spaniards were forced to the ground and the few weapons they possessed were seized. Then they were bound hand and foot, dragged to the edge of the jungle, and tied to trees.

It was late afternoon, and the sun was just reaching for the green waters of the Gulf. The *nacom* ordered evening camp. They would return to the city the following day.

That night, as the moon slid behind somber gray clouds and offered a still darkness, Gonzalo Guerrero (Aalam), and his shipmate Gerónimo de Aquilar, found themselves tied back-to-back against the rough trunk of a coconut palm. Gerónimo, like his friend, was tall with dark hair. His eyes were brown and normally carried a touch of benign deviousness.

A warm breeze ruffled the palm branches and the moon pulled away from a battery of cumulus clouds, providing a soft, silvery light. Somewhere in the distance, a night bird cried mournfully, and another answered. All of this was enveloped by the incessant buzz of the mosquitoes that constantly tormented the bound men.

Gonzalo glanced around, quietly twisting for as much of a view as possible. It appeared that most of the camp—Mayan and Spanish alike—was lost to a restless slumber. A soft wind carried the rumble of snores. There were two Mayan guards that he could see, both leaning against the remains of the lifeboat near the water. He and his people had been given coconut juice and some dried meat. Even their brutal captors realized that the dead make poor slaves.

Gonzalo slowly shifted around to his companion, bound behind him. "Gerónimo," he whispered, "are you awake?"

His friend huffed angrily. “Good Lord, man! How could anyone sleep while being eaten alive by these bugs from Hades?”

Gonzalo couldn’t suppress a smile. “Listen, my gut tells me we are likely destined for the same fate as the captain.” He paused. “We need to escape, before we end up in a pot.”

“No argument there,” Gerónimo whispered. “I’ve been working on my bonds for the last half hour. Those painted cannibals did a fair job of binding me, but I’ve already worn myself down to flesh, and this *sisalana* fiber stretches when wet.”

“True enough,” replied Gonzalo. “Sweat and blood—the recipe for weakening most all. I’m nearly free myself.”

For the next 20 minutes they struggled with the native rope until finally, with a grunt, Gerónimo pulled himself free. He glanced around quietly. One of the night guards was now 50 feet away, leaning against a volcanic rock outcropping, gradually nodding off, then jerking himself back to consciousness. The other was crouched near the bow of the canted lifeboat, staring at the moon over the water.

The Spaniard quietly scooted around to Gonzalo and worked loose his friend’s bonds. When he was finished, the sand next to the palm tree was damp with blood. Silent as wraiths, they slipped into the jungle behind them. And that was the last they saw of their Spanish companions.

Two days later, only slightly refreshed by wild bananas, mangoes, and the water of a small, seemingly bottomless *cenote*, they were just beginning to risk a little hope when they blundered into the patrol of a neighboring warlord. The Mayan soldiers had moved so silently through the jungle that the two Spaniards were surrounded before they knew it. Once again, the men were taken prisoner. It was their second lesson about this unusual but capable race.

(The first being, "never shake a finger and shout at a Mayan *nacom.*")

A couple of days later, they had left the jungle and were traveling on a Mayan *sacbe,* or "white road." They marveled at the remarkable limestone causeways that linked cities and settlements. This time, their hands had been bound in front of them and a rope, held by an attentive guard, was looped around their necks. They were now passing small villages and agricultural areas.

During this time, Gonzalo noticed the absence of beasts of burden, such as cattle or horses, and a distinct absence of the wheel. Here was a society whose means of transportation was singularly limited to human effort.

A day later, they came to their first city, and what a sight it was.

The Mayan commander turned to the two foreigners and pointed to the magnificent city. "Chetumal," he said proudly, adding a handful of words they didn't understand. "Chetumal," he said again.

Twenty-foot-high, white limestone walls with walkways atop them, and a huge wooden gate protected the metropolis. As they entered the city, they found themselves awed by huge courtyards, bustling markets, municipal buildings, water systems, and extensive gardens, as well as palatial residences for the local leaders, and homes for the upper military contingencies. There were smooth stone streets, and remarkably colorful artwork on the sides of buildings denoting nature, rituals, and the lifestyles of the people.

As they were led along the inner causeway, there was no longer any question in the minds of the two Europeans as to the capabilities of this society. But it was also then that great disappointment found them. That afternoon they were forced into a small limestone building with bamboo-barred windows and two guards at the heavy wooden door.

They were offered a jug of water and bowls of reasonable food—a stew of meat and strange vegetables. Then they were allowed a decent night's sleep.

The following morning, a person of obvious presence entered the room where they were being held. The man was accompanied by two powerful-looking guards, both of whom were armed with *macanas*—the same deadly weapon used on the Spanish captain when they were first captured. The Mayan—tall, well muscled, and a long lock of black hair at the side of his shaven head—was attired in sandals, a colorful loincloth, and a beautifully embroidered cotton cape adorned with exotic feathers. The oddity that grasped the Spaniards immediately was the leader's eyes. They were crossed—literally turned toward the bridge of his nose. The Spaniards had no way of knowing at the time, but this peculiarity—the crossing of the eyes—was considered a special distinction of the upper class. As soon as a child could focus on objects around it, the noble families would have a jade bead hung from the forehead, to dangle invitingly. By the age of one year, the eyes of most all upper-class and royal children were attractively crossed.

The nobleman studied the captives for a few moments, then barked a few words in an unintelligible language. When the Spanish failed to respond, he tried once more.

"No comprendo," replied Gerónimo. *"Lo siento. No comprendo."*

The Mayan huffed and spoke to the guards, who immediately held the prisoners as he examined their skin, muscles, and teeth, as if he were buying a horse. Finally satisfied, he stepped back and pointed to Gerónimo. Without ceremony, Gonzalo's friend was bound with his hands behind his back, a rope was looped around his neck, and he was led out by one guard. The upper-class Mayan followed, while the other guard held his *macana* at Gonzalo's throat.

"God be with you, my friend," the Spaniard whispered as he watched his terrified companion being led away. A shove between his shoulder blades forced Gonzalo to the ground, then the other guard exited as well.

The Spaniard never saw his friend again, but history would recount that after being purchased by the Mayan nobleman, Gerónimo de Aquilar survived for a number of years as the man's slave in the Central Yucatan peninsula. He was eventually rescued during the Spanish invasion of the Mayan Empire in 1519. Because Gerónimo had become so proficient at the Mayan language, he went on to serve as Cortez's interpreter for the remainder of Cortez's Mayan subjugation.

The following day another Mayan of obvious importance appeared at the door. Feathers of the exotic quetzal bird were braided into his dark scalp lock, and ritual tattoos adorned his face, arms, and chest. He was wearing a rare, black jaguar cape and a finely embroidered deerskin loincloth. He was tall and muscled, and his dark eyes were slightly crossed In addition, his forehead had been somewhat flattened. Gonzalo couldn't have known, but royal children's foreheads were flattened by tying a board tightly against their head during the first few days after birth—another characteristic of attractiveness and position within the Mayan society. The powerful aristocrat was accompanied by a wizened older man, dressed in a white cotton loincloth and adorned with jade necklaces and gold bracelets, his dark hair braided into a topknot. Both the men's ears were pierced with gold and jade rings. They were accompanied by a brace of powerful-looking soldiers carrying spears and heavy obsidian knives. A troop of 15 additional soldiers stood at the ready outside the cottage, seemingly impervious to the summer sun, waiting for orders from their *nacom*. Gonzalo had no idea at the time, but he was in the presence of Lord Nachán Can of Chetumal, one of the major Mayan warlords, accompanied by his high priest, Bahman.

Gonzalo's life was about to change dramatically.

The two Mayans were fascinated by Gonzalo's pale skin and strange, gray eyes. They asked numerous questions, none of which the Spaniard could answer. They touched and poked him and spoke constantly between themselves. This was a portentous moment, because the shaman had already spoken of dreams he'd had where he saw white gods in their land. He thought this creature would make an excellent sacrifice to the gods, perhaps preventing the presence of any more of these creatures.

Nachán Can wasn't so sure, and it was his decision that carried the most weight. In the end, there was a compromise of sorts. Gonzalo was given to the priest, and for the next few months, the Spaniard became his slave. However, almost immediately Gonzalo refused to submit, to sacrifice his character. Bahman, who often drank too much *pulque* (a native beer made from the maguey plant), had him beaten with split bamboo cane, causing painful wounds, but it didn't change the resistance in the man's eyes. So he was hobbled with *sisalana* rope and watched over at all times by at least one Mayan soldier. At first, Bahman found the Spaniard interesting, but the lack of communication began to dull his interest. Ultimately, this new responsibility became more of an annoyance to the priest than anything else. It took him away from his studies of the stars and their movements, and their relationship to the gods and future consequence.

Gonzalo, while constantly considering escape, found himself somewhat fascinated by this whole turn of events. He knew he was in a dangerous situation, but he somehow found it more fascinating than terrifying. As the weeks passed into months, he relaxed, accepting the situation for the time being while he sought a means of escape. He began to glean a basic knowledge of the Mayan language, which came to him without challenge, and the customs of Mayan people. He was given the name "Ata Aalam."

Gradually, his apprehension paled into curiosity, on a number of levels. To begin with, he was somewhat astounded by the presence of order and decorum in this society. Their rules on theft and dishonor were brutally simple, and usually resulted in the loss of an appendage. The more heinous the crime, the more important the appendage. Their system of writing was remarkably complex, consisting of 800 individual glyphs read from left to right, and their sense of architecture was simply phenomenal—in many cases rivaling the cathedrals and castles of Spain. He came to realize through Bahman's teachings that the Mayans had a bewildering number of gods, with at least 166 named deities. The supreme deity was *Itzamna.* His wife was *Ix Chel,* the goddess of the moon. Aalam also reluctantly came to accept that their knowledge of astrology and astronomy rivaled the wisest thinkers in Europe.

Last, but certainly not least, was the Mayans' knowledge of health and medicine, which was a complex blend of mind, body, religion, ritual, and science. Aalam watched the Mayan medicine men suture wounds with human hair, reduce and heal fractures, and use powerful herbal remedies long before most of these things were even considered in his distant lands. He saw their "doctors" serving as dental surgeons, creating prosthetic teeth from jade and turquoise and filling teeth with iron pyrite; and using "sweat baths" with medicinal additives while Europe was still "bleeding" people who were ill.

On a baser level, he was taken by the vast presence of gold and gems in this society. Even the average household had small, golden statues of gods, and emeralds were common in the jewelry of men and women, adorning bracelets, necklaces, earrings, and amulets. The natural greed of "the conquistador" edged his honor at this point. He found himself thinking, *I could be a rich man if I might escape and take a few of these baubles with me...*

Bahman, the priest, never found any great level of appreciation for the Spaniard. Aalam was more like his dangerous pet. Bahman believed this foreigner to be perhaps an evil spirit that had taken a form similar to Mayan. In an attempt to let the gods decide this whole turn of events, the priest arranged for Aalam to be used as a combatant in the violent contests for the entertainment of the Mayan hierarchy. It was certainly the lesser of two evils for Aalam. He was unaware at the time that almost all prisoners, regardless of where they came from, were sacrificed by the Mayan priests. It seemed that the gods were in continuous need of appeasement.

Nonetheless, arena combat was hardly any better, and the scars on the Spaniard's body were testament to the mistakes he made early on. But he soon became proficient at the *macana* and the flint-bladed Mayan spear, applying the techniques of the cutlass and the Spanish pike, surviving long enough to catch the eye of Lord Nachán Can once again. It was then that his life took a turn for the better.

After a particularly brutal contest, which Aalam had barely survived (two of his less-fortunate combatants lay in the arena, coughing up blood and listening to the last, faltering beats of their hearts), Nachán Can motioned Aalam over to the white stone grandstands. The Mayan lord and his entourage sat in comfortable repose under a colorful cotton canopy, while being fanned by slaves. Nachán Can leaned in, his slightly crossed eyes nearly unreadable, and spoke slowly, because he realized his language was still new to the Spaniard. "You understand, white one, that your life is mine, that I own you, but it seems somewhat of a shame to waste you here in the arena."

"You can kill me at your pleasure, Lord Nachán Can," replied Aalam, "but you don't own me. A person can only be owned if their spirit allows it."

The Mayan leader leaned forward, holding Aalam with his hard, dark eyes. "I see now why old Bahman has found you somewhat displeasing. Perhaps we should give your heart to *Kinich Ahau*, the Sun God—slowly—to see how long it takes to squeeze that arrogance from you."

Aalam shrugged and wiped the blood from his forehead, where a blade from one of his combatants had caught him. "And when my spirit leaves, it will laugh at you."

Nachán Can didn't know whether to be angry or impressed. Few people had ever spoken to him like that. Everyone around him held their breath; they were all too aware of his volatile temperament. The Mayan king ran a hand over his black topknot, then smiled—a rare thing. In the next moment, his somber, stygian eyes lightened and his sloped forehead furrowed, somewhere between enmity and curiosity. "Before the sun sets, you will be brought to the gates of my palace. I will send a detachment of soldiers. Tell Bahman it is my pleasure to 'borrow' you for a while."

The Mayan leader knew he was taking a chance on this white-skinned, powerful stranger, but he was somewhat fascinated by him—like a falconer is with a hawk. *Certainly, his fighting techniques are intriguing...*

There was a part of him that knew he needed to learn more of these white men—where they came from, and how many there were. These were times when enemies abounded, and knowledge was strength. Bahman was lost to his stars and his charts, but the movement of the stars would not preserve Chetumal.

Nachán Can was reminded that until only 50 years ago (1441 AD) the Mayan nation had been unified under one leader, in the great city of Mayapán. But there had been a rebellion, and the city was nearly destroyed. Soon after, it was abandoned. Over the next half century, the powerful Mayan Empire had degenerated into 16 rival states, either constantly at each other's throats, or forming tenuous alliances that failed to survive. If he was to maintain his power, and expand it, Nachán Can knew he must see the jaguar's tail. He must be ahead of his rivals and any potential exterior threats.

What he couldn't have realized then was the exceptional capriciousness of the gods. The timing for the Spanish had been extraordinary. Had they arrived 50 years earlier, they would have faced a unified, almost undefeatable nation, and the history of Central America might well have been vastly different.

So it was that Ata Aalam, the Spaniard from clearly another world, was trained to become a member of the palace guard. Even more remarkable, as time passed, Nachán Can's interest in the Spaniard grew, and he freed Aalam (at least as much as anyone could be free in the Mayan's totalitarian society), and had him attached to his personal guard. He continued to find this strange "European" curiously intriguing, of pure character and not particularly awed by him. This in itself was unique. Nachán was also somewhat captivated by the stories Aalam told of his homeland, and they spent much time exchanging views. (Although Nachán Can considered much of Aalam's conversation to be wild tales—small tubes of metal that could shoot a ball through the air, huge canoes the size of mountains that could traverse the sea, giant animals on which a man could ride, or gunpowder, and cannons…)

More importantly, there was a transformation that had begun to take place within Aalam. At first, he considered escape. But escape to where? He was in a world he knew nothing about, had no idea of where he was, and had no means of leaving. After a while, there was the beginning of a subtle change in the Spaniard. Aside from the turbulent induction to an unusual life, he began to feel strangely comfortable with this new society he had inadvertently become part of.

Granted, the initial transition had taken place in a brutal fashion, but sometimes we find a place that simply captures us; that strikes a distant vision. Swirls of recollection curl around us and what should be difficult or unusual seems natural and easy, and a strange voice within us whispers, "This is my place…" And that's the way it was with Ata Aalam, the Mayan.

So much had changed in the last half-dozen years it seemed like a dream—a tale to be concocted by old men around evening fires. Still, here he was.

From the very beginning, Aalam had found the Mayan language effortless, and now he no longer found himself thinking in Spanish. His mind recorded all in his new language. He found the foods pleasant, the lifestyle physically and psychologically comfortable, and even though some of the customs, such as human sacrifice, were brutal and violent, there was a part of him that countered with the recollection of the brutal Spanish conquests, the Inquisition, and the horrible, mindless atrocities committed by Spanish and English priests. *Are not all religions borne and maintained of pain?* he asked himself. *Is there really any difference between the crucifixion of martyrs, self-*

flagellation, or the Inquisition's torture to produce faith, and the sacrificial Mayan rites? It seemed to him that every form of spiritual refuge brought with it some sort of pain. *Maybe it is a requirement of all gods...*

Gradually, within the process of the last few years, he found the trappings of his old life stripping away, and the garments of his new life—living so close to nature, the wild beauty of the jungle, the absence of the relentless European cold, and none of the diseases and formality that had plagued the Old World—progressively, gradually, converting him to Mayan. He eventually pierced his ears and took to wearing gold or jade earrings. He adopted the hairstyle of Mayan soldiers—a shaved head with only a long lock of hair on the right side (after they had slain their first enemy), and he consented to the ritual tattooing that completed the transition.

With the taking of the jaguar, Aalam had been given the position of second-level *nacom* in the ranks of the Mayan army. (This was after nearly a month of healing.) But the final step, as it is with most men, was a woman…

Her name was Itzel (which related to the Mayan Rainbow Goddess), and she was a handmaiden to Nachán Can's second wife. She was small, perhaps five feet, but she carried herself with a pride of character that almost matched that of her mistress. Her hair was brilliant ebony, and when brushed by the sun it shone like obsidian. She was slim, but subtly sensuous. Her small breasts pointed upwards impetuously through her soft, white cotton shift, and the exquisite motion of her narrow hips had drawn the attention of more than one man in the palace. But she still wore the red shell of virginity around her waist. It was the sacrifice she was required to make in order to serve royalty without distraction. Nonetheless, she had often watched the tall, darkly tanned foreigner, whose white loincloth and jaguar mantle enhanced his powerful physique. He carried many scars—evidence of battles against man and beast—but it hardly lessened his appeal. In fact, they were no more than statements of his capability—and he was a jaguar *nacom*.

Itzel's cinnamon-colored skin gleamed from the oils she applied daily. Her dark-amber eyes were clever, and when away from her ward, they almost always glistened with a touch of mischievousness. (As she was not born of royalty, her eyes were not crossed, nor had her forehead been flattened.) She appealed to Aalam the moment he first saw her in the gardens of the courtyard. It was strange and disconcerting for him. A part of him said the last thing he needed was a complication, that the women of pleasure in Nachán's courtyard were enough, but another part whispered he was well overdue for a "complication."

She gathered flowers from the garden every morning for her mistress, humming softly to herself, and Aalam began to find excuses to be passing by that place at that time. He began offering a smile and she gradually began returning the respects. Finally, he raised the courage to approach her.

"Those are beautiful flowers," he said of the bouquet she was gathering.

She smiled openly, but with just a touch of shyness. "Thank you. Yes, they are."

After a moment of uncomfortable silence, he blurted. "I am called Ata Aalam."

"Yes, I know," Itzel replied. "Everyone knows who you are. How could they not, eh? The remarkable addition to Lord Nachán's bodyguards...the jaguar *nacom*..." She paused. "Some say you come from the other side of the great water."

Aalam nodded. "And they would be right."

She stared at him in such a forthright fashion, it almost made him uncomfortable. “Do you not miss your home?”

He shrugged. “Not as much as I thought I would, to be true.” He smiled slyly. “And not so much today, now that I have finally spoken with you.”

One would have expected her to blush. Instead, she said with a smile, “Well, it has certainly taken you long enough to notice my ‘beautiful flowers.’ I have had to give away numerous bouquets, since my mistress has begged relief from so many blossoms. I was growing afraid I would strip this garden before you heeded me.”

He couldn’t help but laugh at her brashness. *Lord, she is beautiful, and bright she is as well, indeed!*

At first, they met secretly at the beautiful *cenotes*—the natural watering holes at the edge of the city that supplied the populace with water from a system of stone aqueducts. Both were afraid to announce this tryst that had begun to “flower” between them. How would it be accepted? Especially by Nachán Can? But love is such a blinding, careless emotion. As their passion grew, they became less discreet, sneaking into Itzel’s quarters in the palace, or disappearing into the city’s parks for a quiet, romantic meal that Itzel had prepared.

Aalam had never felt such desire, but it was more than simple passion. Itzel had found a place inside him that had been empty for a long time, and she had brought it to life. Up to this point, he had lived for the moment—sailing ships, adventure, and tavern wenches. The future had never been more than a vague dream of wealth or position, earned without his family’s name. Now, for the first time in his life, he found himself dreaming of a home—an existence beyond adventure and hollow conquests. He began to think of a place, and a woman he could return to at the end of the day. He had even begun to think of children. What he hadn’t thought much about was Lord Nachán Can.

They were in his quarters just outside the palace, reclining in his wide cotton hammock, catching their breath, when the door burst open. In an instant, Aalam was stumbling from the hammock, with Itzel tumbling onto the floor behind him. There in the doorway stood Lord Nachán Can, in a jaguar cape, a treated deerskin loincloth, and wearing heavy jade earrings. There was a brace of guards at his back. The Mayan emperor knew he must make an impression. Pain meant nothing to this foreigner, but pride—pride was important.

"You have a choice to make," he said to Aalam, his black eyes flashing, ignoring their nakedness as they struggled to cover themselves with the cotton sheets. "Either commit to this woman, find her a home, and have her bear your children, or leave this entertainment, now. I cannot afford commanders whose minds are lost to their genitals." He huffed as if he was angry, but a small gleam of satisfaction glittered in his dark eyes. He knew a man with a woman was a stronger soldier than a man chasing a woman. "You have one full movement of the sun," Nachán growled, then he was gone.

Two days later, Aalam took Itzel as his lady in the Mayan marriage ritual. Normally, there were negotiations between parents and priests. Items of value were given to the priests, and the husband was required to offer gifts to the family of the bride. But Itzel's parents had been killed by raiders several years ago. Normally, females married at 14 or 15, but because Itzel had been chosen as a handmaiden to the wife of Nachán Can, she had not been permitted to marry. She was now 17.

In keeping with tradition, Aalam dressed in a long, pure white loincloth and soft deerskin sandals. His dark-brown hair was adorned with long, colorful quetzal feathers. He was required to give the bride a *muhul.* This was a package that included a gold chain, at least one emerald, a few wooden barrettes, and a *huipil* (a traditional long, white, sleeveless cotton dress for the ceremonial rite). Nachán Can's personal shaman performed the ceremony, after he cleansed the site with sacred smoke from the copal tree, and the couple bathed in an ancient *temazcal* (sweathouse) for purification.

During the ceremony, their priest told the couple to watch for signs from spirit, blessing them and giving them gifts of the future. The strangely tattooed shaman—long, dark hair past his shoulders and gleaming black eyes lost to peyote—stared at Aalam. "Wings," he said. "The spirits say 'wings' will be your gift from the realms of dark and light."

It hardly made much sense to Aalam, who had rarely found any intrigue in the orthodox faith in his youth. It had all seemed more frightening than spiritual in those early days. But an hour later, as the ceremony closed, he noticed the strangest thing. A small red-tailed hawk had tumbled in, and with a flurry of wings, precariously settled on a low branch of the large mahogany tree above them. It fluttered once more, and fluffed its reddish, dark-brown feathers, picking at the soft down closest to its body, its dark, hooded eyes observing with a strange interest. Aalam knew from its markings that it was a very young bird—a fledgling just out of the nest. Perhaps it had just fallen from its nest. He had grown up in a relatively wealthy family in Spain (*Lord, that seemed like a lifetime ago*), and one of his greatest pleasures had been falconry, or "hawking" as it was sometimes called. He had raised a huge peregrine falcon that could take down a full-grown goose and not even fluff his feathers. It was an incredible thrill to release that bird and watch him soar into the heavens, searching for a target. When his prey was gleaned he would fall, wing-over, with such singular purpose, dropping with astonishing speed, steel-like talons tucked until the last moment.

It seemed remarkably strange, the attention the juvenile red-tail was offering, and the apparent comfort it seemed to have being so close to humans. Aalam couldn't understand, but he remembered it. And he remembered the words of the shaman.

The couple was given the traditional three-day honeymoon, and free now of the guile and secrecy, they used the majority of it discovering a passion neither had ever known. Finally, reluctantly they took a few hours to transfer Itzel's few belongings to Aalam's quarters just outside the palace grounds.

Oddly enough, while they were unloading the last of her possessions, Aalam heard a soft shrill above him, and at that moment the immature red-tailed hawk he had seen at the wedding ceremony settled on the branch of a courtyard tree not 20 feet from him. Tucking in its broad, rounded wings, it pruned itself of some of the last immature down, then cocked its head, staring at him with impervious, dark eyes.

Again, Aalam thought this remarkable, and began to believe in the possibility that the bird had fallen from a nest, and perhaps the first thing it had seen was him. He knew that ideally, to bond with a bird for hunting, you must receive it near infancy, and the process of training was a tedious one, requiring special equipment. One needed a uniquely designed hood for the creature, a perch, long strips of leather knotted to the bird's legs called "jesses," and a "creance"—a long line tied to a swivel on the jesses, then bound to a spindle of line that could be wound or unwound, so the bird was not lost in initial training. The "manning" or training a bird to adjust to humans was difficult. Aalam knew that, unlike pets such as dogs or cats, raptors were generally not affectionate animals. But occasionally, a bird directly from the nest would appear to bond with its handler in a unique fashion.

He was still considering the possibilities of this strange situation, when the red-tail shrilled again and bounced along the limb, a little closer, still staring at him. At that moment, Itzel called to Aalam from inside the cottage. He turned and replied as she came to the door. There was a flutter of wings above him, and the hawk was gone.

When the honeymoon was over, Aalam found himself once again occupied with the whims of Nachán Can. His master intuitively recognized that challenges were coming to the kingdom. Some of his people who lived nearer to the coast and traveled to offshore islands in huge trading canoes had reported seeing a monstrous ship that appeared to be carried by the wind. They told of barrels extending from its sides from which fire burst. The news was disconcerting to Nachán Can—all too much like the stories that Aalam had told him. While he would appreciate the chance to trade and learn from this new, ocean-faring tribe, he knew from experience that when two new groups meet, usually only one ended up benefiting. He called for Aalam, who began an extensive dialogue of what they might expect.

While some might have considered this good news for Aalam, Itzel was terrified. She had heard her husband's tales of these people from across the sea. Most surprising of all was the ex-Spaniard's reaction. He, too, was frightened. He knew all too well what any indigenous people had to expect from contact with the Europeans—death, disease, and destruction.

Without ceremony (which was rare for the Mayans), Aalam began to tutor his king on what he could expect from the ruthless Europeans, and what he might do to defend himself.

"You will be facing an enemy like nothing you have ever seen," Aalam explained. "You must fight them in fashions that will take away their advantages."

"Must we fight them?" asked a cautious Nachán Can.

This was out of his character, but his holy men, including old Bahman, were seeing portents of darkness and fire. The Mayan leader was no fool. He knew that sometimes the priests experienced "visions" to their own benefit. But this was different. The holy men were visibly shaken.

"Could we not trade with them, let the two cultures learn from each other?" he asked.

Aalam shook his head. "These people do not trade, they do not compromise. They conquer. They will strip you of everything valuable—from your gold and your women, to your faith—and when they are done, you will be dust and ashes. They are like rats, like ants. If we do not discourage them, they will come again, hundreds and hundreds. The best you can do is convince them that the price of this kingdom is too high, and perhaps they will leave you be. Perhaps…"

Nachán Can rose from his chair and walked to the window, gazing down on the city below. He stood there for a few moments, then exhaled hard and turned to the man who had not only become a valuable *nacom,* but a friend. "Then we fight them," he growled. "We fight them!"

From that moment on, the Itza Mayans prepared for war with Spain, under the tutorship of a Spaniard.

In the interim, Aalam had developed another remarkable relationship. One morning at breakfast, only a few days after he and Itzel had moved into their cottage, the young hawk suddenly appeared again on the windowsill. It landed with a flutter of wings, cocked its head, and offered a shrill *chwirk.* Aalam knew this was clearly impossible, that surely the gods had a hand in the experience, but for some reason, he had anticipated another encounter. The night before he had found a nest of baby mice in the wall of the cottage. He had captured them, securing the creatures in a wide-mouthed jug. When the hawk landed, he moved to the closet, reached into the jug and pulled out a squirming mouse. With a snap, he broke the back legs of the creature and tossed it onto the wide windowsill. The young red-tail was on it instantly. It paused only long enough to stare at Aalam for a moment and offer a sharp trill, then it was gone, the luckless mouse dangling from its talons.

"I will have no feeding of pets at the table," said Itzel, her face stern, but her amber-brown eyes somewhere near incredulous. "If you keep this up, you may very well become a priest, or a sacrifice—neither of which would please me."

In the spring of 1517, while Aalam and his king were in the midst of their portentous conversations, the Spanish conquistador Francisco Hernández de Córdoba made landfall on the northeastern tip of the Yucatan Peninsula. It was his ship the Mayan traders in their large, 50-foot canoes, had seen. After securing fresh water and some wild fruit, Córdoba sent out a hunting party that shot several feral hogs. Then he continued south, along the coastline, toward Chetumal.

Aalam, who had been with the Mayans now for over six years, began a tutelage of survival for his adopted people. He began with a weapon that had effectively been used against the Spanish—the English longbow. The Mayans had bows and arrows, but they were small. While they killed game (and people) well enough at close quarters, they needed a bow that could propel a heavier, longer arrow through light armor, and perform well at nearly twice the distance of their old weapons. He trained their bowyers to increase the length of the bows by well over a foot, and had the fletchers add six to eight inches on the length of the arrows. He also searched the hills for jadeite, an extremely hard mineral, and it was with this that they made their new arrowheads and spearheads. When Aalam exercised the final product, taking his nearly six-foot bow and driving a three-foot-long arrow through two layers of the Mayans' best armor at 100 yards, the new respect for him bordered on awe.

Oddly enough, Itzel was taken by this unique weapon as well. In the land of the Maya, it was not uncommon for women to learn the arts of war. In fact, CáCalla, Nachán Can's first wife, was an advocate of a woman being capable in the arts of war and hunting. Aalam had a slightly smaller version of his powerful bow made for his wife. Itzel quickly became remarkably adept, much to the surprise of Aalam, who considered himself fairly good. In fact, Itzel became so adept that they began hunting together in the jungle near the city, and it was, more often than not, Itzel who brought home the most game.

Aalam set the canoe makers on the coast to a new project—sails. Up to this point, the Mayans had used canoes up to almost 50 feet in length and nearly five feet wide, complete with thatched palm leaf awnings and up to two-dozen rowers. He had them carve a 25-foot canoe with a small keel, and showed them how to make a primitive rudder and tiller at the flat stern. He used a single mast, a cotton mainsail lightly treated with coconut oil, and a boom, then added simple *sisalana* shrouds. It wasn't a work of art, but when he took the master canoe builder out—a man with serious doubts about this "bird-wing canoe"—the fellow was astounded, falling down in the canoe and kissing Aalam's feet.

Itzel, who had accompanied the king's entourage, was taken aboard the sailboat as well. To Aalam's surprise, she loved "the kissing of the water" as she called it.

The following week, Nachán Can, having witnessed this "bird-wing canoe" perform, ordered another to be built immediately. Aalam, emboldened by his growing position in the community, asked the king for a favor—to have the canoe builder make a slightly smaller one for him and his lady.

"You are growing bold, white one," said Nachán Can, his dark eyes unreadable. "Asking for favors for serving your king…"

"If it does not please you…" said Aalam, eyes down.

"No," said Nachán Can, somewhat harshly. "It does not please me, particularly." Then his furrowed brows relaxed and Aalam could see a glimpse of levity in those strange, crossed eyes. "But those sunburned monkeys who have wasted most of my time drinking *pulque* and building inferior craft should be punished. They will build you an exceptionally nice canoe with wings, or I will give them to the priests." He spat on the floor in disgust. "Priests! Those people never seem to tire of finding reasons to send people on the road to *Ah-Puch*." Nachán Can shook his head. "I swear to you, I think the god of death must grow weary of their requests."

Aalam offered a grim smile. "Trust me, Lord, I have never found one yet, from your land or mine, who wasn't more intrigued with death than life."

During the next month, while Francisco Hernández de Córdoba continued a leisurely course down the coastline of the Yucatan Peninsula, stopping and exploring periodically, Aalam and his king continued to prepare their army. Nachán Can dispatched special scouts called *zabin* (road weasels) along the coast and the *sacbes* (white roads) of his kingdom. He would not be caught unprepared.

While the Mayans did not necessarily maintain standing armies, every able-bodied man, after reaching manhood, was required to participate in regular training exercises with war leaders. There were also units of full-time mercenaries who followed permanent leaders. It was much like the Minutemen of what would eventually become the American colonies. Nonetheless, their armies were fierce, and highly disciplined.

Nachán Can, with Aalam's assistance, now had 200 archers trained with the new English longbow. While the wood in the bows hadn't had the opportunity to cure for maximum tensile strength, they would still serve the archers well. There were another 200 spearmen, who used the notched *atlatls* (a spear-throwing device, generally made from a deer antler, which added power and accuracy), and they had 300 sling men, who could put a rounded stone in a soldier's eye at 50 feet and carried the deadly, obsidian-toothed *macanas*.

The whirlwind of training and preparation was exhausting, but there were still bright moments for Aalam. It seemed that each day he and his lady grew stronger. This bond they had found rose above the exhaustion and quelled the fear. Aalam had never felt more at peace than in the arms of his lady, and once their sailboat was completed, they found themselves escaping for two or three days at a time and heading for the coast. They camped on the beach in a simple, light cotton tent (to dissuade the voracious mosquitoes), and spent their days exploring, greedily sharing mangoes, papayas, and fresh shellfish, and sailing out to the barrier reefs. With the wind in their hair, and misted by the salt spray, they laughed and teased like children, letting the bright sun dash their fears, living on dreams, and for a short time, letting love take the tiller in their lives.

Before returning, they found a shallow, well-hidden mangrove channel and cached their boat among a forest of red roots and yellow-green leaves.

Another remarkable happening, which washed Aalam with a wave of incredulousness, was the hawk. No one understood it, maybe least of all him, but the bird kept returning to the kitchen windowsill, and each night Aalam would find a morsel for her. Then the impossible happened. One morning he was in Itzel's garden, shaking out a cotton towel he used to clean his weapons, when he heard the hawk call shrilly. He looked up and saw the bird circling him, dropping as it did. It landed on the limb of the garden mango tree, a dozen feet from him, and trilled sharply. On the purest of impulses, he wrapped his forearm with the towel and held out his arm. "Come to me, little *Ka'ana' Holcan,*" he called softly, giving her the name Sky Warrior.

The hawk cocked its head, its dark eyes intensely studying the man below.

"Come to me," Aalam said again, still holding out his arm. The hawk chirped, but didn't move. They stared at each other for a few moments, then, disappointed, Aalam shrugged and muttered, "Oh well. There are, I suppose, some things that stretch the graciousness of the gods, eh?" He was starting to bring his arm down when the bird launched from the limb in a graceful glide, and descended onto his outstretched forearm, flaring its wings at the last moment.

Aalam had forgotten the incredible strength of a raptor's talons. Wincing at the pain, even with the towel, he stared at the bird, filled with the joy that this first connection brought—one of the great joys of all falconers.

"I will need a leather armband, my pet, if we're to do this very often," he whispered with a grimace.

The bird chirped back at him, cautious, wary. It backed down his arm, away from Aalam's face (which was comforting for both), then suddenly it launched itself into the sky. The red-tail circled Aalam once, and with a final cry moved off into the western sky toward the jungle.

Itzel came out from the front door and saw him staring into the distance. "Looking for your winged friend, eh?"

"No," replied Aalam with a grin, rubbing his forearm. "She was just here, visiting."

That afternoon Aalam went to a skilled tradesman who worked with animal skins, most often deer, and explained what he wanted. In addition to the gauntlet, he needed two strips of light, pliable but strong leather for jesses, to attach to the bird's anklets. Not something that could become a hindrance to the creature, but something that allowed the handler to control the hawk while it was on the glove, and that could secure it to a perch if necessary. While waiting for the gauntlet to be made, Aalam built a sturdy, five-foot-high perch in the back yard.

A day later, the leathersmith had designed a most effective, laced gauntlet/armguard, and the two jesses for securing the bird. The following morning, armed with his new protective gear and a small bag of mice, Aalam went out behind his cottage and whistled shrilly. He waited a few moments, studying the sky, then called again. He searched the clouds for that telltale soaring black dot. Still nothing. He suddenly realized he was expecting the near impossible. Rarely would a wild hawk exceed the "manning" process and actually bond with its handler for more purpose than just food. "But it has happened," he whispered to himself. "It has happened..."

After another five minutes of calling, he reluctantly gave up, unlaced his gauntlet/armguard, and sat the jesses on the flat board below the perch. Itzel stood in the doorway, nearly as disappointed as her man.

"It is a bird, my husband, and a very independent one at that, eh?" she said. She took his hand and led him toward the door.

Aalam was just entering the cool darkness of the cottage when he heard it—a distant cry. He stopped and stood still. There it was again. He stepped outside and looked up, and there, high in the heavens, was a dot, wings partially folded, sweeping down out of the deep-blue Mayan sky.

Aalam stepped out, grabbed the jesses and the bag of mice off the perch, and quickly drew the laces taut on his gauntleted glove. Holding out his arm, he cried, "Come, Sky Warrior! Come!"

The red-tail spiraled downward, calling back, and this time, without hesitation, it flared its beautiful, rust-colored wings and dropped onto Aalam's outstretched arm. The bird fluttered for balance for a second, then turned to the man, eye to eye, and offered a shrill *chwirk*. It was magical—something so extraordinary that it alters perceptions and draws emotion from the depths of the fertile soil within the heart.

From that moment on, the man and bird were bonded.

Itzel just shook her head in amazement, then she pointed her finger at him and with mock gruffness muttered, "I don't care if you think he's your firstborn, he eats his mice outside…"

"There is no question that they are coming," said Aalam to Nachán Can, who sat comfortably on his mahogany and stone throne, inlaid with gold, silver, and jade. "Our scouts on the coastline have seen their ship at anchor, and they are disembarking with war materials."

Nachán Can huffed, somewhere between anger and apprehension. "The road weasels who have watched them are terrified. They think they are gods!"

"You need to stop this now," replied his confidant. "Send out a proclamation to your warriors. Any man who speaks of them as gods will be executed immediately."

Nachán Can nodded thoughtfully. "Good. It will be done. I will not have fear watering my ranks."

After a respectful pause, Aalam continued. "Lord, we cannot fight them on their terms. We must make them chase us to the place of our choosing—nowhere near our cities. They must not see your wealth, or it will drive them mad to have it, and others will come." Aalam paused again. "Can you tell me of a place that has flat ground, and a surrounding forest? And perhaps a river, eh?"

His king pondered this for a minute or two, then looked down from his throne and nodded. "Where the River Kal passes through the Chur Valley, perhaps half a day northwest of Chetumal. That is such a place."

Aalam returned the smile. "Good. Let me tell you what I have in mind. We should draw them there, make them ford the river, which will break their ranks. Then we will come from the jungle. They will be disorganized and weary when they reach the shore—"

"And that's when we strike!" interrupted Nachán Can, clenching his fists.

"Yes, my lord," agreed his *nacom*. "But we will have some surprises for them."

The Mayan scouts watched carefully as the Spaniards unloaded the last of their provisions and gear. The small vanguard Córdoba had sent inland to explore had been so harried by the guerrilla tactics Aalam's soldiers employed that they soon gave up, and only about half returned to their base at the beachhead. However, they did report that there were remarkable white roads in the interior, which most certainly must lead to cities of some wealth. This news put a fire in the bellies of the Spaniards, especially Francisco Córdoba.

To Córdoba, cities meant gold and other riches. He had come too far to be turned away by the efforts of a few heathens. The galleon that Córdoba captained had a crew of almost 300, and better than half of those, armed with rapiers, broadswords, and pikes, served as soldiers during land excursions. In addition, he employed 120 veteran soldiers, whose arms included halberds, swords, and crossbows. They also had arquebuses—the forerunners of the rifle—but they were heavy, cumbersome, muzzle-loading firearms that had to be fired via a matchlock device, which involved the use of a burning cord that ignited the powder in the barrel. They were painfully troublesome, but being able to knock down an enemy at 50 yards was a huge advantage over having to fight him hand-to-hand. Most importantly, when battling the indigenous populations of Central and South America, the shock effect of the noise and smoke was psychologically worth its weight in gold.

In addition, Córdoba had a dozen horses with handlers, and cavalrymen carrying lances. The horses were a nightmare to load and offload from the ship, but in previous campaigns he had seen the psychological impact of the huge animals on native populations.

By the end of the following day, Córdoba had his full complement of soldiers, horses, and equipment on shore. His campaign for God and the King of Spain (and as much wealth and riches as he could steal) was in motion. Córdoba wasn't much concerned with the information from his scouts. He was certainly not going to be deterred by a smattering of feather-clad, tattooed savages.

When he could, Aalam worked with Sky Warrior. The big hawk's perception was uncanny. It had come to respond to Aalam's whistles like a dog. At first, the *nacom* was certain it was because of the food he offered for the correct response, but as time passed, no encouragement other than a whistle was necessary to bring the hawk to his arm or his shoulder. The two jesses that he had attached to the legs of the hawk proved unnecessary, and he removed them. He didn't need to control the creature. There was simply a mutual bond between two entities. It seemed impossible, existing outside the normal parameters of man and bird, but there it was, and both cherished it. On their treks outside the city, Aalam would point to a foraging rabbit, or a luckless pigeon in flight, then whisper to the hawk, bringing up his arm. In a second, the raptor was in the air. The Mayans under his command watched this with no small degree of incredulity, and Aalam's influence grew.

But the winds of war were rising, and the three horsemen of the Mayan apocalypse, Destruction, Disease, and Death, stroked the flanks of their beasts and smiled...

As the orange sun cut its way through a battery of dismal gray cirrus clouds just above the ocean, and the seabirds greeted the new day with shrill cries, Córdoba sent out his scouts and ordered his company of just over 300 men into a two-by-two marching formation. His soldiers and the small contingent of cavalry protected the front and the rear of the vanguard. The armed sailors formed the inner ranks.

A clear trail stretched from the shoreline of the little bay into the interior. Córdoba, near the head of the column, felt quite confident, although the moist heat of the jungle and the brutal tropical sun made the wearing of even his light armor a truly miserable experience. Regardless, he was on his way to history and wealth. He smiled and straightened in his saddle. Somewhere ahead a bird offered a piercing call, and in the distance, another answered.

As the Spanish entered the interior of the jungle, they were astounded by the wildlife. Jaguars coughed angrily in the trees and slipped away from the noisy columns of soldiers. Multitudes of colorful parrots and flocks of wild turkeys fluttered noisily and disappeared into the foliage, as did deer and armadillos, and an occasional huge black-and-white anteater.

The mood of the confident Spanish was almost jubilant. The trail was good, the weather acceptable, and there had been no signs of savages at all. The small vanguard of soldiers in the lead hadn't seen anything out of the ordinary. Three hours out, they had passed through a small, abandoned village, and one of Córdoba's captains was remarking that obviously the natives had packed up their belongings and fled in fright. It had happened before. The heavily armored Spanish, mounted on their horses, were a formidable spectacle.

They had just begun to relax slightly, Córdoba allowing himself the luxury of a brief reverie, when suddenly a bevy of colorful arrows sprouted from the necks of the front outriders. The jungle in front and to the sides of them came alive with shouts and screams. Colorful, tattooed wraiths dressed in exotic plumed headdresses and loincloths flung spears or released arrows, then disappeared into the collage of greenery. They reappeared farther down the trail, where the jungle began to clear slightly, shaking their lances and bows, and shouting curses at the Spaniards. Córdoba quickly ordered battle formations, and the Spanish, anxious for combat, victory, and the riches that would surely follow, began the chase.

In minutes, it was clear that the jungle was thinning into a valley of agricultural land. Ahead of them, the Spanish could see a shallow river, and on the opposite side was a field, surrounded by the jungle in a horseshoe pattern—the open mouth of the horseshoe toward the Spanish and the river. The small Mayan contingency was still in a skirmish with the Spanish, but they were falling back, appearing somewhat disorganized and frightened now that they were in the open. The Indians, apparently in retreat, scrambled across the river. Shouting curses at the Spanish, they loosed another volley of arrows, then bolted toward the jungle about 150 yards distant.

The Spaniards quickly followed. With Córdoba barely able to control his troops (and the less-reliable armed sailors), it became somewhat of an unorganized rout. The Spanish were using their crossbows, but they had held off on their arquebuses, saving the impact of the weapons—the noise and the smoke—for the most advantageous moment.

But not a hundred yards away in the shadows of the jungle on both sides of the horseshoe-shaped field, Nachán Can's newly trained and equipped army lay in wait. Many of the Mayan soldiers had painted their bodies in traditional red and black, for courage and strength. Most of the officers wore lavish costumes over their hard, compressed-cotton armor, their helmets adorned with the exotic plumes of birds. Traditionally, with Mayan combat, each side blew loudly on conch shells, beat drums, and shouted curses at the enemy as any engagement began. Warfare with the Mayans could only be described as violence with pageantry, and Aalam couldn't change any of this without affecting their spiritual and psychological readiness. But he did have a couple of Old World tricks for the Spanish.

He looked about at his captains, his arms up for silence. He stood there, his exotically tattooed body garnished with a necklace of jade, a deerskin loincloth, heavy leather sandals, and his prized jaguar cape. Many of the captains and their men showed fear in their eyes as they watched the huge, four-legged beasts snort and whinny, splashing at the bank on the far side of the river.

"Hold strong, Mayans!" Aalam shouted. "Today is ours!"

Then he brought down one arm. Two hundred archers stepped from the jungle and loosed a cloud of three-foot arrows.

The Spanish, who had started to cross the river, hadn't expected European-style bows and three-foot-long arrows tipped with jadeite. In their combat with other indigenous populations of the Americas, the combat had been closer, and the enemy arrows of far less quality and strength. It was a costly miscalculation for Córdoba. While not all the arrows were able to penetrate the Spanish body armor, the less protected parts of their bodies paid a price. The armed seamen, generally without much armor, suffered dearly, collapsing into the river and turning the rushing water pink with blood. But the rest pushed on, forcing their way across the tributary toward the enemy.

When the Spanish, led by Córdoba and his cavalry, moved from the water and onto the dry fields in front of them, Aalam was able to control the archers for one more volley. But the Mayans in the jungle on both sides of Córdoba weren't accustomed to this kind of strategy. They preferred traditional mayhem. The foot soldiers in the tree line cried out almost as one, bringing up their obsidian lances and *macanas*, and charged out. Their bodies painted in bizarre colors, vivid feathers in their hair, they roared their battle cries and stormed the enemy. Against all that Aalam could do, the bowmen suddenly tossed their most advantageous weapons to the ground, drew their obsidian knives and clubs, and with the fervor of battle madness, joined their comrades.

It was then that the clever Córdoba brought up the reserve of horses and riders, and his battle-hardened soldiers with arquebuses, and the tide suddenly turned. After the first volley of New World weapons—the roar, the smoke, the Mayans' comrades screaming and dying around them without a single arrow to be seen—the Indians were shocked to terror. Immediately, Córdoba ordered his cavalry into the fray. Six-foot-tall, battle-hardened horses snorted wildly, fording the river, throwing up crests of spray, rearing up on their back legs and charging the terrified Mayans, their steel-shod hooves crushing heads and breaking bones with effortless abandon. It was more frightening than anything even the most resolute *nacoms* had ever witnessed. Truly, they thought they were facing the gods of the underworld.

A second battery of fire from the Spanish arquebuses decimated the courage of the bravest Mayans. Clouds of smoke drifted across the battleground as the Spanish cavalry began to repulse the Mayan infantry. But even in their terror, the Mayans remembered the one thing that had been drilled into their heads over and over: "*Remember the pathways, marked with small yellow flags on the ground.*"

Aalam, who had joined the fray, could see the battle turning for the worse. The plan had been to draw the enemy forward, but the effort was collapsing. His soldiers were turning and running for the safety of the jungle on both sides, not pulling the enemy forward, as was the plan. In a few more minutes, the battle would be a rout, and his epitaph would be that of blood and death for Chetumal and the Itza Mayans.

He recognized that he had one last chance, one final ploy. If it failed, the Mayans of Itza would become a footnote in the history of Spanish conquests. He raised his bloody *macana* and shouted for his three *nacoms.* Two of them managed to reach him, with a few of their men. He quickly shouted over the noise of weapons discharging, horses neighing, men shouting, the wounded screaming, and the smoke from the arquebuses drifting in clouds across the field. But perhaps it was the smoke that saved him; that, and a small contingent of his courageous men who put their terror behind them and charged the Spanish, breaking their ranks just long enough for Aalam to get through to a lone horse and rider who had become separated from the cavalry. Horses were not new to Aalam. His family in Spain had owned a stable, and he was an excellent rider.

He cut down a soldier coming at him with a pike, then snatched up the weapon from the dying man and charged the rider. Two sailors armed with cutlasses would have cut him down from behind, but his first captain, Trogo Catan, and another man, charged in from behind and buried their obsidian-pointed spears in the seamen's necks.

The Spanish cavalryman took a desperate swing at the large Mayan to his right quarter, but Aalam dodged the rapier and drove the point of the heavy pike through the man's chest, dragging him off the horse with the crook of the pike. Trogo Catan cut the man's throat as Aalam threw himself up onto the horse. The creature snorted and neighed loudly, struggling with the new rider on its back, but Aalam snapped the reins around, dug his heels into its flanks, and quickly brought it under control.

All around him now, his men were falling back. The horror of the snorting horses, the smoke, and the roar of the arquebuses was all too much for them. They had never seen an enemy like this. Truly, these strangers had to be gods…

But Aalam knew if his people panicked now and scattered, instead of staying with the plan, all would be lost. He reached to his neck, undid the yellow cotton scarf he wore, and began to wave it. As soon as Trogo Catan saw him, he too pulled out a yellow scarf and started yelling, charging toward the back of the horseshoe of forest from which they'd come. Here and there across the battlefield, the color yellow began to appear, and instead of dispersing helter-skelter in terror, the Mayans began to run in retreat toward the bright-yellow scarves on poles in the center and toward the back of the field.

The Spanish arquebuses were useless now in the melee. They simply took too long to reload and the burning cord used to ignite the powder often extinguished if not constantly attended to. But at this point, it was obvious to Córdoba and his men that the savages were on the run. They had but to drive them into the ground and finish them before they reached the forest.

Unfortunately, in their haste they failed to notice that the Mayans ran toward the jungle from which they had come, until they reached the place where yellow flags had been placed on four-foot-high poles, about 40 feet apart. When the Mayans reached that point, they ran between the flags, and spread out again once they were through the throat.

The conquistadores, lost to the madness of battle and the thrill of an impending victory, paid little attention to the flags as they spread out and charged in a long, curved line, the cavalry leading the way.

The only thing that saved the Spanish leader and perhaps a quarter of his soldiers was their position at the rear of the charge. Hernandez de Córdoba, who was always first in line when it came to the division of spoils, was very rarely first in line when it came to earning them.

Aalam had just reined in his beast and swung around, making sure the last of his people had made it through the throat. Sadly, he realized that they had left many behind, turning the dark Mayan soil red. But the Spanish were close on his heels, spread out in a long line, yelling and charging with a wild bloodlust and the confidence of victory. Then, as the Spanish foot soldiers and the last of their cavalry reached the yellow flags, the most amazing thing occurred. It was as if the earth opened up and swallowed them. The ground under their feet collapsed, and the last of the horses fell headfirst, disappearing. The long line of Spaniards charging alongside and behind them had just enough time to scream before they were shoved forward by the inertia of their comrades at their rear. One moment there had been a wild contingency of conquistadores charging confidently at the Mayans, then suddenly, most were gone, their cries filling the air.

It was then that Nachán Can emerged from the jungle with another hundred archers. His men released a cloud of arrows into the body of the Spanish, trapped and dying in Aalam's cleverly disguised trenches. Then, with a roar, they charged.

In the end, Hernandez de Córdoba survived, thanks mainly to his propensity for being closer to the rear than the front of most confrontations. He and perhaps 50 men managed to avoid the long line of 10-foot-wide and six-foot-deep trenches that Aalam and his men had dug. At the bottom of the trenches, the Mayans had hammered into the hardened ground hundreds of four-foot, fire-hardened stakes, sharpened like knives. Then they covered the open trenches with palm leaves and green reeds, supported by a light bamboo frame.

When Córdoba witnessed the unimaginable disaster manifesting in front of him, he and his remaining men turned and ran under a rain of arrows, fording the river and fleeing for the coast and the ship.

Historians would record this encounter as "a pitched battle in which the Spanish suffered heavy losses, forcing Córdoba to flee with the remainder of his forces and return to Cuba." (This was a kind description, most likely written by Spaniards.) In reality, it was very close to a massacre, and only a handful of the Spanish escaped into the darkening green labyrinth, fleeing in terror, leaving the last of their comrades to be butchered by the Mayan forces.

The sun was reaching into the jungle canopy, casting its last golden trellises through the trees. Nachán Can and Aalam, accompanied by two of their commanders, were surveying the battleground. The wounded were being bound with antiseptic cloths and treated by shamans, or mercifully dispatched if the wounds were too grievous. The few unlucky Spaniards who were still alive were being taken away to be used for sacrifices. In the process, Aalam noticed that his feathered companion, Sky Warrior, was circling above him. He smiled, graced by the knowledge that some things in his life had not changed. He whistled, and the bird cried back.

Among the dead and wounded on that blood-soaked ground lay Carlan Perez, a boatswain for Córdoba's ship. He was gravely injured, his life's blood draining away into a pool of sticky redness at his side. But it was little more than anger now that was keeping him on this side of the great divide. His life was gone, lost to a congregation of miserable, godless heathens. No gold, no riches, only death. As he lay there, shrouded in pain and disappointment, he heard voices approaching.

Nachán Can and Aalam had dismissed their protective contingency. They were surveying the battleground, searching for survivors.

Perez knew he was dead, destined for sacrifice if he lived long enough. As the three men passed him he subtly drew his knife, then suddenly rose to his feet and grabbed Aalam by his long, black skull lock, jerking his head back and putting his blade to his captive's throat. "In the name of the Holy Spirit, I will at least take one of you with me," he growled.

"Is this what your god teaches you," replied Aalam in Spanish. "To kill if you can't satisfy your greed?"

The boatswain started, completely taken aback. But he pulled Aalam's head back tightly and drew blood. "Speak in any tongue you wish, heathen. The workings of the devil shall not deter me."

Aalam glanced up and saw his hawk breaking its circle high above. Nachán Can and his guard stood stock still, watching for an opening.

"We will let you live, if you free my *nacom,"* said Nachán Can, knowing the man didn't understand, buying time, tensing for a leap.

Aalam whistled, not overly loud.

The hawk folded its wings and dropped in a single-minded dive.

"Come, devil," rasped the Spanish sailor in his captive's ear, his arm tightening for the slash. "I'll walk you through the doors of Hell."

But at that moment, a black-and-brown feathered thunderbolt came barreling in on the Spaniard's blind side, striking his head hard enough to nearly snap his neck, talons ripping across the man's eyes, tearing out one orb completely.

The boatswain screamed, instinctively raising his hands to his face. Nachán Can pulled out his obsidian knife and buried it in the Spaniard's heart.

Afterward, they all stood there, catching their breath, both angry and grateful at the capriciousness of the gods.

Nachán Can exhaled, a mist of incredulousness in his eyes. "I have seen many things," he said. "But I have never seen something like that. To draw a creature from the wild and have it do your bidding…"

Aalam shrugged with a grateful smile. "I can only beseech. She does what she wants."

The Mayans celebrated their narrow victory for three days, drinking copious amounts of *pulque*, chewing wild peyote beans, and dancing in the streets to the music of flutes, drums, shell horns, and gourd maracas. Conch trumpets at all corners of the city sounded blessings, soldiers boasted of their courage, and grateful wives made copious offerings to the gods. And the priests, of course, reveled in the glory of blood sacrifice. The gods were rarely ever satisfied.

During this time, Córdoba and a smattering of survivors had stumbled back to the small bay, loaded aboard their ship, and sailed away. But before the priests could kill the few Spanish prisoners who had been taken, Aalam was allowed to interrogate them. It was then he gleaned that it was Francisco Córdoba, from Hispaniola via Madrid, who had landed on the coast with plans to attack the Mayan people. He remembered distinctly how strange it was to use his old language again as he stumbled over the words. The three prisoners were astounded.

"How is this?" muttered one. "Are you Spanish?"

For a moment, Aalam was taken aback by the question. Then suddenly he exhaled softly and smiled. "No," he said with a sudden conviction. "I am not a Spaniard…"

Two days after the battle, Nachán Can ordered Aalam and his wife to his chambers. The Mayan king straightened up in his ornate throne, drew a breath, and tilted his head, staring at Aalam. "Was it hard?" he asked.

"Was what hard, my lord?" replied his *nacom,* puzzled.

"You came to us a Spaniard," his king replied. "Yet you killed your own people to save our nation. How is that?

Was it not painful?" He paused, still staring at Aalam. "I wondered, through it all, at what moment you would find your heritage greater than your new alliance. I trusted the jaguar not to rend me." He shook his head incredulously and smiled. "And most amazed and pleased I am to say, that I bear no wounds." He held his hands out, palms up. "How is this?"

Aalam also drew a breath and sighed. "My king, I have come to realize that sometimes life can be more improbable than the tales of old men lost to peyote." He paused. "It is true, I lived my life in a faraway place. But..." He put his arm around his lady's waist. "I found my heart in Chetumal." His eyes glistened with the emotion that is only found in the passion of love and truth. "Yes, I was born in a distant part of this world," he said. "But in here," he touched his breast, "I am Mayan."

Nachán Can held his friend's eyes, and neither man flinched. "Then it is good that I tell you these words," the king said. "It is written in the teachings of the god, *Kukulcan*, that sacrifice beyond faith, and above courage, shall receive reward of equal proportion." Nachán Can struck his golden scepter sharply on the arm of his chair. "It shall be written as of this day that the jaguar n*acom* Ata Aalam shall bear the official rank of Counselor to the King."

Aalam exhaled, unable to contain his surprise. "My lord…this is not necessary—"

"For once, can you just be silent and gracious," growled Nachán Can. "And allow me some ceremony!"

Aalam bowed and silenced himself.

Nachán Can held up his golden scepter and motioned his jaguar *nacom* forward. "Let it be known throughout this city and this province that you carry this scepter with my blessing, and your word is second only to mine!" He grinned. "Or maybe mine and CáCalla, my first wife." He sighed. “She is such a jealous...how do you say in your language... *perra?* But by all the dark gods, the woman can satisfy every craving I have ever had!” The king rose from his throne and handed the scepter to Aalam with both hands. “Carry this with pride and do not misuse it, or I will take it back, along with the hand that held it.”

In the days that passed after “the Great Battle,” life seemed to glow for the people of Chetumal. The warm winds and gentle rains of late spring brought life to the fields. Hunters returned with the great bounty of the mountains and jungle. Life was good. Only the aging priest, Bahman, seemed unsettled. In the readings of the stars, he saw a shadow growing. Bahman had made his living reading the stars to the best of his ability and making up what he couldn’t divine. Yet for one of the first times, the old man was frightened.

But no one wanted to hear malevolent tidings—not when the nation seemed so blessed with prosperity.

During this time, Aalam and Itzel would often escape to the coast in their little sailboat, which Aalam had improved by redesigning the keel slightly, strengthening the shrouds and the rudder, and adding a small jib sail. With paddles, they would work their way out of the mangrove channel, then raise the sail. Aalam loved the cry of delight from Itzel as the wind found “the wings” and the craft heeled over, skipping over the blue-green waters as if it were alive.

Aalam and Itzel purchased an attractive home at the edge of the city and hired servants. Aalam could not bring himself to own slaves. When asked why, he replied, “A mind that is expanded by dramatic experience cannot go back to its prior dimensions.” He ended up purchasing three slaves, then freeing them and hiring them to work for him. Ultimately, he had created employees who would kill for him, and die to keep him safe. The logic didn't escape his soldiers and his friends, and his image grew.

What few people knew—other than Aalam and the king's second wife, whom Itzel tended—was that Itzel had studied the Mayan system of writing for years, recording, by her liege's request, the life of Nachán Can's primary wife, and on Itzel's own time, recording her life with Aalam. The Maya had the most advanced form of writing in the Caribbean Basin. Manufacturing paper from the inner bark of the amate and ficus trees, they pounded the bark flat, bleached it with lime, and cut it into strips, much like the people had done on the distant Pacific islands. Itzel's history with Aalam was carefully preserved on these sheets and stored in waterproof clay jars.

But as their love, and their plans for a new life grew, so did the shadow old Bahman had seen in his dreams and among the stars.

Unfortunately, to the everlasting regret of the early cultures in Mexico and Central America, the Spanish introduced a single hideous element. It was an insidious ingredient in history that would change the equation of life and death for that entire region. A small contingency of Córdoba's troops had only recently arrived in Havana via Northern Spain, where the populace was battling a growing epidemic of smallpox. No one could have known, but three of Córdoba's men had just begun to display symptoms prior to the battle, and during the worst of the combat, their blood spray found its way to the wounds of two Mayan soldiers.

The indigenous peoples of the Americas had never been exposed to communicable diseases. Their resistance, via heritage, was virtually nonexistent. It started subtly. Two or three soldiers became ill, suffering with a general malaise that evolved into fever, backaches, and vomiting. The families offered small sacrifices to the gods. When that failed to produce positive results, they sought the services of a local shaman, who offered special concoctions and rarer exotic sacrifices. By this time, those afflicted were showing signs of rashes on their faces and hands, which quickly developed into pus-filled sores.

Then the family members began to fall ill, and their friends as well (because many people pulled their water from the wells within and just outside the city). In a short time, a great anxiety began to spread, and indeed, it had captured Ata Aalam.

It had been a long time since the Spaniard-turned-Mayan had prayed. He found himself caught between an old god that seemed totally capricious and mostly ineffective, and a new set of gods who greedily demanded sacrifices for the slightest of situations, and were just as ineffective and arbitrary.

Regardless, he had seen the two Mayan soldiers before they died—the sores, the failure of breath, the eye color. He knew what it was. Aalam had witnessed the symptoms of the disease and the end result firsthand, when it killed his mother and one of his brothers. It was originally called *"variola vera"* by the Spanish, but as it raged across Europe, it became known simply as "the pox," or smallpox. He was a brave man, but at the very thought of losing his beautiful, loving wife, he became craven and weak. He could not, would not, watch someone he loved so much, die in such a hideous fashion ever again.

One evening, after prayers on the ramparts of the city wall, Aalam turned to his wife. The red sun was just burying itself in the shadows of the distant jungle. In the background, they could hear the cries of supplication in a desperate city. Above them, Sky Warrior circled listlessly, as if the hawk could sense the trauma that besieged Chetumal.

"We must leave," Aalam said quietly, staring up at his hawk. "I know this curse. I have seen it before, when I lived far away." He sucked in a breath and exhaled, angry and desperate. "We must pack up what is most important and run, or this monster will eat us too."

Itzel looked at her husband, her beautiful, dark eyes frightened and uncertain. "If we do this thing, where do we go? What do we do, eh?"

"We will take the sailboat," he said, with more confidence than he felt. "I have talked with the traders here many times—the ones who own the large trading canoes. There are islands toward the rising sun, many days by their canoes. They will give me a course. There are few people on these islands, and the Spaniards have not found them yet, or they are too small to interest the Spaniards, which is good." He exhaled. "We will find a place there, in the jungle, by the shore. We will start again, someplace where we can raise a family, and make ourselves part of these new peoples." Aalam offered a struggling smile. "I will fish and hunt, and you will make us beautiful babies."

She sighed heavily. "But our friends, our life…"

"It is what we make it, my wife," he offered, watching the hawk carve the darkening green sky in arcs behind her. He turned back to his lady again. "I would prefer a new adventure over an unquestionable disaster…"

"What about Nachán Can, eh? He will not be pleased."

"That is a chance I have to take," Aalam replied. "I cannot just run in the night, like a thief. I must face him and tell him."

And so it was that they began to quietly gather up a few treasured and necessary belongings—tiny statues of Itzel's favorite gods, a small box of medicinal herbs and binding for wounds, fishing twine with hooks made from gold or silver, freshwater jugs, dried iguana meat, smoked pork, avocados, plantains, squashes, potatoes, tortillas, and dried fruits. Aalam spoke with the three men who worked for him, explaining that they would need a device to carry their possessions, and together they began to construct a small, wheeled cart (the concept of which Aalam had explained to Nachán Can, but the leader saw it more as a diversion than a practical application, and there was very little use arguing with him).

The one thing that did catch Nachán Can's attention, along with Aalam's, were the horses that had survived the combat. All of the riders had been killed, but four of the horses escaped without injury, galloping away in the frenzy. Aalam caught two after the battle and found the other two in succeeding days. Nachán Can was enthralled by them, showing almost no fear, and wanted to ride them immediately. Within a week of working with Aalam, Nachán Can was proudly riding his horse, a dark stallion, through the streets of Chetumal, terrifying and awing the citizens, which was exactly his plan. When his first wife, CáCalla, asked if that was really necessary, Nachán Can replied cleverly, "My dear, a king can never have too much awe."

Within two days Aalam and his helpers, along with a talented woodworker, had completed their wheeled transportation in a secluded location just outside the city. The cart was primitive but functional, complete with a bench seat in front and a box in the back for goods and supplies, with two spoked wheels, a simple axle, and a collar, shaft, reins, and a girth for the horse. Then, knowing that he had to, Ata Aalam went to the palace.

He knew he was risking everything to take this chance on the capriciousness of the most powerful person in the province, but for him, there was no alternative. He had studied this from all angles. He knew the secret—the smallest chance to save the city—would be to shut down the wells for Chetumal, boil all the water that was used for anything, and keep the sick quarantined. But the Mayan society, as magnificent as it was, had no understanding of communicable disease. Some would listen, and try to do what was right, but most would consider the concepts of quarantine, of boiling water, and the children not dipping the same family jugs into the same well, as simply bizarre, and the disease would spread.

It was early morning and the sun was just breeching the windows of the palace. The voices of people in the bazaars and on the streets of Chetumal could just be heard. Nachán Can sat on his throne, sullen, and hostile. "After all I have given you, all I have done for you and your woman, you would leave your city and your ruler in the midst of this calamity?"

Aalam shook his head sadly. "My lord, if I could save you and your people by staying here and fighting this thing that is coming, I would. I would do that gladly. But this is not a jaguar, or an army of vengeful enemies. It is not something you can battle and destroy. It is a plague," he said, holding his hands out in forlorn desperation. "It is an evil spirit that comes to you silently on the wind, invisibly, and takes most everyone you love. You cannot defend against it, you cannot kill it, you can only run from it, and pray that just the tiniest vestige of this insidious demon has not found its way to you, or those you care for.

"I owe you my life, my lord, but I do not owe you my lady's," he continued. "You are a man easy to anger, but you are also a man of integrity. I pray that you will understand the passion I have for my woman—that you would understand I see what is coming…" Aalam paused for a breath. "For as much as you are my friend as well as my lord, I would pray that you and your family secret away some of your wealth, to a place no one knows of, and be prepared to leave here on a moment's notice to a place of safety, because, at the end of the course with this disease, laws of gods and men can collapse quickly…"

Aalam expected the usually contrary Nachán Can to explode with anger and a conflicting response. Instead, he sat there for a full minute, drumming his fingers on the arm of the throne. "I have a place. Not a palace by any means, but an acceptable escape, and almost no one knows about it," he said quietly. "I use it to find pleasure with women other than my wives. CáCalla, my first wife, she can be…selfish about my affections sometimes. It is just into the jungle, near the limestone cliffs of the River Cha, at the base of the mountains, barely one sun from here." He paused. "There is a place, cleverly cut from the rock floor in the bedroom, where I keep some things that please me. In the center of the floor in that room, carved into the stone, is an image of a jaguar."

The king stopped and stared out the window with a slight smile, his eyes distant. "It is the right eye that holds the most value," he said. "It needs but a touch…" He straightened up and shrugged. "Maybe I will take a few slaves and add to the possessions in that room. But I need with me one man I can trust. A king and a handful of slaves in a jungle is not a comfortable combination. If you insist on leaving your king on this wayfaring of yours, then you can pay your fee by guarding me one last time." Nachán Can smiled, not so pleasantly. "And now you're asking yourself, 'if my king would divulge this secret, has my life become cheap?'" He sighed strangely. "The answer, my friend, is no. You have done much for me, and for Chetumal. You deserve your life."

For the first time in all the years that Aalam had known him, his king's face softened.

"We will do this thing, then I will let you go, to find yourself another life with your hawk and your woman, in your winged canoe. Ultimately, it is the least I can do for you. I will find my way, as will Chetumal. Whatever the gods will, eh?"

Then the king straightened up in his chair, his face stern once more; that of a ruler. "When this is all past, perhaps we will meet again, on the other side of the darkness."

A day later, Aalam, Nachán Can, and four slaves headed out quietly through a lesser-known exit of the city. Each slave carried a cumbersome hide pack strapped to his back. By late afternoon, they came to a large river his king called the Chur, and continued along the edge of the river for another day, following a convoluted trail that only Nachán Can knew, winding their way west, along the jungled shoreline to a battery of huge limestone bluffs. Cleverly built into the soft rock near the bottom was a narrow opening, appearing to be nothing more than a natural cleft, but inside that cleft was a small but remarkable corridor that widened out into a great room, a bedroom, and a simple bath fed by an underground stream. Ducts chiseled by slaves provided air and acceptable light. Aside from Aalam and a few long-gone women of pleasure, no one in Chetumal knew of it. The laborers who had built it had long since found their way to the realms of darkness or light.

Nachán Can and Aalam deposited their packs, which contained little more than some dried iguana, mangoes, and bananas for the trip, on the living room table, then went back to the bedroom. The slaves followed with their heavy packs. Nachán Can had told them to stack their baggage against the bedroom wall, then return to the living room and partake of the fruit and iguana—that they had earned it, and that afterward, they could sleep. It was unusually gracious, and Aalam was pleased to see his king showing some simple consideration.

Moments later, as the two men stood alone in the bedroom, the ruler of Chetumal turned to his compatriot. "Move the bedding away from the floor," he said. When Aalam had complied, Nachán Can pointed to the incredible relief of a jaguar in the center of the rock floor. "Push on the right eye," he said calmly.

The sun was setting and the shadows were growing on the granite walls as Aalam bent down and pushed on the rock eye. As he did, it gave, receding inward an inch. Suddenly, the three-foot by three-foot, three-inch-thick rock square that contained the jaguar relief slid backwards, under the adjoining rock square, displaying a small, eight-foot by eight-foot room under the bedroom floor. The Mayan chieftain struck a piece of flint on an adjacent hunk of iron rock and the spark lit a tallow candle. He motioned Aalam to follow as he moved down the stone stairs.

Even for a man accustomed to seeing wealth, Aalam still gasped. There were heavy reed baskets and mahogany boxes, all filled with precious gems such as jade and emeralds. Better than half of the boxes were filled with gold and silver necklaces, and many others contained small golden statues of the gods, solid-gold calendars, and a king's lightly plated golden armor.

One at a time, Aalam took the heavy packs, which had been transported by the slaves, and lugged them down the steps into the eerie dimness of the single candle. The backpacks possessed exotically designed gold jewelry, jade, and emeralds—wealth well beyond the means and dreams of the average Mayan. When they were done, and had stepped up from the room, Nachán Can touched a lever under the square jaguar stone, and pulled the stone back into place in the floor with a satisfying click.

It had been a long day. After bidding his king's permission, Aalam offered a prayer to *Xaman Ek*, the god of travelers, then took a portion of the bedding and curled up in a corner.

The following day, when the airshafts offered a little light from a pale morning sun, Aalam awoke and moved into the main room. There he found all four slaves sprawled out on the floor, dead, a dried yellow foam staining their mouths and their chests.

He turned and found Nachán Can, standing in the doorway of the bedroom.

"You poisoned them."

Nachán Can nodded. "Good thing you decided not to eat the iguana."

There was a pause, suffused with anger on Aalam's part, and indifference on his king's.

"Did you really think I could let them return?" said Nachán Can. "With the knowledge they possessed?" He shrugged. "Even they knew their fate." He nodded toward the entrance. "You are free to go now. I will stay for a while, amongst my trinkets, then find my way home." He brought up his hand and placed two fingers on his heart, a strange touch of sadness in his eyes. "Until the darkness finds us..." he said.

And that was the last time Ata Aalam ever saw the great Nachán Can.

When Aalam returned to Chetumal, Itzel almost smothered him with affection borne of relief. "I was so afraid…" she cried, allowing the implication to go unsaid.

"I, too," he whispered. "More than I care to admit. We must move, before the wind shifts."

Aalam spent the next day locating and speaking with the masters of the large, 50-foot trading canoes—particularly the one who had spoken of an island perhaps five to six days out, if one stayed in the direction of the morning sun. He said the island was populated by a simple people, similar to Mayans, who did not seem aggressive, and looked forward to trade.

While Aalam worked at preparing for the voyage, Itzel was busy gathering foodstuffs and collecting ink and sheets of treated and bleached ficus bark paper, knowing that where they were going, there might be no means to process bark. This endeavor of saving her and Aalam's personal tale had become a passion, and like every true wordsmith, she captured every detail of value, even Aalam's journey to the limestone cliffs off the Chur River and the king's hideaway, as he had related it to her. She stored their history, along with additional paper and small bottles of ink, in three waterproof clay jars, sealed with cork plugs and rubber tree sap. Finally, she used thin strands of gold to tightly bind the cork to the mouth of the glazed jars.

Two days later, as the sun cleared the rolling jungle to the east, Aalam and Itzel, and the two of the three men they had freed, then hired a year earlier, set out on a trail to the sea. The men wore little more than deerskin breechcloths and heavy sandals. Itzel wore a cotton breechcloth and halter top, her long hair knotted down her back.

Their horse and the little carriage they built performed admirably, carrying the heavier articles such as Itzel's clay jars with the history of her and Aalam's lives, additional weapons, water jugs, and foodstuffs. By evening they had reached the coast, and the beach Aalam and his lady had claimed as theirs so many wonderful times. They could smell a change in the air—a heavy, rich, salty flavor—and heard the seabirds crying, while the waves tumbled softly onto the yellow sands. It called to the adventurer in Aalam, and he smiled.

The only situation that clouded the event was that he had not seen Sky Warrior all day. Not a sign since they had left the city. *Perhaps the bird realized we were going,* he thought. Who knew, but it left a small measure of emptiness in his heart.

The following day, one of the men helped Aalam retrieve the sailboat from the mangroves and bring it around to the beach. The converted Spaniard exhaled a considerable sigh of relief when he saw his boat, still there, still intact. As he and his man ran the boat tightly along the coast, Aalam watched the sky, but there was still no sign of his feathered companion.

After pulling the sailboat into shallow water and anchoring, they began to carefully secure their supplies and equipment. Aalam began by checking all the sails and storing extra lines and fittings. (Their cleats and pulleys were made from gold, as there was no iron in the Mayan nation.) They had filled their water jugs from a small spring on the way the day before. The incredible gift from Nachán, the golden scepter of the king, was bound to the mast, and the water jugs were stored amidships to maintain balance. With the food, water, cooking utensils, fishing gear, and Itzel's clay jars containing their remarkable history, it was a fairly crowded affair. There were, of course, weapons as well—Aalam's *macana*, their obsidian knives, a spear, and both Itzel's and Aalam's bows, with arrows.

By the time the sun was nearing its apex in the cloudless sky, Aalam and Itzel were ready. They, with their men, knelt in the sand and offered prayer to *U Kux' Kaj,* the god of wind, storm, and fire. Then, with no more than a brief embrace, Itzel and her man climbed aboard, and their companions waded out, guiding the sailboat into the green-blue sea. Aalam hoisted the sail, the offshore winds snapped it full, and even as loaded as the craft was, she lifted proudly up onto the sun-gilded surface. Aalam, at the tiller, ran a hand through his shoulder-length chestnut-colored lock of hair and sighed, smiling at his wife. Itzel sat on the bench seat amidships, her reddish skin darkened by the days in the sun, her dark eyes filled with as much excitement as trepidation.

"I love you," he said quietly.

"And I you, heart of my heart," she replied.

About 500 yards out, Aalam brought the craft about, dropped the sail, and let her drift for a moment. They both stared out at the land of the Maya—the country that had given birth to one, a new life to the other, and had made them both Mayan.

After a moment, Aalam reached for the sheet line and the tiller, staring out across the sky one last time. Still no sign of his hawk.

Itzel read his mind. "We must all go our own way at some point, my husband."

He nodded, smiling sadly. "Strange to feel this way about a creature that eats mice on my windowsill."

His wife shrugged. "Love has many colors, and each creature sees those hues differently."

"So it is," Aalam said, as he brought the sheet tight again, and the little craft responded briskly, heading out to sea.

They had been sailing for just over an hour. Aalam had finally settled into the little cockpit at the stern, the tiller under his arm, staying with the course he'd been given by the old trader. The horizon was engulfed by heavy, gray-and-white cumulous clouds, and there was no sound but the gentle slapping of the waves against the hull. Itzel was just pulling up the makeshift cotton canopy amidships, for some relief from the sun, when Aalam heard it—that shrill cry—high and distant, just out from the land behind them. Itzel stared at him, a gleam in her eyes.

After a few moments of craning his neck, Aalam saw it—a dark dot high in the sky above the jungle, heading out to sea. He whistled. Nothing. He whistled again—more hastily than his pride was comfortable with—but the dot didn't change course. He recognized that it was too small to be his hawk. The bird was probably a young petrel, a little farther offshore than it should be. He reigned in his disappointment and reluctantly returned to the tiller. He was about to take his eyes from the bird when he saw another dot, high in the heavens, above the petrel. Suddenly, the dot began to fall, and he heard that familiar, harsh cry.

Aalam turned to Itzel, and she was smiling. Together they watched the huge red-tail hawk fall on the unsuspecting petrel. By the time the smaller bird realized it was in trouble, there was that fatal collision and an explosive puff of feathers. There was a moment of tangled spiraling as Sky Warrior gained control of his kill, then continued downward, toward the sailboat.

Knowing he would need his deerskin gauntlet, Aalam started to shift forward from the tiller, but Itzel was already holding it in her hand, moving toward the stern to pass it to him. He smiled. "How lucky I am to have a woman who reads my mind," he whispered.

Itzel just smiled. "I live to serve, master," she said, her dark eyes flashing sarcasm.

Sky Warrior fell in a circling dive, throwing out his wide wings at the last moment, and flaring into what could only be called a flamboyant landing on the bow. It fluffed its wings, tilted its head, and purled loudly, still clutching its kill.

"It's not my fault you're late," said Aalam as he let out the breath he'd been holding. He brought up the arm with the laced gauntlet, and without hesitation, the hawk dropped the petrel on the deck and flitted from the bow to his forearm.

"Do you think we could get back to the business of finding a new home now, eh?" asked Itzel.

Aalam chuckled, his gray eyes sparkling. "Yes, my lady, I think we can, now."

During the journey, the gods blessed them with kind seas, but by the fifth day, they were sunburned and weather-beaten, and weary from constant shifts at the tiller. They were still blessed with sufficient food, although they were down to the last two jugs of water. Aalam had captured a dozen mice before they left land. These, and an occasional luckless bird, kept Sky Warrior content.

Aalam had to mark their course at sunrise each morning, aiming their bow two points north of the newborn sun, then holding that course as best as possible through the day. As the sun set, they watched for the Dog Star as it rose above the darkening horizon, which provided their course for the night.

The old trader had said that in approximately five cycles of the sun, they should watch for the bluffs of a plantain-shaped island. He said that this island would consume the distance of a day's paddling in one of his large canoes.

By the morning of the sixth day, the sea was still empty, but the western horizon was darkening behind them, as far as the eye could see. The sailor in Aalam recognized that sky, and it frightened him. The Mayans called the great storms that came off the water *"hunraqans."* (Later, the Spanish would adopt the name from the Mayans, calling them *"hurac'ans."*) But at this point it mattered little what they called it, death on the wings of wind and water was headed their way, and they both knew it. But the gambler and the optimist in Aalam was reminded of an expression by the old priest, Bahman: “Sometimes the gods will challenge you, just for entertainment. It is then that you will find yourself in the worst of situations, suddenly seasoned with the most remarkable of chances. You see, if the gods didn’t occasionally throw us a bone in the most impossible of circumstances, humans would soon tire of the game.”

Aalam was looking for a bone…

They quickly threw everything overboard that wasn’t absolutely essential—cooking pots, empty water jugs, duplicate weapons. Then Aalam drew the mainsail and the jib taut, hoping to run a tight quarter on the edge of the storm and skirt the worst of it. At least, that was the plan.

The sky darkened, and the winds rose from robust and challenging, to a howling whine, and rains came in vicious sheets. In the process, Aalam saw Sky Warrior lift off the stern, away from the storm, and disappear. Aalam laid the craft over tightly, struggling with the tiller, while Itzel sat on the bench amidships, hugging the mast with one hand, and bailing furiously with half a coconut husk in the other. The rain continued in stinging blasts, hammering the sea, and all but blinding them. But remarkably enough, in the process of all this terror, the gods threw them a bone.

Suddenly, the blinding deluge eased for a few moments, and the clouds gave just enough to allow a bleak sun to penetrate the fury of the storm. There, to the port side, a breach in the holocaust offered a brief view of…land! It was miserably distant and only a gambler or a fool would take the odds of making it. But it was land.

Aalam fought for control, his muscles knotted and aching as he tried desperately to keep the craft moving toward a cove on the distant island. Itzel bailed until she could no longer lift her arms, then simply collapsed, her eyes an amalgam of fear and anguish. By then they had entered the mouth of the small bay. But just as they made the shallow waters and began to risk a glimmer of hope, it happened—a freak wave, driven by the undercurrents as the skiff hit the sand and coral shelf just offshore, drove the boat over and into the foaming crests. The craft furled to the starboard, the sail and battered mast caught the sea, and the sailboat rolled. The last thing Aalam remembered was reaching out for his lady as the heavy boom swung into him and everything went dark.

There was something bright above him—a pale light that slightly diffused the still darkness. He could hear moaning, filled with desolation and anguish. He felt something touching him, something cold and terrifying. Aalam could only surmise that he had reached the dreaded realms of the dead and the vile god *Kisim*, the deity of death and decay, had come for him. He tried to move, but his hands wouldn't rise. The creature moved closer, blocking out the light so it could take him, its narrow-fingered hands touching his face and throat. He tried to cry out, he tried to resist, but he was simply too weak. His last thought was of Itzel…

"Aalam! Aalam! You cannot leave me!" said the creature, its voice choked with emotion. "Don't you dare!"

The hands were squeezing him, shaking him.

"What kind of seedy, witless husband would do such a thing, eh?"

A small smile cracked Aalam's dry and battered lips, and he opened his salt-caked eyes. The rising sun was just etching the palm fronds with gold along the curved beach. "What kind of a lazy wife would take so long to retrieve her husband from the doors of the Underworld?" he croaked. "Eh?"

Both Aalam and Itzel were battered and weary and desperately in need of sustenance, but for the first couple of hours, the most they could do was hold each other gratefully. Aalam finally made it to his feet and found a bevy of coconut trees along the shore. Many of the trees had been blown down and the fruit was ripe. By some miracle, Aalam still had his knife tucked into his belt. He stripped back the husk at the top of the coconuts, then punctured the soft spots on the top of the hull, and they drank until they were sloshing.

In the process, Aalam assessed what was left of their lives. The onshore waves had driven the shattered hull of their little sailboat into the shallow water, about 100 yards offshore. It lay askew, a portion of the bow still above the surface, but the mast was broken off about midway up. There was not much in the way of foodstuffs that could be salvaged. The dried iguana meat and smoked pork was lost, but some of the avocados, plantains, squashes, and potatoes had drifted onto the beach. By some extraordinary gift of the gods, Itzel's three waterproofed clay jars containing their history (and that of Nachán Can and Chetumal), had floated onto the beach of the horseshoe cove. Even as exhausted as she was, Itzel quickly pulled them past the high-tide line.

While Itzel was busy with her projects, Aalam swam out to the boat and found his obsidian-toothed *macana* and their longbows, with a sheath of arrows still bound to the inner hull of the boat. The cottonseed oil on the wood had preserved them nicely. He also discovered another bone from the gods. The golden royal scepter of the Itza Maya empire, which had been securely bound to the base of the mast, had also somehow survived. With the water level barely at his chin, Aalam simply dove down and cut it loose from the remains of the mast.

Once they'd had time to ascertain their location, they realized it was really a perfect place to be shipwrecked or otherwise abandoned. A freshwater spring gurgled on a hill just inside the jungle. There was a multitude of tropical fruit, even wild sweet potatoes, and the bay teamed with fish. It looked as though they had survived the worst. The only thing missing was Sky Warrior. Aalam knew that terrible storms often killed birds, and they had been well out to sea when the worst struck. Each morning he watched the sky, listening for that familiar cry, but the silence taunted him.

Aalam and his wife sought the highest ground they could find, a bluff a quarter mile east of the cove where they were shipwrecked. The view made them realize that they had most likely found the island the Mayan trader had spoken of. It appeared to have the right shape and size. Itzel found a cave that looked out over the eastern sea. The mouth was wide enough for air circulation and there was a perfect place for a hearth just outside, under a slight ledge. It was there that they decided to settle, and there that they dug into the soft coral and buried the glazed clay pots that stored their history. It was a remarkable accounting of their first meeting, the coming of the Spanish, and the incredible story of the golden scepter given to Aalam by Nachán Can. Itzel had also included Aalam's final days with the Mayan king, and the tale of a treasure cached in the floor of a secret room, inside the limestone walls off the river Chur. To Aalam, this all seemed a great deal of trouble, but Itzel saw it as the greatest story of all time for their children—an heirloom that would tell how remarkable their father was.

After some consideration, they chose to bury Nachán Can's remarkable golden scepter there as well. As Aalam had said, "Who do we need to impress, eh? Besides, things that shine draw greed and envy."

Two days later, as the evening sky swallowed the sun and they sat around their cooking fire, Itzel and Aalam saw shadows moving hesitantly out from the dark labyrinth. Half a dozen men and a few women stopped at the edge of the jungle. An older man stepped forward and offered a salute, two fingers across the heart, which was used either as a greeting, or a term for goodbye among various Mayan tribes.

As it was, their languages were similar, and with a little sign language they were able to communicate well enough. Within days they learned that the people on the island were fairly primitive. They had a few stone buildings, but most lived in the coral caves along the higher shoreline of the island. It became clear they were not of a violent nature, but they were, without question, wary. The Spanish from Cuba had just begun to raid the Central American islands for slave labor. One of their villages had been attacked two moons ago. Strangers were to be dealt with at arm's length. No one trusted a ship with a sail.

That resolved, the only issue that left Aalam disconcerted was the loss of Sky Warrior. Each morning he would walk along the beach where their boat had foundered, and call, then whistle, but the silence still taunted him.

One morning, as the sun had begun to cast its light across the island, Aalam was returning to the cave in which they had taken residence, when Itzel stepped out, a strange look on her face. "You found nothing, I suppose."

Aalam shook his head, reaching up with his left hand to release the binding of his deerskin gauntlet. (At this point, he wore it more as a gift of memory…an emblem of fading hope.)

"Don't take it off," his wife said, as she casually glanced above him. "Call one last time."

Aalam swung around, scanning the sky, then suddenly he stopped. High above, at the edges of the shallow thermals underneath the cumulus thunderheads, was a dot. And then he heard the cry.

Aalam instantly called back, his heart hammering. It wasn't just for the creature itself, although he carried more affection for that bird than he would care to admit in any of the *pulque* taverns of Chetumal. But his feathered friend represented survival against all odds—against the challenges of life and its victories, large and small.

Again he called, and suddenly the dot began to fall.

Sky Warrior called out with a vibrant, shrill cry, and the big hawk's wings flared as she broke into a glide. In moments, Aalam felt the rush of wind from the wings and the solid grasp of talons as the bird settled onto his arm. He saw tears in his lady's eyes, and strangely, he felt that same moistness on his cheeks. Quickly wiping his face, he ran his fingers down the thickly feathered back of his friend.

His wife smiled. "Sometimes, the gods, they throw you a bone…eh?"

Over the next few days, life began to settle down. It had been well over two weeks since they had left the coastline of the Itza Mayans. Aalam had managed to find their jadeite ax in the sand near the remains of their sunken boat, and had begun to fell a tree for a canoe. Itzel had started to work the shorelines for crabs and crayfish, and began to collect fruit from the jungle. It wasn't long at all before Aalam had his small canoe trimmed and hollowed out, and had produced two small paddles. This opened them up to a variety of foods and exploration, and they began to enjoy their sojourns into the bay and the mangroves.

Ostensibly, all seemed good, but as the days passed, there was something about Itzel—something in her eyes. They seemed to lack her normal enthusiasm, and she was easily fatigued. When Aalam asked her, she said it was nothing, just a headache, but when he held her at night, he noticed the heat coming from her skin, and her lower back was tender to the touch. His concern began to slide from apprehension to fear. He'd seen those symptoms before, when his mother and his brother had fallen ill…

During their last days at Chetumal, Aalam had prayed to every god he knew, *Just give me this one thing, let us escape this wretched malady. Let us be gone before it overwhelms the city and the province. Please…* He had gone to the shamans and offered sacrifices. He had fallen to his knees and prayed in the few Latin words he still remembered. And it appeared that the gods had listened. But in the end, they hadn't—because they were gods, the most capricious of beings within Heaven and earth.

Then, as if the gods were taking pleasure in his misfortune, they added one more ingredient to this stew of misery. The following morning, as he stood on the bluff that offered such a beautiful view of the sea and the perfect natural harbor below, he saw them…sails! As the Spanish caravel came about down below him, dropping its sheets and weighing anchor in that perfect little bay, the sun glinted off the hatch grates on the deck. It was a slaver!

"My God!" he whispered quietly, filled with terror. He was suddenly reminded that the Spanish could not find themselves satisfied with simply taking the wealth of the people they came upon. They wanted their pride and their dignity as well. They insisted on enslaving them.

He returned to the cave a man bitter and lost. His world was ending. His hawk called to him plaintively, circling him, but he didn't have the energy to reply. When he told Itzel, he could see the life drain from her. She was growing worse. The first of the blisters that gave "the pox" its dreaded name had begun to show on her skin. He knew what this meant for himself as well. They had kissed, they had held each other, and they had made love. It was only a matter of time…

She coughed lightly, then drew a ragged breath, staring at the distant ship. "Is there nothing we can do? After all, my love…we have nothing to lose."

Aalam calmed himself and gazed out at the sea in front of the cave. "I know every pitch and yaw to a caravel and I know her just as well below decks. They're carrying no slaves now. Their hatch grates are up to cleanse the air of the slave pens. They're on a run and our little island is their first stop." He huffed angrily. "They're about to introduce these people to hell."

He squeezed her hand and fell pensive. "The caravel is a swift, well-fitted craft, but its primary weakness is the powder room. It's built too close to the upper deck. With a little luck, we might be able to take advantage of that." He paused, studying the craft in the distance. "They've probably sailed from Cuba. They'll enjoy themselves today, get their feet on some land, but tomorrow they'll prepare for a raid of the shoreline villages."

"So it is tonight, my husband, eh?" said Itzel, her soft eyes filled with determination.

"Yes, my lady...most of the sailors will be ashore. Only a skeleton crew will be onboard." Aalam sighed and squeezed her hand. He paused for a moment, then spoke quietly. "This is what I have in mind…"

The orange moon was just coming off the horizon. The crew had taken the two launches to shore. The few disgruntled guards aboard the caravel were well on their way to being seriously drunk, regardless of what the captain had ordered. After all, why should the others get the first choice of the women and the liquor in the village? They never noticed the small canoe that slipped quietly across the bay as the moon briefly buried itself in the ashen clouds.

While Itzel held the canoe fast against the bow of the caravel, Aalam tossed a looped rope over the fluke of the anchor and scrambled up over the anchor and rail, then onto the deck. In moments he was a shadow. In his hand he carried his *manaca,* and his deadly obsidian knife was tucked into his hide belt.

One of the three guards was already slipping into a drunken stupor near the portside bow. He hardly felt the knife that cut his throat. But the two near the bow heard the man's death gurgle, and they moved forward from the quarterdeck as cautiously as their drunkenness would permit. Aalam slipped out from behind the mainmast and practically decapitated the first man, but as he did, his foot caught on a pile of rigging line and he lost his balance. The third guard, less inebriated than the others, had his rapier out in a heartbeat and drove it into Aalam's side. The sailor ripped out the blade and was about to complete the coup de grâce when the bloody point of an arrow sprouted from his chest. His eyes, still filled with incredulity, faded to indifference and he dropped to his knees, then collapsed face-first onto the deck. At that moment Itzel was there at her man's side, holding the bow he had taught her to use so effectively.

Unfortunately, they had failed to notice one final man, aloft, on the main spar of the mizzenmast. He began yelling like a banshee.

Aalam turned to his lady. "Do you think you can do that again?" he gasped, holding his wound and nodding to the weapon in her hands.

Itzel never answered. She just pulled another arrow from her hide sheath, nocked it, and let it fly. The

Spaniard's attempt at warning ended in a short shriek, and a second later, his body struck the deck.

But at this point, all stealth was lost. Those on shore had heard the cries and were stumbling toward their launches on the beach. Aalam sat leaning against the mast, holding a hand over the wound just under his ribs, blood pulsing out between his fingers. Itzel knelt next to him, gasping for breath. She had all but exhausted the last of her resources, her hollow eyes pale in the moonlight.

"One thing left, my lady," Aalam whispered painfully. He glanced across the deck at the glowing lantern. "Help me up. We must get the Spaniards aboard or around the ship, before…"

Itzel could see the blood coursing down his waist, soaking his loincloth and his legs. His breath was coming in sharp gasps. The Spanish rapier had torn into his vital organs, and time was now at a premium.

Aalam pointed at the glowing lantern in the rigging. "Bring it to me. I have to make the hatch...the powder room. You, my love, must buy me time, but at the last, you must let the Spaniards in the launches get aboard…"

Itzel moved quickly to the rigging and undid the lantern, then carried it back to her man. Aalam took it and pulled her into him with one hand, the glow of the lantern illuminating them. "I love you, my lady," he whispered hoarsely. "And in the name of *Hun H'unahpu,* the god of life, I will find you beyond the darkness—again."

With that, Aalam kissed her fiercely, then tore himself away and stumbled across the deck and down the steps of the hatch, into the bowels of the ship and the powder room. He opened the heavy door and sat the glowing lantern on the floor. With the last of his energy, he drew his knife and battered open the lid of a small keg, kicking it over, the gunpowder spilling across the floor.

Above him, the Spaniards' launches had made it to the caravel and the sailors were crawling up the heavy netting at port side, crying out and drawing their weapons. Itzel killed the first three to make the deck, and that immediately dampened their enthusiasm. But soon there were a dozen onboard, firing their crossbows in the glow of the moon, cursing and shouting. A bolt from a crossbow found her, burying itself in her shoulder.

Itzel was at the end of her strength. The disease and the wound had finally eaten away the last of her reserves. Everything was blurring, and the last of her breaths were coming in gasps. All she wanted was to hold her man one last time. She lurched across the deck and stumbled down the dark stairs to the dimly lit powder room. There she found Aalam lying on the floor, the glowing lantern in his trembling hand, the last of his life's blood draining onto the weathered planks.

"You came for me," he whispered, his eyes glazing.

"Of course I did, my love," she sighed, as she eased down next to her man, wrapping her arms around him. With a final, almost peaceful breath she whispered, "It's time for us to go now, heart of my heart. The gods are waiting…" Then she pushed the burning lantern over, into the gunpowder…

Far above them, a hawk sailed across the face of the yellow Mayan moon, and it cried…

October, 1967
Just South of the Yucatan Channel in the Gulf of Mexico

Monstrous seas were tumbling around them like foaming avalanches. The old freighter creaked and groaned against the onslaught of a vicious, unrelenting ocean. The storm had a name, but it hardly mattered now. The captain, pale white and soaked to the bone, stubbornly clutched the wheel. The windows on the forecastle had been blown out by a thunderous wave not 10 minutes ago. The first mate was sitting against the wall in the corner of the wheelhouse, trying to tie off a gash on his arm, the blood from the wound draining down his wrist and melding with the sloshing waters in the wheelhouse.

The ship had left Port Harcourt in Nigeria two weeks ago, carrying the usual cargo of palm oil, unrefined rubber, and canned animal foods, to be delivered to Miami, Florida, and Vera Cruz, Mexico. They also had an unusual delivery for a somewhat eccentric millionaire in Vera Cruz—a man who found pleasure in bizarre things. But now they were a hundred miles off course, and none of them were likely to see Miami again.

"Most of the crew's gone, sir," said the first mate as he stood shakily. "Washed overboard while trying to get the latches on the life rafts released. Don't think this old girl is gonna hold together much longer, and the rafts are gone."

"Not a damned thing we can do about that now," muttered the captain, as another huge wave battered them on their right quarter. The ship rolled, then crashed down hard.

"Sir, what do we do about thems that are in the hold?"

The captain huffed out a bitter breath. "Well, I think it's safe to say they ain't never gonna see Vera Cruz." He offered a grim smile. "Hell, neither are we..." The fellow paused and wiped the water from his face. "Let 'em go. Just unlock the gates. They might as well have a fighting chance."

The first mate blanched slightly. "Even the…"

"What does it matter?" the captain replied bitterly. "Nothing and nobody on this ship's gonna see land again. No creature deserves to be locked away and watch the water come up at their face. Even that one…"

CHAPTER ONE

There's nothing more provocative than the promise of gold...

—Dan Hendrix

Twenty-two Years Later...
Key West, Florida – March 1986

The closed black casket rested somberly on a long table in front of the bar. The people at the surrounding tables were involved in quiet conversation, waiting for the preacher. Who would have dreamed, Crazy Eddie ending up like this? It just didn't seem possible. He seemed to be too full of life to go out like this.

The reverend came stumbling out of the bathroom, pulling up his Dockers shorts and tucking in his flowery Hawaiian shirt as he moved over to the casket. He shooed away a clique of Eddie's favorite girlfriends, then turned to the congregation at the surrounding tables. He reached for the bottle of tequila and the glass on the coffin, poured himself a shot, and hammered it down. He held the bottle aloft.

"To Crazy Eddie!" he cried.

Then, to the responding roar of "To Crazy Eddie!" he took one last solid hit of José Cuervo, turned, and broke the bottle on the casket. The crowd raised their glasses, and with a final hurrah, knocked down their liquor.

"The man always did have a style about him," muttered Will with a morose smile.

At that moment, while everyone was cheering, the casket opened, the lid fell back, and Crazy Eddie came crawling over the top of the soft velour crypt. He missed the grip on the bronze rail and tumbled to the floor, but managed to preserve the bottle of tequila in his hand. Eddie dragged himself to his feet in the midst of the enthusiastic ovation and raised his hands.

"Who would'a believed it?" shouted the preacher, hands out. "Our favorite bandit going legit!" Over the ovation, the preacher continued, "We're here to celebrate Crazy Eddie, or Mr. Edward Jackson Moorehouse, Key West's newest legitimate businessman, and the newest bar in town!"

And, as they say in the movies, the crowd went wild.

A couple of hours later, Crazy Eddie was sitting on the bar (not *at* the bar, but *on* it) by the beer taps, so he didn't have to go far for a drink, yet close enough to the crab races table to be able to throw lime wedges at the crabs he didn't like. No one complained, and for good reason. He owned the place. "Crazy Eddie's Bar and Swill"—that's what the plaque over the door said. As far as the lime wedge thing, no one cared. He hadn't hit a crab he was aiming for all night. Eddie was an occupational hazard for the gamblers, and he added another dimension to the crab races.

Supposedly, Eddie had taken his share of the money from the last "impossible gig" he and his friends had recently survived, and had gone legit and invested it in a bar. Rumor had it that they had actually found Pancho Villa's lost treasure in Mexico. But then, who knew for sure? Eddie and his buddies always seemed to be involved in some sort of outrageous scheme. Besides, exaggeration and drinking were the town's primary entertainment. Half the best-selling writers in Florida practically lived at Key West's bars, just to pick up ideas for their next yarn. Everywhere you looked there were smugglers, gamblers, sly-eyed pretenders, and midnight riders; those who were buying time, those who were killing time, and many who had done time. The damned place was like a Hemingway novel.

Eddie had spent a number of years in the southern islands back in the old days, leaving him with a distinct black Caribbean vernacular flavored with 1960's Haight-Ashbury slang. He was in his mid-40s, tall and gangly, and rarely seen in anything other than khaki shorts, fruit-juicy shirts, and weathered leather sandals. He had a short beard, long, sun-bleached hair, a thin, slightly bent nose (the consequence of a disagreement somewhere in the past), and he wore a black patch over one eye (also the result of failing to duck quickly enough). Eddie had a ruddy tan and an easy smile, and he most always wore a Jimmy Buffett "Margaritaville" ball cap that he claimed was given to him by Jimmy himself. Eddie was a laid-back dude, without question, yet he was one of the best pilots I had ever known. He owned an old Grumman Goose, and he could make that baby moan and groan, and put it in places that would give the average pilot a permanent case of the hives.

My friend Will Bell and I were sitting in the corner by the back wall, trying to coax two ladies from Miami into letting us give them a "tour of Key West." Will, tall and lanky, suntanned, blond hair to his shoulders, and clever blue eyes, was telling them that we were treasure hunters—practically best friends of the famous treasure hunter, Mel Fisher. (Mel wouldn't know us from Dolly Parton, but the reference didn't do any harm.) I was sitting back and letting him run point. He did that fluid conversation thing really well.

In looks, I was pretty much the opposite of my friend—nowhere near his height, sun-bleached brown hair not quite as long as Will's, and hazel-brown eyes. I did spend a lot of time at the local gym and that was a plus for me, but the truth was, our constant competition for women was generally a neck-and-neck run. We were attired in our usual

Key West hunting trip outfits—tropical shirts, Dockers shorts, and Kino leather sandals. We'd been living in the Keys ever since getting out of college. Several years ago, we came down here for a pleasure diving vacation and we never left.

At the table to our right were the other esteemed members of "The Hole in the Coral Reef Gang"—ex Special Forces pilot William J. Cody (Cody Joe to his friends); his lady, the tenacious but beautiful Max Delane; and former Vietnam helicopter pilot Captain Travis Christian—all bona fide hunters of old, shiny things.

The trouble with being an authentic treasure hunter was, once you found anything old and shiny, the Feds were up your ass like a bad case of hemorrhoids. The truth was, almost all the transactions that had gone well for us had taken place in poorly lit backrooms or in the hulls of seedy fishing boats, where even the cockroaches carried pistols and nobody wanted to know names.

While Will and I were in the process of a fairly good performance with our barroom princesses, I noticed a couple sitting at the table to my left. The lady was definitely attractive. She was in her late twenties, about five foot five, with a nice figure. She had Mediterranean-colored skin, gray-blue eyes, and long, dark-red hair. But she also possessed a slight overbite, which softened her sense of austerity and made her more approachable. Will would have called her a "natural beauty." The guy accompanying her had the same Mediterranean skin, curly brown hair, pale-blue eyes, and a slim build. But oddly enough, he possessed fairly well-defined muscles. He was probably 25 or 26, no more than five foot four inches tall, and unassuming to the point of being practically invisible. She was drinking margaritas. As far as I could tell, he was on his second orange juice. The lady was dressed in a colorful tie-dyed skirt and a sleeveless yellow blouse. Her smallish companion was wearing blue jeans, sandals, and a Bull and Whistle T-shirt. She ordered their drinks from the waitress, and was doing the talking. He replied with shrugs and subtle movements of his hands.

I also noticed a couple of Stock Island ruffians sitting at the table next to them. They'd evidently crashed Eddie's celebration and decided they might like to get to know the little lady better. The two guys (dark tans, tight T-shirts, blue jeans), moved over, uninvited, and pulled up a couple of seats. After a few moments of borderline polite conversation, asking the usual questions, the larger of the two, who called himself Ryker—shoulder-length black hair and a bandito black mustache—leaned into the lady. His eyes glittered slightly.

"Why don't you give your little brother some change and let him find the gumball machines?" He reached out and put his hand on her arm. "We could take a walk, maybe go somewhere and play some grown-up games. The night is young…"

Little brother's eyes flashed ever so slightly as he glanced at his sister, then he went back to his orange juice.

The woman didn't flinch. She didn't even move her arm. "Thank you, but no. We're enjoying our own company."

"You sure?" the guy replied, pulling her arm a little closer to him. "I don't think you're sure." He winked at his buddy, a heavily built Cuban with long hair and lots of tattoos. "I don't think she's sure, Truz," he said, then he turned back to the lady. "You could have two for the price of one…"

Truz smiled, but there was nothing nice about it.

"You have no idea how out of your league you are," she said, shaking her head cynically, still staring at the first fellow. "I would like you to leave us alone now, or I'll turn my little brother loose on you."

Ryker pulled back slightly and looked at his friend. They both chuckled, confident and malicious.

Little brother hadn't even looked up. He was quietly sipping on his orange juice, watching the crab races.

More drunk than smart, Ryker tugged the woman toward him, standing, pulling her up. "C'mon. Quit playing hard to get. Junior can watch your purse while we dance for a bit."

I shot a quick look at our friends. Travis glanced at Cody Joe. Cody nodded, and they began to rise. I looked at Will. My dive buddy shrugged.

"What the hell," he said, not terribly happy about being interrupted, and generally far more content with talking his way out of situations.

But at that point, the woman's brother stood up and carefully pushed his chair in with almost methodical attention.

The big guy, still holding the woman's arm, stared at the little fellow in front of him. He put his hand out, his index finger almost under little brother's chin. "Sit down and drink your lemonade, Tinker Bell. We'll call if we need you."

The small man's soft blue eyes suddenly went glacial. Fast as a viper, he grabbed the guy's extended forefinger and snapped it upwards. The crack was the kind of thing that twists your stomach just a little. It took a moment for the pain to reach Ryker's befuddled mind. He stared at his finger, which was pointing straight up at the ceiling (the rest were still pointed the other way—not a desirable situation). He shrieked, trying to move back, but little brother wasn't having it. He ground the broken finger in its socket and the guy screamed like a newborn, falling to his knees.

Faster than you could blink, the small fellow kicked his opponent in the head with a solid roundhouse. Another definitive crack echoed as the man's jaw shattered, and he crumbled to the floor. The contest was over.

"Whoa shit!" muttered Will incredulously, certainly echoing the opinions of the people at our tables.

The woman had moved back, showing very little, if any, concern. It seemed strange to me at the time, as all of us still stood by our tables, somewhat amazed.

Truz, the Cuban across the table, grabbed his beer bottle and broke it on his chair back. Cold and malevolent, he came around at "Tinker Bell," weaving the jagged glass in front of him.

As the Cuban stepped in, the little guy didn't move. Didn't even blink. Actually, the corners of his mouth turned upwards in what looked like a smile, and his pale-blue eyes, for the first time, came to life. I thought maybe he was demented, but there was something about his look of anticipation that made me a little uncomfortable. Too bad the other guy didn't feel the same way. Truz slashed at his opponent's face, but by the time the bottle reached its intended destination, the smaller man was gone. He'd done some sort of magic act, dropping toward the floor, then gyrating on a heel and coming up beside the Cuban, hammering the man in the right kidney with a spinning back kick. All the time, there wasn't a moment of concern in the young man's eyes. He was confident and comfortable. Hell, the guy was enjoying himself.

This circus had finally caught the attention of the bar. The Cuban was fairly heavy, ham-fisted with respectable arms and shoulders. This wasn't his first rodeo. He got up and charged. Just as he reached his adversary, the small fellow grabbed one of his arms and pivoted. Using his antagonist's inertia and a hip throw, he bounced Truz off the floor like he was a ragdoll. The staggered Cuban was just coming to his knees when the guy stepped in and caught him with a sidekick to his ribs, caving in two of them. (It was another one of those sounds that you remember. Especially Truz.) Before the Cuban could suck in a painful breath, his opponent moved in and caught him with a stiff-knuckled punch to the carotid artery on the side of his neck. That was "end-game."

The little fellow wasn't even breathing heavy. He nodded to the woman, that half-smile showing itself again. He paused and glanced around, then casually began picking up the chairs at his table and setting them carefully back in place. At that moment, somebody started to clap. Within seconds the whole place was applauding.

Cody looked at Travis, a good degree of appreciation in his eyes. "Pretty damned impressive."

Travis nodded, his green eyes smiling. "Ya, mon," he said. "Eddie's only been open three hours and he's already had his first bar fight. That's respectable for Key West." He glanced over at the little guy picking up the chairs, as calm as if he were at a lawn party. "Let's help him straighten up. There's sure as hell nothing else he needs help with."

As they moved over, the guy stood, adopting a calm but defensive pose.

"It's okay man, we're on your side," said Cody, hands out. He nodded to the two on the floor. "Just thought we'd help you throw out the trash."

The man with the curly hair smiled and nodded.

Once the "trash" had been dumped out back, the two ladies from Miami that Will and I had been "coaxing" decided to move on. So, we invited our new friends to join us, and they accepted. We pulled two tables together, and after introductions, we all sat down.

"Talia" Tesca looked at me. "Kansas Stamps," she said. "How is it you were named after a state?"

I shrugged and offered a slight smile. "I've been told my parents were passing through Topeka, Kansas, when I was conceived. Topeka would have been a lousy first name."

Talia was quick to explain that her brother, Benji, was unable to speak, and had been that way since birth. He was, however, highly proficient at sign language. During the next half hour, everyone got to know each other, the challenge of Benji not being able to communicate verbally having very little effect on the evening. He would sign to his sister and she would reply for him, and he also possessed a soft, unique whistle when he wanted to get your attention.

As it turned out, Will had a cousin who was unable to speak, and he had studied signing for over a year, becoming relatively proficient. It wasn't something done so much out of kindness. The girl was an absolute knockout—long blond hair, blue eyes, and a figure that could stop traffic. And she was a very *distant* cousin…

We soon discovered that our new acquaintances were an interesting pair. They were from Israel, but had been visiting the States for the last two weeks. Talia explained that her father was a martial arts instructor for the Israeli Defense Forces. Benji was an expert in several forms of martial arts. Had it not been for his inability to speak, he would have become an instructor, like his father. Talia had a college degree in Middle Eastern history, and had also studied the various arts of self-defense with her father for years.

"Well, that certainly explains the little floor show moments ago," said Cody, whose expertise with his hands and feet was well respected.

"You study too," Talia said to him. It wasn't a question.

Cody shrugged. "Yeah, but not so much anymore. How'd you know?"

Talia smiled slightly. "The way you move, and the increased size and scarring on your first and second knuckles—much time on the heavy bag and makiwara boards, eh?"

Max, Cody's lady, spoke up. "Don't let his modesty fool you. He's very good—at *everything* he does." She ruffled his hair affectionately, subtly staking her territory. She knew all too well the effect those blue eyes and that long blond hair had on women.

Talia got the message loud and clear, and switched directions, turning to Will and me. "I couldn't help but hear some of your conversation earlier, with the two ladies," she said. "About you being treasure hunters. Is that true?"

We all glanced at each other, and I nodded. "A little…except the part about knowing Mel Fisher. While we've been successful, we don't relish spending as much time talking with the government as Mel."

"It's kind of a hobby," Will added.

"Well, that's somewhat remarkable," said Talia. "We share your enthusiasm for antiquities. Benji and I have done much amateur archaeology in the Middle East, although I stress, amateur. We're here in the U.S.—the Florida Keys—for a few days of tourism before we fly out of Miami for Roatán Island, off the coast of Honduras."

"Haven't spent too much time in Honduras, but had an interesting couple of weeks in Mexico last year," said Travis with a grim smile, recalling an adventure we had all shared concerning gold coins, Pancho Villa, and a cabal of nasty bandits.

"Did you find anything?" the lady asked.

"We don't know you that well," I replied.

"But we'd like to…" said Will with a smile.

Damn! He was such a crotch snake—always trying to wiggle past me in the race for new and interesting…

"Anyway," Talia continued, "Benji and I are members of the International Federation of Archaeological Clubs. It is an international nonprofit organization formed in 1984.

Each year they choose a historically significant but not well-known area for an international 'group hunt.' Not only do many major metal-detecting companies give away thousands of dollars in equipment as prizes, but there is a $5,000 cash prize to the one who finds the gold coin the company sequesters somewhere in the hunting field. The hunt lasts only one day, from sunup to sundown, but it's an exciting affair, I promise."

"Sounds like fun," I said.

"It is," Talia replied enthusiastically, as her brother nodded. "This year it's being held on the Caribbean island of Roatán. Registration on the island starts Monday, three days from now. The hunt begins the following day. It costs $200 per person to enter." She paused and looked at Will and me. "If all that you have said about yourselves is somewhat true, it may be below your standards of entertainment. But who knows, eh? Perhaps you would like to take a shot at it, just for fun?"

"After our last experience in Mexico, I think I've had enough treasure hunting for this decade," said Cody.

"Hate to be a spoil sport," said Travis, leaning back in his seat and running the fingers of one hand through his long, dark hair. "But I've had all the adventure I want for a while. Besides, I've got bonefish charters booked solid for the next three weeks. You start canceling on clients and they find someone else, and they tell their friends."

Will looked at me. He offered his typically mischievous smile, and his eyebrows did that little "Groucho Marx" dance. "We could take the 310," he said. "I've had some carburetor work done on the port engine, but they'll have it finished tomorrow." Will got that funky smile again. "The greatest pleasure in being a successful scoundrel in the business of shiny things is that you can make your own hours." He paused, looking at our new friends. "How about we save you an airline ticket? Our little twin can make the hop, no problem."

Benji glanced at his sister and their hands spoke for a moment, then Talia looked at us. "I hate to sound too cautious, but we're suddenly talking about flying away with two people we've just met. How do we know you're not scoundrels of some sort?"

Will chuckled. "We are scoundrels, but I'll tell you what we'll do. I'll give you the phone number to our banker. The password is Blowfish. And also the number to the head of the DEA in Key West. You can call them tomorrow, or go by and meet with them. At that point you will have discovered that we're 'reputable rascals.'"

About that time I saw Eddie working his way over to us from across the dance floor

"*Hola*, my funky brothers and sisters! Was' happenin'?" He looked at Talia and Benji, then pointed to Will and me. "Don't believe more than about half the shuck and jive these dudes are sellin'," he said with a confidential smile. Eddie glanced out at the dance floor, where Benji and Talia had decimated the two characters earlier. "By the way, very impressive floor show." Then he turned to the rest of us. "So, funky brothers of restlessness, shiny baubles, and mayhem, whatcha think of my new gig? Crazy Eddie's Bar and Crab Races! 'Where you can find a nimble crab with almost no effort, and a nimble companion with almost no crabs!'"

That brought a round of chuckles.

"Well, I hope this doesn't mean we can't invite you and the Goose on an occasional venture," I said.

"No, no, man!" huffed Eddie. "Hell no. I'm just trying a new gig. You gotta remember, brothers and sisters, you're under no obligation to be the same person you were yesterday!" He exhaled and offered a pensive smile. "The truth is, average people collect *things*. But folks like us, we collect *moments*, and they get turned into stories, and when it's all said and done, the person with the most stories wins."

"Damn, what a great expression," I muttered. I raised my glass and the others joined me. "Here's to The Hole in the Coral Reef Gang—and stories," I said.

"Hell yes!" yelled the others. "Hell yes!"

CHAPTER TWO

You either answer the compelling call of chance, and roll the dice, or you don't, and live with the eternally maddening question—What if?

—Bill Green

As it was, Travis, Cody, and his lady begged out on the idea of a vacation to a Caribbean island (it sounded an awful lot like their present life), and Eddie was way too busy trying to birth his new child.

Honestly, trying to find pre-planted gold on a small, poorly developed island was a little mundane for Will and me. But damn, Talia was a really interesting lady—clever, gutsy, and just short of knockout beautiful. Key West had a lot of women. Hell, there was a constant procession stumbling off airplanes and buses hourly. And I know this is a strange thing to say, but for my partner and I, sometimes life just seemed like a scene from an old Bob Hope and Bing Crosby movie, over and over again. Somehow, we kept finding somebody with a situation, and usually, we ended up getting our asses in a fix before we got laid. *If* we got laid.

I would have never believed it a few years back, when we first stumbled our way into the Keys, but taking a real vacation on a tiny island with nobody chasing us seemed like it might be a fun thing. Besides, Roatán had a remarkable history of English and Spanish pirates—and, supposedly, buried gold. Okay, okay, there was the beautiful girl, and that helped add some flavor. That, of course, would mean the inevitable competition between Will and I, but I could live with that. I had a handful of Ex-

Lax and sleeping pills to slow him down. Messy, but effective…

So, there we were the next day, having breakfast at Two Friends Restaurant. I had just gotten off the phone with Talia. She had checked our references, and it was a go.

"Just a simple, uncomplicated vacation," said Will, holding up his hands, palms out.

"Yeah," I agreed. "A simple, uncomplicated vacation."

The following morning, as the brilliant red sun was breaking through a barrier of pink and white cumulus on the horizon, turning the salt ponds behind Smathers Beach into slate-gray and blue pastels, we were fueling at Key West International. Our gear was loaded, and we'd run over the charts the night before. Will's little Cessna 310 would handle the trip comfortably. We'd lift off the island and shoot west, across the blue-green waters of the Gulf, into Cancun. After refueling, it would be due south for a little over 300 miles (about two hours) to Roatán.

Will, the historian of the two of us, had done some quick research on the small, banana-shaped island off the coast of Honduras. As we sailed along in the blue stillness, mesmerized by the drone of the big Continentals, he filled us in on the island.

"One thing's for sure, it's had an interesting history, especially for treasure hunters," he explained. "The Spanish were the first to discover it, but they didn't really have much use for it other than raiding the indigenous population occasionally for slaves. Later, the British settled there and built plantations, but British pirates also discovered it was a good location for raiding the Spanish shipping lanes. For over a quarter century, the pirates in that area had their way with shipping and local plantations, until the Spanish amassed an armada and wiped them out in

1650. The pirates had built a fort near the island's east end, in a perfect little bay—"

"That's the place the treasure hunt is being held!" interrupted Talia. "Old Port Royal. The International Federation of Archaeological Clubs thought this was as genuine a location as could be found. The property is actually owned by a very rich Texan, who allowed this invasion in order to promote the island." She smiled. "Who knows, might be a real piece of eight out there somewhere…"

Benji whistled in agreement.

Two hours after departing from Cancun, Will reduced power and dropped 20 degrees of flaps for landing. Below and ahead was Roatán, the largest of the Honduran Bay islands—a thin, fairly mountainous ridge of sand and coral about 48 miles long and a half-mile wide, sitting smack dab in the center of the largest barrier reef in the Caribbean.

The runway at Coxen Hole, the largest town in Roatán, just slid off into the ocean, into a huge expanse of crystal-clear, iridescent blue and green water, strewn with wildly shaped, orange-colored reefs. Not much room for error there. Over the years, Roatán had become a haven for divers from around the world. With dozens of shipwrecks around it, the ruins of buccaneer strongholds, and a history of lost gold and silver (as well as a couple quiet little airstrips and easily accessible coves for burlap-wrapped, midnight deliveries), it possessed an undeniably exotic mystique.

After clearing Customs at the airport, we rented a little Chevy Chevette, loaded up all our gear, and headed toward the motel we'd booked. There's only one main road that runs along the edge of Roatán from one end to the other. It does a little circle at the western end, passing through Coxen Hole, the capital city, and dissecting West End (a laid-back, very tropical community, which is probably the most popular place for tourists), then heads east to the less populated part of the island, where Old Port Royal is located. Along that road, you'll find beaches and most of the tourist shops, restaurants, motels, and of course, bars. Lots of bars. You'll never find an advertisement in a travel magazine that reads, "Beautiful tropical paradise with no bars." You'd be out of business in a week, and if Jimmy Buffett heard about it, he would have at least two songs on his next album about "No Margaritas in Paradise."

We found our way to the Coconut Breeze Motel just outside of West End, got checked in (a two-bed room for Talia and Benji, and the same for Will and me), and after an opportunity to clean up, we were back in the car and headed into West End. It was five o'clock somewhere…

Our first stop was a weathered, gray-planked bar and restaurant whose deck and small pier extended out just over the ocean. You could hear the waves rolling in under you—very "in the islands." At the few tables on the deck were a smattering of tourists and locals. The people of Roatán are a bawdy union of English, Spanish, and Black Carib descent—the Black Carib being a combination of Carib and Arawak Indians, and African slaves. In the end, they called themselves "Caracoles."

The sun was slipping into billowy, gray-and-white cumulus clouds on the horizon, burnishing their edges with bronze and gold and painting the sea a rich silver—all my favorite colors. We watched a V of pelicans gliding in onto the calm water in front of the pier, poised and stately in flight until that last ungainly moment of what can only be described as a somewhat orderly crash.

Our waitress showed up—an attractive lady whose heritage represented the amalgam of peoples on the island—coco skin, large green eyes, and long sable hair, all packaged in a clinging island muumuu. Very nice. I even saw Benji taking several appreciative looks, signing to Talia. She grinned and slapped his hands.

Will and I immediately began our perennial competition. I was already subtly checking my pockets for the Ex-Lax and sleeping pills.

We had a great dinner and a couple of cocktails each, Benji knocking down three or four screwdrivers. (When we first met him at Eddie's bar, we thought he was drinking orange juice, but it turned out the boy had a serious passion for screwdrivers.) But just about the time we began to loosen up, Talia insisted on being taken back to the motel. The contest officially began at nine the following morning. Registration was at eight, and we had at least a half-hour drive to the horseshoe-shaped bay at Old Port Royal.

"Sorry to be a spoilsport, boys, but I don't want to be anything but sharp tomorrow morning," she said. Then she aimed a strange, but without question, promising smile at us. "Some pleasures are perennially available, but some have an expiration date." Her eyes sparkled mischievously. "One pleasure at a time gentlemen, eh?"

Without another word, she turned and headed for the car, her brother following behind her, whistling pleasantly.

Will whispered. "I don't know about you, but that sounded an awful lot like an invitation. Although I'm pretty sure she was looking at me when she said it."

I shook my head. "No, no, she was definitely looking at me." I put my finger to my right nostril. "Couldn't have been you, not with that huge booger sticking out of your nose like a chinchilla worm."

"Booger? What booger?" shrilled Will, instinctively brushing his nostrils. "Jesus! There's no booger!"

"There was!" I said seriously. "It was so big the blind guy playing congas saw it. Maybe it just crawled away."

"Jeez…" moaned Will, still rubbing his nose then looking at his hand. "A booger…"

Benji smiled as he walked away.

The next morning, when we reached the gate to the dirt road that led down to the bay, there was a collection of automobiles backed up along each side for a quarter mile. Hundreds of treasure seekers from across the Western Hemisphere had come to pay their respects to history and Lady Luck. Will parked the car, we ambled down to the gate, and completed the registration process at a small stand. From there we headed toward the niche in history that had fascinated so many people.

After about a 15-minute hike we came to a small, picture-perfect horseshoe bay, with golden sand and calm water, protected from the wind on three-quarters. But most significantly, there were the two small islands that sat just offshore near the mouth of the bay and the very narrow channel that led into it. This is what made Port Royal such a valuable find for pirates. With cannons mounted both on the islands at the mouth of the narrow channel, and on the surrounding cliffs of Roatán, it was damned close to impossible for anyone to bring an unwanted ship into that harbor without being decimated. The Spanish had been defeated twice there, before eventually taking the fort.

As we neared the remaining ruins, I could see the other element that made this location so valuable—a freshwater spring that bled out of the hill into a pool at the edge of the jungle. It was an incredible experience—remarkable, almost entrancing to look out over that emerald-blue water encompassed by a nearly perfect horseshoe of sand that led up into a bevy of jungle-covered hills. I could almost see the rugged stone walls that once protected the warren of ruthless, but highly enterprising buccaneers. I imagined the caravels, the Dutch flutes, and the converted merchant ships that had been taken as prizes, bobbing on the bay, gilded by the sunlight of an earlier time. I could almost hear the voices…the merchants that gambled their lives and their wares at the pirates' pleasure, the hawkers, the shills, and the whores who, like hoards of lemmings, somehow, unerringly found their way to illicit havens such as Port Royal.

At the sound of the starting whistle, we decided on a grid search, beginning at the beach on the far side from where we came in, then working upwards toward the crest of the hill. From there we'd work back down to the beach, then back up, continually moving eastward, back toward the entrance. Will and I used White's Electronics metal detectors. Both Benji and Talia preferred Garrett Company detectors. As anyone knows who hunts the relics of other times, metal detectors are as personal as weapons or cologne.

An osprey circled high above, watching the invasion of his terrain with detached curiosity as we entered the thick growth of the hillside. The palms on the beach gave way to an interior laced with sea grapes, copses of buttonwood, and gumbo limbo trees. Mottled lizards scuttled across the leaf-covered ground beneath our feet, and the last of the morning mosquitoes bombarded us with dogged persistence before fleeing into the leafy darkness of the jungle. The air was heavy with the sweet-sour smell of wild mango, salt, and decaying vegetation. I looked at Will and I could see the buccaneer's gleam in his eyes. Once again, we were doing what we loved. No one can ask for more on this journey of life. And then there was the girl…

Talia paused to wipe the sweat from her forehead with the back of her hand. The sun seeped through the boughs, brushing her with strokes of gold and amber, and once again, I was taken by the simple allure of this woman. Even in a khaki shirt and blue jeans, with her hair pulled back in a ponytail, there was a freshness about her, and a subtle sexuality that didn't rely on coyness or fragility. She was, however, a little on the independent side. She caught me looking at her and our eyes held for a moment.

"If your tongue starts to hang out and you begin to drool, I'm gonna be far less impressed," she said.

Benji smiled.

Will, just coming into the clearing, adjusting the chin strap on his canvas hat, looked up. "Did I miss something?"

"Nah, not at all," I answered with a smile.

The competition was limited to a half-mile-square area, the boundaries marked with red flags every 50 yards, but it was damned near like a circus with 300 people. There were hunters arguing with each other about terrain and finds, folks yelling when they hit one of the smaller finds, and judges dashing back and forth across the hillsides and the beach confirming hits. But no one had hit the big one yet.

Throughout the day, we dragged ourselves up and down the hillsides to the beaches, running our detectors across every conceivable likely location, but nothing produced. There were occasional, excited shouts from contestants here and there as they hit small caches. But still no one had hit the big find.

Near the end of the day, we were exhausted, sweat-soaked, and raked bloody by thorns and brambles, but we had yet to find anything with a golden sheen. The four of us were sitting on a large rock outcropping near the eastern boundary, trying to find a breeze, removed from the majority of the contestants, when Will excused himself for a call of nature. A few minutes later I heard my partner yell from a bluff just below and about 50 yards from us. There was something in his voice that caught my attention.

Roatán had experienced a tropical storm the week before that was just short of a hurricane. With it had come a good deal of rain, washing out roads and changing the topography here and there. Will was standing by a section of hillside that had been washed away. What had been a shallow cave perhaps hundreds of years ago had collapsed and opened up, spilling dirt and rocks down the hillside, and widening the sides and floor of the original cavern. It had probably been a fairly large cave, but centuries of erosion had added a foot or two of dirt to the floor. Water from storms past had eroded the soil above and weakened the root systems of the trees over it. This last storm had finally collapsed the remaining roof veined with roots, and flushed the soil from top and bottom out of the enlarged entrance. It was no longer a cavern, but a partially covered wash now.

Will stood there, holding something in his hand. He had wiped it off with a handkerchief and its chipped black surface reflected the sun. As we walked over, he held it out—an obsidian knife blade. The bone and leather handle had deteriorated, but the rock blade shone brightly.

"Lord, that's incredible," I muttered, just a little jealous that Will had made such an unusual find and become the center of attention, as everyone had to handle this unique antiquity. But after a few moments, I noticed how it caught Talia's attention in particular. I watched her face as she held it. Her eyes seemed to become distant and cloudy as she ran her fingers over the bright black stone. Finally, she stepped back, still holding the artifact in her hand. She exhaled, and her eyes cleared, but she still seemed puzzled.

"I did considerable research on this island," she said. "There is no obsidian in Roatán, at least none has ever been found to my knowledge." She brought up the blade, almost reverently. "This was imported from some other culture. Most likely Aztecs or Mayans, eh?"

I quickly glanced around. None of the other contest competitors were anywhere near us. Given the red boundary flags that I could see, it appeared we were just outside of the contest's parameters.

"Where there's one thing, there may be more..." said Will, taking the words from my mouth. "I think we need to get away from here, right now. Come back tomorrow, when everyone's gone..."

I nodded. "Real good suggestion. Who knows what's buried here. Could make this vacation really interesting. Let's get out of here, now."

As we reluctantly trudged away, Will muttered one of Crazy Eddie's expressions: "It's harder to leave an ancient find than it is a new lover."

"Amen," I grumbled.

Above us, a large hawk circled listlessly in the cumulus thermals. It cried out, then rolled a wing and fell away.

CHAPTER THREE

Pound for pound, nothing holds more omnipotence than gold. Nations have been bought with it, honesty and integrity have fallen to its luster, and far too often, truth has been smelted into a more desirable shape—all for the possession of this lustrous, malleable metal. Such is the power of the yellow shine…

—Stanley McShane

The treasure-hunting contest had been quite a success. Almost all the hidden prizes had been found, and a couple from Fort Meyers, Florida, had found the grand prize just a half hour before it all wrapped up. It mattered little to us. The real prize for us was the discovery of the cave and the obsidian spearhead, which was "floody bucking amazing," as Will put it. And then, of course, there was Talia, who was right near the top of the list when it came to prizes.

I was lying on my bed, and Will was in the bathroom, shaving. We were to meet Talia and Benji at the motel tiki bar on the beach at seven.

"I'll flip you for her," I said. "Winner take all. Then we wouldn't have to go through all this Bob Hope, Bing Crosby *Road to Zanzibar* thing, which inevitably ends up with one of us wiped out on Quaaludes and locked in a bathroom somewhere." I exhaled heavily. "I don't know why this always seems to happen to us. I can hardly remember us meeting two girls and everything going smoothly. It's always one…"

"There were two in Panama, Kansas," said Will, washing his razor. "But come to think of it, they did try to kill us."

I couldn't help but smile. "Maybe we're getting too far

ahead of ourselves. Who's to say she's even remotely interested in either one of us?" I sighed angrily. "This whole freaking thing would be a whole lot easier if we just ran into ugly girls. Then you could have them all. Truth is, it's distracting, perplexing."

Will offered that goofy smile of his. "I hate to see you perplexed. Why don't you just remove yourself from the competition, and I promise to tell you about it, huh?"

All doubts about giving up on our perpetual competition were swept away when we reached the tiki bar and found Talia standing in the sand on the beach, watching the sunset. She had on a loose-fitting, almost sheer floral shift that definitely outlined her finer qualities, along with leather sandals, and a beautiful yellow hibiscus perched behind her ear. With her dark-red hair framed in the final, glowing rays of the sun, she looked like an advertisement for a Caribbean rum.

Benji was sitting at the bar, appearing very much the tourist in his Dockers and his fruit-juicy shirt, already into his second screwdriver. The boy had a distinct passion for Russians when it came to alcohol.

It was a great evening. After dinner at a perfect little seafood restaurant, we found our way to a funky Caribbean bar that had nice music and a little floor show. The whole thing was marred only by the incessant competition with which Will and I were cursed. Toward the end of the evening I was beginning to slur my words, thanks to the Xanax Will slipped into my rum and Coke; and Will found himself struggling with an untimely case of "the runs." (Nothing like Ex-Lax to quell the ambitions of the most ardent admirer…)

Talia was no fool. Finally, after Will had just returned from the bathroom, again, she leaned forward, elbows on the table, and looked at us. "I hate to disappoint you two, but I'm not looking for a relationship, and I know a one-night stand with one of you would put a wrench in the works for all of us."

"How about a one-night stand with both of us?" asked Will. "I could live with that."

She shook her head. "I don't think so. Not my thing."

"Well, shit! That sure takes the fizz out of the Coke," I muttered.

"Who knows?" Talia continued. "We might be onto an important find. Let's be content with that, and not make this any more complicated than necessary, eh?"

"A simple, uncomplicated vacation, huh?" mumbled Will. Then he got up and made another run for the bathroom.

The sun had barely crested a pale-blue horizon as we parked the car behind a stand of mimosas, well off the road. No point in drawing attention—the treasure contest had been held on private property, and like it or not, what we were doing was illegal. My conscience might well have gotten the better of me had I known this was a serious find, but for nothing more than an old obsidian knife, I'd let the devil take the wheel.

As we arrived at the site, rocks, dirt, and roots lay spread across the wash. The last of the cave roof was split in several sections and collapsed. Ironically, nature, and the recent deluge that had come through, had done most of the work for us, having cleared the floor and entrance area. Before the storm, I doubt anyone would have looked at it and considered it anything but an anomaly of nature. After a quick perusal, we all took out our metal detectors, did a brief ground balance for best performance, and began working from the outside in.

There was little time for suspense. Not 10 minutes later Will's detector chimed. He ran the head of his machine over the spot several times to get a pinpoint, and by that time, we were all standing around him. Will pulled his "digger" from his belt and probed the damp ground. Almost immediately, he hit something hard, but it didn't feel like metal. (We'd been doing this long enough to develop a sense of what was metal and what wasn't.) Nonetheless, he was getting a nonferrous metal signal from the machine, and that was a good sign.

Benji brought over a military folding shovel and locked it open. While Will prodded, providing the target area, Benji began to dig carefully around it. It wasn't long before the top of a pottery jar appeared. The first, most significant thing was the emergence of its wide, cork cap, carefully bound with what appeared to be gold thread to protect the integrity of its contents. Apparently, a resin-like substance had been poured over the seal at the mouth, for preservation, but after all these years it had grown hard, cracked, and brittle.

In moments, with hearts hammering that familiar locomotive beat, we carefully began to dig around it, pulling the dirt away with our hands. Everyone was excited, all speaking at once. All but Talia, I noticed. There was an excitement and anticipation in her eyes, but there was something else. She possessed a profound, almost reverent countenance. Her eyes seemed lost to distant memory as she knelt and ran her hands through the dirt, and she alone reached down and lifted out the 18-inch-high, remarkably detailed pottery jar. I have no idea why, but I know the others felt it too. At that moment, we knew it had to be her.

"By the remarkable detail and the calligraphy, it's Central American, probably Mayan," I whispered.

"Whoa shit..." whispered Will, almost reverently.

My friend was reaching for the end of one of the gold binding threads when Talia stopped him.

"We can't open it here. The humidity or heat might adversely affect what's inside." Her eyes were still distant, and her breathing heavy. "We don't want to lose what they hid so long ago."

Will glanced at me and I read his eyes.

She said, "They hid"...

Benji whistled softly, reaching over and picking up his detector.

"He's right," said Will. "Let's get at it. There may be more."

In the next two hours, we found two more pottery jars, exactly the same as the first, all carefully sealed with gold caps and thread, and all within a few feet of the original find. But near where the mouth of the cavern must have been, we also found remnants of clay cooking utensils, obsidian arrowheads, and the deteriorated remains of wooden spear shafts. But the gods saved the best for last.

We were getting set to call it a day, when Talia took a deep breath and exhaled slowly. "There's got to be something else. I don't know why, but I just feel like we're missing something."

"I don't know about you, but I've had a pretty good day," said Will, as he was breaking down his detector.

"No..." she said quietly, almost to herself. "Something more..."

She flipped on her detector and slowly walked back into the cave. There was a flat rock in the very back, against the cave wall, large enough to have been used to place objects upon, perhaps. Her eyes were getting that distant gleam again. I don't mind telling you, it was just a little eerie. She started pushing on it, oblivious to us. Will, closest to her, rose and helped, and they slid the rock over about two feet. The rest of us were watching now, captured in some sort of mystical stage play. After they had moved it, Talia picked up her detector.

It didn't take but moments and her machine was chiming. We all moved in, around the two of them, and began clearing the dirt.

"It's a solid hit," muttered Will. "A couple feet long, at least."

"Careful with your digging," whispered Talia, her eyes still holding that strange gaze. "Don't damage it..."

Will looked at me and mouthed, "Don't damage it?"

At about a foot and a half down, Will's digger hit something, and at Talia's urging, we used our hands to remove the last of the dirt covering the elongated object. We were all on our knees now. At that point, the sun broke through the clouds above us. Its rays struck and held.

You could hear the mutual gasp, like the hiss of a punctured tire. Once again, Talia reached in and carefully lifted the object out, her eyes filled with exhilaration and awe.

"Mucking fagnificent..." whispered Will almost reverently, easing back on his haunches.

As Talia carefully wiped the dirt from the object with her handkerchief, it was as if the air had been sucked from our lungs. Whispers of lost history captured our fantasies as she reverently lifted out an incredible golden scepter, carved with exotic figures, inlaid with jade, and possessing a huge emerald mounted at one end. The sun embraced it, the emerald gleamed, free from the earth after so long, and our imaginations took wings.

"My God...it's beautiful," I muttered, thoroughly in awe.

Talia slowly nodded. She held it out to us, pointing to the golden knob at one end. "It bears the seal of Nachán Can, the last ruler of the Mayan city, Chetumal."

"And you know this how?" Will asked.

Talia shrugged. "I must have read it or seen the seal somewhere. I've done a good deal of research about the Mayan Empire."

"You're sure?" Will asked.

Her eyes suddenly changed again. There seemed to be a mystical certainty about them. “How does a moth know it’s springtime, after a long winter?” she whispered, staring at me. Talia exhaled, her gaze returning to the scepter, gradually coming around. “I’m sure I must have seen it somewhere…”

Fortune having been more than kind to us, we decided not to push our luck. It was time to go. Besides, we had worked the area around the cave fairly well. Once we knew more about what we’d found, we could always come back.

CHAPTER FOUR

There's no such thing as a bad treasure…
—Bobby D'Antonio

After having a chance to clean up, we met in Talia and Benji's room, and examined our finds more closely. We all realized there was some chance of damaging whatever was in the three heavy pottery jars, but we simply couldn't resist opening one.

Very carefully, Will and Benji gently pulled away what appeared to be ancient, hardened sap from around the mouth, then carefully worked the gold wire loose from the throat. Gradually, they pried back the weathered, deteriorated cork lid, then gently pulled it from the wide mouth. Talia stood beside them, watching every move, that strange look in her eyes again. When the lid had been removed, she peered inside.

"Papyrus of some sort, it looks like," she whispered. "Sheets of it, rolled up together." She paused, and her eyes went distant again. "No…it's bark that's been flattened and treated with lime," she said quietly.

Will just looked at me, eyebrows up. He shrugged. "Okay, if you say so…"

She turned to us questioningly, not quite sure what to do.

"Well, we've come this freaking far," said my partner with his usual laissez-faire attitude. "Be gentle, baby, but let's have a look."

Talia looked at us nervously, then slowly slipped her slim hand into the mouth of the jar, grasped the rolled papers bound with leather strips, and carefully pulled them out. She moved with a deliberate caution, carefully laying the bark paper on our little table. Benji pulled the knife from his hip and handed it to her, and she delicately slit the bonds that had bound those words for over 400 years.

With the meticulousness of a surgeon, she carefully separated each of the four brittle sheets, then took the first and spread it out on the table. "I'm barely a novice at Mayan writings," she said, staring at the calligraphy. "I'll be lucky to pick out a few words…"

Finally, after several minutes, the silence was broken by Benji, who whistled and signed impatiently.

"I'm with him," muttered Will. "What the hell's this all about? Are you getting anything?"

Talia sighed. "I don't really know. I'm picking up the same pronouns in several places, and I'm seeing references to Chetumal several times also. There is a symbol for sickness and a symbol for the sea used, as well." She looked up, obviously frustrated. "There is no way I can decipher this. I just don't have the knowledge. But if I were to make a guess, I would say it is an accounting. A story of some sort."

I sighed, somewhat let down. "So, where do we go from here?"

Talia tapped her fingers on the table. "We need someone who has a handle on ancient Mayan."

"Oh, great," muttered Will. "Wait, I'll just get the phone book and look under 'Mayan calligraphy translators.'" But he caught himself and turned to me. "Hold on, Tonto. We might just know the guy for the job." He snapped his fingers. "Hell yes, our old buddy, Dr. Benton Larner of the University of Miami. The son of a bitch specializes in Central American history and languages!"

Damn! I couldn't believe it. He was right. Larner was the dead opposite of the archetypical older professor with a pipe. He was a selfish, chain-smoking, egotistical prick with a secret penchant for cocaine and hookers, but damned if his specialty wasn't historical Latin American languages. He wasn't inclined to go out of his way for anyone, but we had inadvertently saved his bacon one night in Key West—an affair involving a bag of white powder and a Haitian hooker. We weren't actually in the habit of saving people from themselves, we just happened to be in the right place at the right time, and he owed us.

An hour later, we had carefully returned the writings to the jar, and I had Professor Larner on the phone. When I explained the circumstances of the find, he huffed angrily. "And what makes you think any of this is legitimate? If you had any idea how many times I've gotten calls from idiots who think they've discovered the rest of the Dead Sea Scrolls—"

"First off, we're not your average idiots," I replied, cutting him off. "And secondly, we have an archaeologist with us who has been able to decipher enough of this to verify it's some sort of retrospection of an historical experience."

"Christ!" muttered Larner. "And I'm supposed to drop everything, the lectures I've got scheduled, and dash out to some rat's ass little island—"

"Roatán, off the coast of Honduras," I said, starting to get pissed. "Listen, if you don't want to have first look at this, I'm betting I can find someone who does."

There was a moment of pensive silence.

"Okay, okay. I'll fly out tomorrow," Larner gritted. "I'll call you back when I've got the flight schedule. Book me a room. A *good* room."

"I'm assuming you mean one without cockroaches," I said, jerking his chain. "They're hard to find. You wouldn't think there would be so many cockroaches, with all the rats to eat them…" I smiled and hung up just as Larner began to sputter.

That evening revolved around wild speculation and a terrific seafood dinner at a little place just outside of town. As delicious as the food was, the speculation was even more entertaining. Talia had been drawn back to the scroll she had opened, explaining she was almost certain it was a recollection, a story, as there were names that kept coming up—Itzel, Ata Aalam; Chetumal, one of the capital cities of the Mayans; and Nachán Can, without question one of the kings of Chetumal.

"It might well be one of the most significant firsthand accounts of life with the Mayans discovered in modern times," she said. "For God's sake, we found a golden scepter with it! A king's scepter!"

"You gotta admit, that sure as hell supports her argument," said Will.

The following morning we located a print shop and had copies made of every page, just to be on the safe side. We hid those under the rear seat of our rental car. That afternoon Dr. Larner arrived at the airport. He had rented a bungalow less than a mile from us, but he drove directly to our motel.

We were all waiting in Talia and Benji's room. I had given Larner the number. There was a knock at the door and Will opened it.

The professor was a tall, lanky man with prematurely graying hair, arrogant blue eyes, bushy eyebrows, and a wide mouth that turned at the edges, as if the taste of life had disappointed him slightly. He seemed older than I remembered—perhaps his early 50s—but there was hawkishness to his personality, hard and unyielding, demanding, and truly pleased with very little.

We invited him in, and as soon as introductions were completed, he settled into a chair at the small dining table and pulled out his reading glasses.

"All right, let's get to it," he said. "The sooner you

show me this magnificent find of yours, the sooner I can be impressed."

The rest of us found seats in the adjoining living room as Talia brought out the suitcase in which we had transported the clay containers. She took out the one we had already opened, and passed it to him. Larner accepted it respectfully with two hands, studied the outside for a few moments, nodding with some reluctant approval, then carefully removed the deteriorating cork plug and took out the four sheets of bark paper it contained. He looked around at us.

"You may as well make yourselves comfortable," he said. "If there's anything to this, we're going to be here a while."

I watched the man as he perched his reading glasses on the bridge of his nose and slowly, meticulously, began reading the four sheets. Gradually his face morphed from a casual interest to being reluctantly captured. He tried to hide it, but he failed. Twenty minutes later, he finally looked up.

"You have my attention," he said grudgingly. "Give me the next."

In the next 20 minutes, he didn't even look up, but there were moments when his eyes inadvertently lit up, then he seemed to catch himself. When he had finished those pages, he was reaching for the last four before Talia could hand them to him. It was in the early part of those last four pages that he inadvertently sucked in a breath, and I saw his eyes change. He tried to conceal, it but there was something that really grabbed him by the short hairs. I glanced at my partner. Will didn't move, but his eyes said he'd caught it as well.

When the professor was finished, he lit a cigarette and blew a pall of smoke at the ceiling. He looked around at us, then began to speak. "Well, I can't say it isn't interesting from the aspect of describing Mayan life. But it doesn't provide any new revelations. This recollection was apparently written by a Mayan woman as some sort of description of her later years. Her name was Itzel and her husband was a soldier for Nachán Can, the ruler of Chetumal." Larner took a breath, and continued. "She and her husband evidently left Chetumal because of a plague-like scourge of some sort. They sailed to Roatán, somehow, and settled here. While it obviously possesses some insight, it unfortunately doesn't describe anything that historians don't already know."

He glanced around at us again, and offered a shrug of indifference.

"It has some value in terms of antiquity, though, and I recognize that." He paused. "If it can be authenticated.... You wouldn't consider letting me make copies of these, would you? So I might study it for the historical aspects, and perhaps even find you a buyer?"

"You're right, we wouldn't consider it," said Talia. She'd picked up on this guy as well.

The room fell silent.

Talia exhaled hard, coming to a decision. "There's one other thing we found..."

Larner's eyebrows rose slightly. "One other thing?"

"You sure about this?" I said to Talia, and she understood completely, but we needed as much information as we could get, especially now.

Talia excused herself, went to the bedroom, and returned with the scepter wrapped in a pillowcase. She gently took it out and I heard Larner inhale sharply.

"This was with the writings," she said, as she handed it to him.

He took it as if it was his firstborn, running his hands gently over the golden, jade-inlaid shaft, and almost caressing the huge emerald at the end. The man was actually breathing heavily. After a moment he said, "Obviously, this changes things. It bears the symbol of Nachán Can, and of course, lends some credence to your little tale."

"We know," said Talia.

"Well," said Larner. "I suppose I might be willing to purchase these items from you. For my collection..."

"You'll be the first one we'll call if we decide to do that," I replied, and the congeniality fell away from Larner's eyes.

"Well, sorry that we dragged you all this way for nothing," said Talia.

Larner waved her off. "Not to worry. I probably needed a few days away from the rat race. I'll relax a day or two, then return. Besides, I can write it all off. Research..." He paused once more, his eyes slipping back again to the scepter in Talia's hands. "You're sure you wouldn't like to—"

"We're sure," I said.

On that note, the professor rose and we gathered our papers, securing them once again in their containers. Talia put the scepter away, and without much more than an additional apology, we bade the professor goodbye.

As soon as Doctor Larner reached our motel lobby, he placed a call to a phone booth across the street, where a fellow who had come in on the same flight as he, was waiting. "Ironically enough, there might be something to this one," he said. "But they're not cooperative people. So we do it your way."

CHAPTER FIVE

Never underestimate the power of pain. It has no conscience...

—Attila the Hun

Actually, Dr. Larner's summarization of our find didn't discourage us at all. There was something about the man that was slippery. Beyond his intellectual façade, I got the feeling he could have fit well as a barker in a carnival.

"He was just too anxious to leave after reading the papers," I muttered as we sat in Talia and Benji's second-floor room. "And when he saw the scepter, I thought his tongue was gonna fall out of his mouth like Wile E. Coyote's."

Benji signed and Talia chuckled. "Benji says the guy's a toad. The whole time the professor was here, he wanted to step on him."

"There was something in those documents that caught our boy's attention," said Will. "Somewhere near the middle of the last four pages."

"You're absolutely right," chimed Talia. She took the third container and opened it carefully. "I have a rudimentary knowledge of Mayan words. You don't major in ancient civilizations and not come away with some understanding. Let's have a look at that section and see if there's a word or two that comes up consistently."

As she carefully laid the bark papers out on the table, I saw her eyes change again—shadowy and distant, almost reminiscent. Talia turned to the third page and began running her finger along the calligraphy. A few minutes later she muttered, "Hmmm," and a moment or two later she did it again, then sighed. As she moved along, her eyes lit again. Finally, Talia set the papers aside and looked up at all of us.

"I've got an inkling of why our professor buddy got the sparkly eyeballs when he reached the third page," she said. "I don't know much for sure, but on those last two pages, the word 'gold' comes up three times, and the Mayan word for 'hoard' or 'cache' comes up twice. Also, 'Nachán Can' is there a couple of times. And the name Chur." She took a breath, her eyes clearing some. "I'm not certain, but I think there is a river in the Guatemalan jungle, well over 60 miles to the west of the original city of Chetumal, with a similar name. We need to check the Mayan name." She eased out a breath, her dark eyes shining. "Not the Chetumal in the Yucatan—that came later—but the original Mayan city of Chetumal, which was located where the city of Santa Rita is now located in Belize." Talia shrugged. "Not too much left there of any archaeological value. Some ruins for tourists to ogle." Again, she gazed around at her friends. "It would be interesting if there was a river there, to the west."

"But now, what we need most of all is someone to tell us what the rest of that document says," said Will. "There's a key in there somewhere..."

Benji whistled softly and signed to Talia. She smiled. "He says, 'man does not live by conjecture alone. Food is also necessary, and sometimes liquor.' It's time for dinner."

Still chuckling, Talia stored the suitcase under the bed in her room, and we all headed out to a seafood restaurant across the street.

About a hundred yards away, a man leaned against a palm tree by the resort parking lot, watching. He smiled.

After a relatively quick dinner of coconut shrimp and sweet potatoes (our excitement outweighing our appetites), we headed back to the motel, determined to track down a lead in Belize that could decipher the information we lacked. We were just starting across the street when we saw a man coming out of Talia's room, carrying our suitcase.

He glanced at us just about the time we saw him, and he bolted for the stairs. As the thief turned the corner to the stairway, he ran smack into a guy coming up—a big guy, longish dark hair, tanned, in blue jeans, a Van Halen T-shirt, and canvas jungle boots. The vandal, thinking the man was trying to stop him, didn't hesitate. He took a swing, catching the man solidly on the temple and dropping him to his knees. It was a punch that would have taken out most guys. The fellow with our suitcase started to vault over his opponent, but the downed stranger grabbed him by his pant's leg and jerked. The thief tumbled to the cement stairway, dropping the suitcase. He quickly managed to make it to his knees, but before he could regain his balance, the big guy rose and hammered him with a vicious roundhouse, catching the thief on his jaw, practically lifting him off his feet. That was the end of the fight.

The thief was still out cold when we reached them.

The large fellow pushed our suitcase over to us. "I'm assuming this is yours. You want me to call the police?" he asked with a Central American accent, hardly fluxed by the whole thing.

Talia glanced at Will and me. "No," I said. "We've got issues here. One of them being nobody steals from us."

The guy took a moment to look us over, then shrugged. "Your business, not mine."

While Will and I grabbed the thief and quickly dragged him into our room, Talia looked at the stranger. No, actually, she was staring at him...*strangely*. "I guess we owe you a thanks for stopping this guy. You took quite a shot."

"Yeah," he said, rubbing the side of his head gingerly. The fellow held out his hand. "Santino Roso. My friends call me Santi."

She took his hand without taking her eyes from his.

Warm. His hand was warm and calloused. *Not a paper-pusher*, she thought. "Talia," she said.

There was an awkward pause. "You're visiting here, I assume," Santino said hesitantly, obviously trying to preserve the conversation.

"Yes. Me, my brother, and a couple of friends. We came here for the recent treasure-hunting contest out at Old Port Royal."

"Ahh, yes, I know about this," the fellow replied, holding up a finger. "Did you find anything in the contest?"

Talia pursed her lips. "Sort of…" (God, she liked his voice. It was charming and strong—like a familiar sound coming from shadows.)

At that point, I returned, and damned if it wasn't obvious that I was interrupting something.

"You're going to have to forgive me," she said awkwardly to her new acquaintance. "It's as my friend said, we have issues." She paused, trying to find a way to explain, not exactly wanting this stranger to go away. "Not of our making, but unfortunately, it's something we have to resolve."

Santino put up his hand, palm out. "No problem. As I said before, it's not my business." (Damn, he didn't want her to go away. It was the strangest thing…)

There was another of those pregnant pauses. I felt like a prop in a movie scene.

"Well, perhaps I'll see you again," he said finally. He smiled disarmingly and brought up his hands, speaking with them as Latinos do. "Maybe after you have resolved your difficulties..."

"Maybe," Talia said.

With that he nodded, then turned and walked down the stairs. We headed for our room.

The burglar was conscious, but Will and Benji had bound his hands and legs with some cords from my jungle bag, and thrown him on the bed. He started to yell, muffled as he was. Benji stepped over and slapped his face hard enough to make his ears ring.

Talia stepped up to the bed and looked down on the man. "We want some answers about several things. I'm going to take the gag off now. Whether you see the sun tomorrow depends on what you say."

When she had removed the gag, the man glared at us and spoke with a sneer. "I'm not going to tell you shit. A bunch of bush-league amateurs trying to play in the big boys' leagues."

I was about to speak when Benji signed to Talia and Will. "Benji says he wants a long hairpin from my bag," Talia said. "And we're to gag him tight, then you two will go in the other room for a few minutes. I will stay with Benji...to ask questions…"

We could hear the man screaming through the gag, then periods of quiet conversation, then more screaming. I turned on the television. Fifteen minutes later, Benji and Talia came out with some notes they'd made while questioning our friend. Talia explained the details to us. The man was still whimpering in the bedroom.

"Larner told the fellow that the third page contained passages where the woman explained that her husband was a *nacom* for the Mayan king, Nachán Can," Talia said. "There apparently was an outbreak of plague—probably smallpox after an encounter with the Spanish—and the king wanted to secure a little of his wealth in a secret place away from the city. He took her husband with him, and some slaves to carry the treasure. Apparently, there were no exact details of where the cache was hidden, but there was supposedly a series of white limestone walls on the Chur River, and it was there that the treasure was cached. It sounds like the king had built a secret quarters—sort of a man cave—inside the limestone, and that's where they hid the gold and jewels they were carrying."

"Benji got that guy to tell him all this?" I said. "Do you think it's true?"

She smiled. It wasn't pretty. "There's a lot more to Benji than meets the eye. Aside from being proficient in a variety of martial arts, he worked in Mossad's interrogations community for a while. He knows how to hurt you in ways you can't imagine. Trust me, the guy told the truth."

Will shoved a thumb toward the guy in the bedroom. "So, what do we do with him now?"

"There's a small freighter in port right now at Coxen Hole," I said. "From Venezuela. I saw it when we came in. It's a long shot, but the truth is, freight companies never pay captains enough. I've met very few independent captains who weren't interested in an extra dollar. Give Will and me an hour."

As it was, I was dead on, and our timing couldn't have been better. Two hours later, our battered thief, bound like a turkey for market and locked in a large shipping crate with a couple bottles of water, was on his way out of town. I had given the captain a story about the man trying to rape my daughter, and being a married man with children, he suddenly became quite cooperative. The *Zuela Queen* was just weighing anchor, bound for Caracas. The captain said he might let the fellow have some "air time" once they were well out to sea, depending on what kind of mood he was in.

Now we had the key. We knew there was a Mayan treasure at stake here. But our buddy, Dr. Larner, knew it too.

"None of this means that the treasure is still there," said Talia, trying to calm us down. "Four hundred years is a long time. And then there's that bastard Larner…"

"You're right," said Will sarcastically. "Let's just go home and forget about it. I've got knitting I'm behind on."

Talia shot him one of those "if looks could kill" stares.

"The good news is, we have almost all the equipment we need with us, thanks to the treasure-hunting contest," I said. "But we'll need some supplies and equipment when we get to Belize. I've been looking at our maps. We would probably have to come into Belize City, then travel south to Santa Rita, the town built over the ruins of the actual Mayan city of Chetumal. At that point, everything else is a guess. It appears we would have to go west, into Guatemala, into a State reserve area called Reserva de Biosfera Maya, but like I said, it's still a guess. However, it seems that there definitely is a river that runs west, once you get into Guatemala. El Chuj."

"That's pretty damned close to 'Chur,'" Will muttered excitedly.

I grinned. "Yeah, it is. But if we are to pull this off, we're going to need a guide."

"That adds another person to the pie," said Talia.

"Nobody goes into jungles in the middle of nowhere without having someone who knows where the hell they are and what to expect," Will said. "I'd rather share the rewards than have someone sharing my entrails and beating my bones on a hollow log."

"Well, that's certainly graphic," said Talia sarcastically. "But I guess we'll worry about that when we get to Belize. Which might as well be tomorrow. Let's not forget that Larner knows everything we know, and probably more. If we're going to beat him to the white limestone cliffs of the Chuj River, we have to move."

"Just a simple, uncomplicated vacation," muttered Will.

Benji signed again, and Will translated. "He says all this talk about how rich we're going to be and whose going to eat us has made him thirsty, and it's almost five o'clock somewhere."

I couldn't help but smile. The more time I spent around

Benji the more I liked him and the more I respected him. "The man's got a point," I said. "We can just as easily plan our new adventure at the tiki bar."

No sooner had we settled into a table at the edge of the bar, with our railing facing the beach, than Santino, the fellow that had taken out the thief, came strolling in. He still had on his blue jeans and jungle boots, but he had exchanged his Van Halen T-shirt for a white, Cuban-style Guayabera. With his long hair and dark eyes, the guy looked like something out of a freaking commercial. Talia had already zeroed in on him. She waved casually and he headed our way.

Santino paused in front of the table and smiled. "Well, I see you no longer have your sticky-fingered companion. I hope he is not floating somewhere now."

"No, he's not," Will said. "But that would have been my first choice."

"Would you like to join us?" said Talia. "If you stick around for a drink or two, maybe the alcohol will loosen our tongues and we'll tell you where we buried him."

Santino started for a second, then he saw the gleam of humor in Talia's eyes and relaxed. "Sure, why not," he said, pulling up a chair next to the wooden railing of the bar, and next to Talia.

Cocky son of a bitch, I thought.

Will shot me a glance that said he totally agreed.

After a round of drinks had arrived, Talia asked, "So, are you from this area?"

Santino shook his head, setting down his glass. "No, actually, I'm here on a work-related project. I'm from Belize."

Talia tilted her head slightly, her eyes still holding him. "So, what do you do that takes you to exotic places like Roatán?"

"I work for the government of Belize, in wildlife

management. My degree is in ornithology—the study of birds," he replied. "I am here on loan from Belize." He took a sip of his drink. "There has been a disease that has infested the hatcheries of herons on this island—a mite that attacks newborns and fledglings. Sadly, it is nearly 50 percent fatal. I was sent to try to determine and repair the situation, if possible. It has been a challenging affair, but we have defined it, and the Roatán Game and Fish people will begin dusting the rookeries this week with a formula that kills the mites." He shrugged. "Unfortunately, I will be leaving directly. My agency is sending a plane over for our crew. We fly out tomorrow."

"Too bad," said Talia, but something in her eyes offered a double entendre. "This is certainly a wonderful place."

"It is indeed," said Santino, but as he spoke, I saw him scanning the horizon, behind Talia, looking out toward the beach.

Hmmm, maybe he has a girlfriend… I thought. *Someone he picked up to keep him company on the island. Wouldn't surprise me.*

He turned to us. "Excuse me, but I'm looking for a friend who should have arrived by now, although she doesn't actually take orders all that well sometimes."

Ahh, enter the girlfriend. Most guys like this one are never far from a pair of shapely legs…

Just then, the absolute strangest of things happened. He stood and whistled shrilly out toward the ocean. I was about to comment on his unique method of training girlfriends, when a huge hawk of some sort came soaring out of the sky with a screech, flaring its wings and landing on the railing behind him. It screeched again and threw out its wings once more for balance, its fierce eyes riveting us. I have to tell you, it was a startling damned thing, having a wild creature that large—and dangerous—just plop down next to you. The hawk folded its wings, shook once like a dog, and settled not a foot from Santino's shoulder.

"Whoa shit!" blurted Will, inadvertently sliding his chair back.

I have to admit I pretty much did the same. Talia, on the other side of the table, was equally startled.

The hawk had a deep golden color at the base of its distinctively hooked bill, with thick, swept-back black feathers, and yellow legs, but its eyes were remarkable—a rich amber iris surrounding an intelligent but conscienceless, midnight-colored pupil. It called out again—a raspy caw, but not necessarily aggressive.

Santino immediately slid over and stroked the bird with the backs of his fingers. "Ahh, Pixan, always the one for an entrance."

"Jesus!" I muttered. "You know him?"

"Her," said Santino. "And yes, we have been friends for a long time. We have been together since I found her, freshly fallen from her nest, down-covered and squawking, not even a fledgling yet. There was no way to put the bird back in the nest. The mother wouldn't have accepted her with the lingering scent of a human on her feathers." He smiled. "So I became Pixan's mother. That was two years ago. I will tell you, I have rarely seen a creature so intelligent. She's like a dog with wings. Because I raised her practically from the cracking of her egg, there was simply no need to go through the laborious food/command training process. She was mine from the beginning. I do, however, have to have a leather gauntlet for my forearm." He pulled the 10-inch, worn leather band from his back pocket and slipped it on his forearm, tightening the strings. "With her size, the talons are nearly strong enough to crush bone."

It was an amazing thing, for sure, but of the four of us, it was Talia who was the most taken. "Pixan," she said, still staring at the bird. "What an unusual name."

"It means 'spirit' in ancient Mayan."

"She came with you? I mean, you brought her to Roatán with you?"

Santino nodded. "I 'hood' her when we travel, and remove the hood when we get where we're going. Other than that, she is relatively independent. We don't have the normal bird/human relationship. I was practically the first creature she saw and she identifies with me as family. There is no need for the standard anklets and jesses—the leather straps to control or contain her. She lives her own life. She simply chooses to be with me. She does what she pleases in the daytime and comes home to me at night. Of course, the fact that I feed her, and we hunt together, helps with the bond."

"That's absolutely amazing," whispered Will. "Floody bucking incredible…"

Talia was just sitting there, strangely quiet, staring at the hawk like a lost child. She blinked a couple of times. "That's remarkable," she said quietly. Her eyes cleared and she asked, "What kind of hawk is it?"

"She's a Great Black Hawk," said Santino. "Known for their strength and intelligence. Like most women," he said with a smile. "Eh?"

As we sat and drank, we talked, learning about each other. I must admit, regrettably, that the majority of the conversation was between Talia and Santino. He was a native of Belize, born and raised in a small town called San Ignacio, in the western part of the country. He had come to know that area of western Belize and eastern Guatemala well. His father was a Mayan Guatemalan, and was killed in the civil war that had been raging there for years. It was one of the reasons Santino was stationed as one of the few Belize rangers in the Mayan Biosphere Reserve—a huge, remote area of surrounding jungles. He often coordinated with the Guatemalan government while living in the small town of Melchor de Mencos, on the border of Guatemala and Belize. He explained that it was somewhat of a lonely job, but he loved the jungle and the mountains around it, and he escaped to Belize City every couple weeks to let off some steam.

As he talked, explaining where he was stationed, the hair on the back of my neck stood up. I glanced over at my companions, and the coincidence had not eluded them, either. *The son of a bitch was a ranger for the very area we had to go into!*

CHAPTER SIX

If you're not lost occasionally, you're not much of an explorer…

—John Perry Barlow

"The jungles of that area, although known for their dangers—poachers, bandits, and more than one dangerous creature—seem more like home to me than the city," Santino explained. "I grew up in them. I love the smell of the jungle after a rain, the steam rising off the floor, and the taste of the air. The calls of the animals and birds are exotic. It's like a dangerous paradise. I suppose I know the Reserva de Biosfera Maya as well as anyone." He smiled, almost reminiscent. "It is like a woman—beautiful at times, dark and moody at others, always intriguing and always slightly perilous. And you never really know what to expect next."

Talia chuckled. "I should probably take offense, but that's actually pretty accurate."

"This is like in the freakin' movies, Kansas," Will whispered to me. "This just doesn't happen in real life. This guy knows, works in, the very area we have to go into. I can't freakin' believe it! I'm beginning to feel like a marionette—like there's somebody above me working the strings."

"Could be there is, my friend," I said quietly, while Talia talked with Santino. "Could be. Have you forgotten how many times the Big Guy upstairs has pulled strings for you and me? There's no bloody reason in this world why we should even be here, but we are." I exhaled hard. "Let me tell you something. Three-quarters of the people in the world would listen to this conversation and say it's bullshit—that things like this just don't happen. But one-quarter—the incredibly lucky, the right-timers who stepped out of foxholes still alive when the bullets quit flying and the blood had been spent; the ones who crashed airplanes and walked away without a bruise; the sailors who fought the best Mother Ocean could throw at them and still lived to lift a Red Stripe at the next palm-fronded bar...those who are either blessed or cursed with a reason for being here—they would listen to this and smile. Because they know that there's somebody above all this madness that pulls the damn strings. Don't be so negative, my friend, and just be freaking glad He's pulling ours today!"

Will drew back slightly. "Man, that's a mouthful, but I'll be damned if you don't have a point. This freakin' world is like a chessboard for the gods." He grinned. "You're saying the same thing that Rufus, our old Jamaican buddy, says: 'May your life egg break cleanly and the Great Tortoise grant you a moonlit path to the sea…'"

And we both laughed at the graciousness of what we called *luck*.

I looked a Benji and Talia, who had already picked up on the remarkable coincidence as well, then turned to Santino. "Would you excuse us for a moment? I need to have a word with my friends."

"No problem. I need a refill anyway," our new friend said, holding up his glass.

As Santino ambled over to the bar, I turned to the gang. "There's not a stupid one among us here. You all realize what we've just had dumped in our laps. Here's a guy who knows, and knows well, the area we're talking about going into. You've got to realize what an asset he would be. He could certainly help us find the river we're looking for. Hell, my guess is he'll know exactly where it is. He may even know where the limestone cliffs are located. And he appears capable, to say the least." I took a breath. "The downside is, it's another slice of the pie, and if he turns out to be a 'goody two shoes' he may tell the authorities—"

Benji interrupted me with a sign or two. Talia interpreted.

"Benji says, 'If you don't find anything, you get no pie anyway. Some pie is better than none, eh?'" She paused. "And I agree with him, and you. This guy could be a huge help. I mean, what a thing to have happen, to have this fellow fall into our laps the day before we leave. It's almost spooky. I say we take a chance and tell him what we're up to."

I looked around. Everyone nodded.

"Okay, let's talk with him."

The truth was, it was a short talk. There was no question that Santino was a man of character, but he was also a man who put in hard, long, sometimes dangerous hours, and whose monthly salary was the equivalent of a night desk person at an American Motel 6. He truly wanted to help his country, to make it better and stronger, but he realized he could probably do that better as a rich man.

After he had heard our pitch, there was silence for a moment. He ran his finger around the top of his glass, and it made that little squeaky sound. His hawk shifted restlessly and chirped. Santino laid a couple fingers across the bird's back, then slowly turned to us. "You are obviously not new to adventure, but you are new to Belize and Guatemala. There is one last thing you should know. Guatemala is embroiled in a civil war that has been going on for 25 years. It ebbs and flows at its own discretion. There are times when it seems like any other Central American country, but it's not." He sighed angrily, caught in a moment of passion. "The people of Guatemala, especially the true Guatemalans—the Indians who carry a proud Mayan history—have had their land taken, usurped by interlopers. So now, they fight to have at least some of it returned.

There are times when there is blood in the streets."

I glanced at Will.

"Terrific," he muttered.

Santino continued. "Guatemala, or I should say, the Guatemalan authorities, are not as kind as those from Belize. Belize has a huge tourist trade. If Belize authorities begin 'roughing up,' as you say, tourists, they would go out of business in a year. But Guatemala is a poor country that is, in truth, envious of Belize and its beautiful tourist-oriented coastline. They have many social difficulties, including the most dangerous prison system in the Southern Hemisphere. They are not above trumping up charges on foreigners to allow for bribes to free them. The problem is, few Americans can survive the horrors of a Guatemalan prison for very long."

"Now that part nobody told me," said Will, holding up a forefinger. "I would have remembered."

"Just bear this in mind as you travel into Guatemala," Santino said. Then he relaxed. "The good news is, once you get through the checkpoint at the Belize/Guatemalan border, you should be fine. Where you're going, even the mean Guatemalans don't like."

Santino was talking about "you" not "we." It looked like we'd called this wrong, that we were really screwed, when he took a deep breath, and released it slowly, then looked at us and smiled. "Okay then, I have made my little speech. So when do we leave, eh?"

Fortunately, Santino's department owed him a week's vacation time. He could probably stretch that to 10 days. If we hadn't found anything by that time, we were probably screwed anyway.

The following morning, I took Talia and her brother to the local bank and we purchased a safe deposit box, where we left the scepter. There was no point dragging that with us through Central American Customs. An artifact like that would set off bells the moment someone saw it. Then we all gathered at the Coxen Hole Airport and loaded our bags in the nose compartment and the rear of the plane. Santino gently slipped a soft leather hood over Pixan's head and set her on a perch in the back seat by him. Will took the left seat up front and I took the co-pilot's slot. Talia and Benji had the middle seats. After a few moments with the tower for wind direction and runway, we were skipping down the strip, then leaping out over that colorful medley of gin clear, blue-green waters and staggered orange reefs. We were off on a new adventure.

I felt like one of the age-old buccaneers who had coursed that coastline 300 years before, off on another sail for brown-eyed girls, yella gold, and the pure damned excitement of it all.

It was just a little over an hour's flight to the main airport in Belize City. After landing, we taxied over to the Flight Based Operation, and they directed us to a tie-down on the tarmac. We cleared Customs without a hitch. The Customs people knew Santino well, so there was no problem with his hawk. We rented a heavy-duty Toyota Land Cruiser at the FBO as well, offloaded our gear into it, and no more than a half hour after touching down, we were on our way along St. Thomas Street. We made a right on Northern Highway and found a little hotel that Santino had recommended. We took four rooms; one for Santino, one each for Talia and Benji, and Will and I shared a double room.

My buddy and I shared a pint of tequila and discussed plans for this upcoming gamble of ours. But it had been an exhausting day, and before long, Will bid me goodnight and crawled into his bed. I was tired, but not ready for sleep, so I decided to step out and visit with the moon in the courtyard of the hotel.

Benji had finally wound down from the previous day's activities. He didn't like hurting people. It wasn't part of his nature, but like many a good soldier, he had to accept and understand the occasional necessity of violence. He had known more than one man who had become lost in the demarcation zone between sadism and duty. He was tired, and after a quick shower, he hit the sack. He was asleep before Talia had finished her shower.

Talia, however, was still hyped from the day. So much was taking place so quickly—a new course to an ancient treasure, the excitement of new intrigue and the possible danger, and that man—unassuming, apparently good-natured, and handsome. But there was more. There was a strange connection that was totally unexplainable. It wasn't just the looks. Hell, she'd had her share of handsome men. It was something else. His voice...his damned voice was so...*familiar*, and every time she got close to him, she wanted to take his hand. It wasn't that animal magnetism that she'd stumbled across once or twice; it was more as though she felt at home. Safe. Damn, it was like some sappy romance book—stupid as hell, and she sure didn't need that right now.

She wasn't really tired at the moment, so Talia slipped on a pair of shorts and a light blouse, and quietly crept out of the room to commune with the starlit night for a while.

Santino had caught a rat in an alleyway behind the hotel and had fed his hawk. After a shower, he lay on his bed—no shirt or shoes, just his pants—staring at the ceiling. He couldn't get her out of his head. His life was going well now. He was doing what he loved, exactly what he dreamed of, and soon, if he desired, he would be rising in the ranks of the Ministry of the Interior, which was good on a number of levels. It wasn't that he didn't need a woman now and then, but he wanted those that came with no attachment right now. He had a couple that always smiled when he turned up at their doors. But mostly he wanted to be part of the "new Belize," a modern country taking its place in the world, yet he saw the need to preserve its animals and its wilderness. Santino had seen too many countries become tar pits—stripped of their natural resources so a small handful of unconscionable people could become wealthy. He knew that to fight this, he had to rise to a position of power in the Ministry.

But suddenly, this woman shows up. And from the moment he saw her, he wanted to say, "So good to see you again!" Those eyes, that smile, and that voice—so familiar. *Dios!* He needed to be strong. Women were easy to find, but he might only get one chance in this life to become something important—not just for Belize, but for himself and his birth country, Guatemala. Only one chance. He would be strong.

Santino stretched out on his bed and read for a while—a nature magazine he'd picked up in the FBO at the airport, when suddenly there was a knock on his door. He had called the front desk, as there were no towels in his room. He got up, walked over, and opened the door.

There stood Talia, holding his towels. "The concierge was just about to knock," she said with a smile. "I told him I'd take care of it for him."

They stood staring at each other, captured in the moonlight like pale Greek statues. Santino didn't say a word. He simply stepped in and grabbed her around the waist, drawing her into him and kissing her gently, the passion of the kiss taking on a life of its own. The towels fell to the ground as Talia wrapped her arms around him and pulled him to her, and they stumbled backwards into the room. Santino kicked the door closed and drew her to the bed.

"Son of a bitch..." I whispered harshly from the

shadows of the patio. “Son of a bitch!”

When I told Will the next morning, he blurted a string of expletives that would have made a Tijuana whore blush. “You know, Kansas,” he said bitterly, “this is a hell of a lot like our last trip to this area—Mexico, if you remember—when Cody ended up with the beautiful Max Delane.”

“Yeah,” I muttered bitterly. “Way too much like it.”

Will shrugged, then sighed. “Well, we’ve still got the opportunity of a great treasure hunt, and as Crazy Eddie would say, ‘some far-out barroom tales.’”

I grinned. “When it’s all said and done, the person with the most stories wins.”

The following morning, Santino explained that he would have to meet with the Ministry of the Interior for permission to take a leave of absence. “It shouldn’t be a problem,” he said. “But it is still necessary. I should have it taken care of in a couple of hours.”

You didn’t have to be paying serious attention to notice the change in Talia and Santino. It was sort of a magical transition in the eyes and the attitude. It’s like everything was “okay.” Something that would have made a soul disgruntled yesterday is “okay” today. The air smells better, the sun is kinder, colors are brighter, and you’re just a more tolerant human being. That pretty much described Talia and “Santi” now. (To Will and me, he was still Santino. He wasn’t ever going to be “Santi.”) They were politely doing their best to muffle it, but it was hard to miss the little touches and that effervescence in their eyes.

I hated them.

No, I didn’t hate them, but I sure as hell wasn’t happy.

Will was standing next to me as Talia and Santi crawled into a taxi, headed for the Belize Ministry of the Interior. Talia had just suddenly decided she’d like to see the

Ministry.

Yeah, right...

My partner, rarely a gracious loser, issued a bitter expletive under his breath as we waved at them.

"Why do all the dark-eyed handsome guys get the girls?" I muttered.

"Because they're dark-haired handsome guys, asshole," Will hissed.

By midafternoon Santino and Talia had returned from the Ministry. Santino's department was evidently pleased with his work in Roatán, and they gave him the 10 days' leave he wanted. We headed to a store that Santino used for his outings and bought tents, lanterns, a portable gas stove, a few pots and pans, utensils, sleeping bags, mosquito netting and spray, some dried food, a few canned goods, and especially a top-notch two-way radio with two additional handsets.

It was the bare essentials, but with any luck, we hoped we'd only be in the real wilderness for a few days. The final item we needed was some dynamite. Like Will had said: "Four hundred years is a long freakin' time and Nature has a habit of changing her face occasionally. It would be a bitch if we found the limestone cliffs, only to discover that the entrance we needed wasn't an entrance anymore, and needed fixing."

Fortunately, with Santino's connections at the Ministry of the Interior, he managed to procure two sticks of dynamite along with a handful of blasting caps and cord—another one of those things that would have been impossible had we not run into him. Given the civil war Guatemala was still involved in, things that went "boom" just weren't easily available to the populace there or in surrounding countries. I was becoming a serious believer in Will's concept that we are all little more than chess pieces for the gods.

Santino had spent years in the area where we were headed. To our amazement and infinite joy, he said he thought he recalled a section of foliage-covered limestone walls along the river called El Chuj. But he wasn't certain. If we got lucky, this could be a "short, cool gig," as Crazy Eddie would say.

Will always carried weapons in secret, insulated compartments built into the engine cowlings of his 310, including a 9mm Smith and Wesson in each compartment, with several boxes of ammunition. They were almost impossible to locate, yet easily accessible, and no one paid attention to a pilot checking his engines. While Will occupied Customs in the FBO at the airport, I "checked the engines" and subtly put them in my toolbox.

Fortunately, with Santino's connections, we were able to clear possession of our pistols with the Belize State Department, through the Ministry of the Interior. It took an entire day. Without Santino, it might well have been impossible. We were going to have to gamble once we got into Guatemala. The Guatemalans didn't like their own people having guns (could have had something to do with a 25-year civil war…), but like Will had said, things that go bang were a necessary ingredient for this little gig. We didn't want to have someone "sharing our entrails and beating our bones on a hollow log."

At the end of the day, we were sitting at a little downtown restaurant, sharing possibly the best tacos I had ever eaten, and drinking margaritas. (The generous portions of tequila in the margaritas may have contributed to my opinion of the tacos.)

Santino paused and looked at us all. "I know this all seems like a wonderful adventure, but you should know we are going into a very remote area. To quote a British author, it is 'the heart of darkness' in Guatemala. There will be no one to save us if something goes wrong, and I wish not to scare you, but it is an odd place. This Reserva de Biosfera Maya is several hundred square miles of sparsely populated jungle, occupied by primitive natives and cursed with difficult terrain that is truly dangerous, and it is the meat of strange stories." He drew a breath. "The loggers who cut raw, crude roads into that area gave up long before they took the trees they wanted. The natives harassed and killed many of them, and they came out talking about strange experiences with an animal of some sort. The people of that area say there is an animal that lives in the jungle—a dangerous creature. They call it *La Araña de Plata*—the Silver Spider. Those who have caught glimpses of it say it is a huge silver beast that moves through the trees like a spider. Many of the deep jungle villages have prayer poles they worship in hopes that it leaves them in peace."

"Well, that's just great," muttered Will. "Sounds like a Stephen King novel."

"It gets worse," said Santino. "Over the last couple of decades, many people have disappeared in this area. Most recently, in 1983, a group from the University of Belize lost two people—one a professor. He was quite a well-known man—an anthropologist. Apparently, they somehow got separated from the main group during a storm and were never found. Victims of *La Reserva de Biosphere Maya.*"

While Santino was speaking, Talia wasn't interjecting much, but she was subtly studying him – his movements, the way he used his hands when he spoke, the way his eyes filled with expression. It all seemed strangely familiar. *Like trying to touch a shadow. You can see it, but you can't grasp it.*

Santino paused. "Many of those who come through this area claim they have heard 'the trees quaking in fear, and strange roars and cries at night.'"

"Well, it's the jungle," said Will. "What did they expect?"

Santino did that shrug of his. "That is true, but the stories are consistent. A heavy thumping, screams, and roaring. The part about trees quaking, I don't know." He eased out a breath. "And there are bandits as well, along some of the better-traveled roads. Life is hard there."

"And yet you chose to make your livelihood out there in the jungle?" Talia asked.

The big man with the dark hair sighed and a small smile curved the corners of his lips. "Yes, strange, I know. But I love the jungle—the smells, the birds, and the animals, and the ruins of the old ones. I feel at home there." He paused and a strangely distant look crossed his face. "It's as if it is a place I *came from*, not that I *go to.*" He shook his head, the distance in his eyes faded, and Santino was back. He grinned. "Besides, what else could I do to have no boss on my back and make my own hours, eh?"

"Why didn't you tell us this earlier—about the weird creature, the disappearances, and the bandits?" asked Will.

Our Latin friend smiled. "Would it have changed your minds?"

CHAPTER SEVEN

It is in the compelling zest of high adventure and creative action that men (and women) find their supreme joys.
—Antoine de Saint-Exupery

Professor Benton Larner waited out the rest of the day in his Roatán bungalow. His man hadn't come back. Hell, he'd just disappeared. That wasn't good, but it didn't deter the good professor. The stakes in this game were too high. After having read the writings the woman had shown him, he realized this might be "the big one" he'd been looking for. It was still a long shot, but the directions were there, and the landmarks. He had been to Guatemala several times. He was aware of the river that was mentioned, El Chuj. He was certain that was the one, given its distance and direction from the original Chetumal. All he had to find was the limestone walls.

He would need a crew to pull this off, and a guide from the area, but that wasn't a problem. He had people in mind already. There was no doubt the Reserva de Biosfera Maya was a difficult place. It would require hardy people. He picked up his address book and made two calls—calls to individuals he had used on prior "excursions"; folks who weren't particularly concerned about removing obstacles.

An hour later, he was at the airport, booking the next available flight into Miami. By the following afternoon, he was sitting in the back of a bar just off the University of Miami campus, exhaling a blue cloud of Marlboro smoke at the ceiling, when two people walked in. The first, in khaki slacks and a black polo pullover, was tall and heavily built, with nearly shoulder-length blond hair. Balac had that Slavic look—square, heavy face, and pale-blue, somewhat indifferent eyes. Not stupid or haughty eyes, just detached. Simply a look at the man warned most people that, in a situation with him, discretion was the better part of valor.

The other was definitely the more interesting of the two. She too was tall—easily six feet, half of her legs, and everything in just the right places. But if you looked closely, you could see the tight muscle groups in her arms and legs, as if they'd been chiseled by a sculptor. Her name was Serina—at least that's the name she used with Larner. She was dressed in a green tube skirt, which clearly defined her stunning figure, along with simple leather sandals. Her eyes were a cautious, hard gray, but Larner knew they could soften sufficiently to steal the attention from a newborn kitten. Her hair was a rich sable, cut to an innocent pageboy style. She would have been more remarkable with long hair, but in her business (that of getting "difficult" things done for people), long hair could be a liability.

Serina was as deadly as a viper, but she could do that "schoolgirl" act and turn men into putty. Moreover, she was a fixed-wing and a small-class helicopter pilot. She was from South Africa and had worked with their Special Forces. Unfortunately, she got into an altercation with an officer during a mission. One night he decided they should become better acquainted. She disagreed, and shot him in the leg. It compromised the operation, and cost Serina her career. Nonetheless, she was very handy...*if* you could get past her temper.

Larner nodded and they came over, taking a seat at his table.

They spoke quietly, leaning into each other for about 10 minutes. Then Larner laid out a small map on the tabletop, which was followed by more cautious conversation. In the end, Larner glanced from one to the other.

"This is not going to be an easy one," he said. "While I may hire a handful of 'expendables' for the heavy lifting, there's absolutely no guarantee..."

"There never is," said the woman quietly.

Larner continued. "But it could have a big payday, and I can promise you, it won't be boring. I am telling you, these people have the scepter of the Mayan king, Nachán Can." He paused, his eyes growing flinty. "But you understand, if it comes to pass, we're the only ones who come home."

The eyes of the big man grew animated and he spoke with a Slavic growl. "Business is business."

Larner leaned back and took a swallow of his whiskey, satisfied. "Get your gear together. We leave tomorrow."

The following day, while Larner and his people boarded a plane at Miami International using false passports, we were loading aboard Will's 310. There was no point in just stumbling into this whole affair when we could spend a day studying the Reserva de Biosfera Maya from the air. We could view the roads going in, determine where the checkpoints were, and most of all, we could get a look at this Chuj River, which supposedly had a battery of limestone cliffs somewhere. In addition, while Will flew, Santino and I could plot the most sensible ground course for our expedition.

Santino had explained that he was going to board his hawk at the Office of the Interior for the day. "That Pixan," he said with a grin. "She is such a jealous little *perra*. And I don't want my two ladies fighting."

It was a gorgeous, early spring day, with bevies of gossamer white stratus clouds drifting across a clear, azure sky. A southwest wind at 10 knots would offer us little competition, and the temperature was a perfect 76 degrees. We lifted out of Belize International and took a southwest course, following one of the few major roads as it moved across miles of rolling land, passing through some of the small towns—La Belmopan, San Ignacio, and Melchor de Mencos, the official border crossing from Belize into Guatemala. Then we turned northwest into the thick, green labyrinth of the Guatemalan jungle—the heart of darkness.

About 20 miles into Guatemala, we started seeing rivers crawling across the jungle floor. Santino unfolded his map and we began to coordinate, to determine which one was El Chuj (which, strangely enough, was one of the ancient names for the Mayans).

We hadn't been in the air an hour when Santino pointed ahead and down to a small river that made a distinctive S bend. He slapped his map excitedly with a finger. "That's it!" he cried. "That's it! It matches my chart exactly. Take us down!"

The river meandered down in slow curls from the northeast, but at one point it made a very distinctive series of S bends over perhaps a quarter mile.

"Take us down, Will," I said. "Like Crazy Eddie says, 'Treasure don't come bangin' on your door. You gotta chase it, knock it out, and drag it home by its feet!'"

Will smiled as he rolled a wing, banking us downward in a casual turn. In minutes we were soaring along, just above stall speed, about a thousand feet above the river. Unfortunately, after running the series of S bends up and back, there was no sign of any limestone walls. I exhaled hard as Will pulled us up to 2,000 feet and backed off his throttles to a slow cruise.

"Well, that sucks," he grumbled. "I'd hate to think all this bullshit was for nothing."

"Do it one more time, and put us right down on the water," I said. "I've come all this way. I'm not leaving until I'm damned sure we're wrong."

Will sighed, somewhere between frustration and anger.

"Why not? I've paid my money, and I wanna see a naked girl."

So, we did it again—so low to the water, I swear I could have opened my door and scooped up a handful. But the results were the same. No limestone walls.

"Could we be in the wrong place?" asked Talia. "I mean, maybe this is not the only curve in the river."

"I sure as hell didn't see any other S curves from up there in the clouds," said Will bitterly. He turned to me as he drew the plane around and started climbing up and away. "You got any more suggestions, Tonto? Because we're burning daylight."

I would have probably countered with a jab reminding him that I was the Lone Ranger, and he was Tonto, but there was something nagging at me. On the last pass, I noticed that at one point, for about a quarter mile, the interior of the jungle on the starboard side changed slightly. It went from the helter-skelter variety of trees, plants, and a variety of contours, to vine-covered greenery mixed with shrubbery that began more horizontally, then turned vertically. The plants and small trees in that particular stretch turned upward, toward the sun, but if you were paying attention, you could see that the trunks started out horizontally, then turned upward. The plant life was so thick on that sloping hundred yards that it was difficult to see the subtle change. If I hadn't been looking for it, I wouldn't have noticed the patches of gray-white limestone behind the vertical greenery. With a start, I suddenly realized what had happened. After a few hundred years, the jungle foliage had literally grown out of the limestone cliffs and covered them.

Will banked up and out as I explained what had happened, then he threw us over and brought us by the location once again, just above stall speed. This time, when everyone knew what they were looking for, they recognized the shadowy gray outlines of the limestone walls behind the verdant exterior of plants and small trees.

"Floody bucking amazing," whispered Will, slightly in awe.

"We found them!" I muttered. "We found them!"

"Well, that's step number one," said Talia quietly, somewhat amazed, while Benji whistled and gave us a thumb's up.

Santino just grinned and shook his head in amazement. "*Fantástico, amigos! Fantástico!*"

Later that evening, we spent an hour at our motel poring over the best maps money could buy and trying to locate the old logging and mining roads that were used before much of Guatemala became government reserves (and logging was somewhat limited). Assuming it was still there—and that was somewhat of a stretch—one of the reasons this little treasure of ours would have remained undiscovered was because it was too difficult to get to. Ten miles past Tikal was the last vestige of civilization, a hole in the wall called Uaxactun. After that, there was nothing but jungle and old logging roads, hopefully one of which led to the Chuj River. There were no guarantees, but we had nothing to lose.

When we finished plotting a course, I sat back and looked at my friends, then turned to Will. "Listen, I know we have no right to do this, given the fact that our Crazy Eddie has just embarked on a new career, but I'm getting the feeling that we need somebody from our old team to know what we're up to, and Eddie would be the logical choice, because he's got that Grumman Goose. For one thing, that floatplane can easily get into the Chuj River. And in a pinch, it's big enough to get us all out, with maybe some shiny stuff, if we got so lucky."

Will tilted his head, thinking about it.

I turned to Talia and Benji. “You’ve met Crazy Eddie. He was the one with the new bar, the night we first met.”

They both nodded in recollection.

“He seemed like a good man,” said Talia. “A little strange…but good.”

“Yeah, he’s both of those things,” said Will.

I reached for the phone.

“So, you’re tellin’ me that my funky brothers are on another wild gig, and you didn’t even invite Eddie? Huh?” said our old friend.

I could hear music and the raucous murmur of voices in the background.

“Jesus, Eddie! You just semi-retired from the wild life and started a legitimate business three weeks ago!” I moaned.

“Shit, man, a dude needs a vacation every once in a while.”

“We just need to put you on call, in case we get into trouble.”

“Then you freakin’ might as well send me over now. You two can’t drain your dragons without splashing your feet.”

There was a pause.

“Okay, okay,” said my friend. “Eddie’ll cool his jets. But you better hurry up and get into trouble. I’m gonna go smoke a disappointment doobie, and find myself a pair of firm but gently upturned breasts to take my mind off this bummer. Then I’ll be in a better mood while I’m waitin’ for your call. Over and out, funky brothers.”

When I finished with Eddie, I turned back to my friends. “Now, I think we need a safety valve here. The radio we have won’t reach out of the country. But if we string up a high wire antenna out in the bush, it will probably reach Belize City. I’m thinking if we get into serious trouble, we need someone who can contact Eddie."

"I have a cousin on my mother's side—Petie," said Santino. "He lives here in Belize, just outside of the city. It just so happens he's a ham radio operator. Actually, I was going to mention him this evening, as a backup for us."

"Perfect!" I said, slapping the table. "Call him!"

"Now?" asked Santino.

"Right now."

Ten minutes later, we had our safety valve. A good ham base station had up to a 600-mile range—far more than what we were dealing with. We set contact times of eight a.m. and six p.m. daily, and we gave Eddie's phone number to Petie. That solved, we decided it was time for a really nice dinner. It might be the last decent meal we'd enjoy for some time.

While we were celebrating at one of Belize City's better restaurants, Larner and his two associates had safely managed Customs and were settling into their rooms at the local Marriott. During the day, Larner had stopped by the airport and loosened a tongue with a 100-dollar bill. He now knew what his competition was driving and where they were staying, and that they had seemed "excited" today when they returned from a flight into the interior of Guatemala. The manager at the FBO also heard them talking about leaving for the interior on Western Highway tomorrow morning, and the town named Uaxactun was mentioned. The manager was a very observant fellow. More than once, he had paid his rent by paying attention. Larner was pleased. Once again, a little money had bought him valuable information.

Benton Larner had connections around the world. During his life he had stolen more antiquities than a legion of 4th century Huns. His connection in Belize was an unconscionable but clever bandit named Chico Rogale. Chico operated just outside Tikal, in Guatemala, which was just about smack dab in the middle of where we were headed. But then, that's why Larner chose him.

Rogale was tall and lanky with a slightly hooked nose and shoulder-length, ebony hair. His left eye was pewter gray and his right eye was outer-reef blue. Having a good deal of audacity, he had billed himself the most handsome and dangerous bandit in Guatemala. "Startling" might have been a better description. You didn't have to be stunning to make the "most handsome bandit" list. If you had all your teeth, you were in the top five right away. But to reach even the top 20 "most dangerous," you had to be a heartless bastard son of a bitch, void of any socially redeeming qualities. The truth was, Rogale pretty much qualified there too.

He had the majority of the authorities in the more remote northwest portion of Guatemala in his pocket, and as long as he didn't kill too many people, they looked the other way. Chico Rogale, a big fan of American Western movies, liked to refer to himself as "the John Wayne of Guatemala," although no one could figure out why. He had never rescued a woman in his life and he hated horses. But he had killed a number of people with the six-gun he carried, so nobody argued the point. Larner had already contacted him and set up a meeting. In fact, Chico the bandit had spiffed himself up, donned his favorite boots and cowboy hat, and driven into Belize City. He was headed up the elevator at the Marriott at that very moment.

The four of them—Chico, Larner, and the "Dick and Jane" of ruthlessness, talked for the next half hour. Two of Chico's men—gorillas in jeans and leather—stood quietly, one on each side of the room. Larner explained that he was on a hunt for a unique bird, found only in the backwaters of the River Chuj. It was a very rare, valuable tropical bird, and if he could bring one out alive, his client would pay him $20,000 dollars, American. Unfortunately, his client had hired one other group for the same task. He gave Chico pictures of the individuals (which he got from a "helpful" member of the American Embassy in Belize City) and told him he needed his competition "distracted." If Chico was successful, he would split the $20,000 with him.

"Dios!" Chico exclaimed. "Twenty thousand for a freakin' bird? Da little son a bitch must shit gold!"

Larner shrugged. "Different strokes for different folks. What can I tell you?"

Chico paused and cocked his head. "How distracted you want dese people?"

"Mortally," replied Larner, his expression unchanging.

The bandit thought about it for a moment. "Five thousand, up front, nonrefundable, and five more when I bring you proof. You want fingers, heads?"

"Heads would be just fine," said Larner without even blinking.

"Works for me," replied Chico.

Larner reached into the breast pocket of his coat. The big men in the corners of the room stiffened and slid their hands inside their jackets.

"Easy, easy," he said. "Money. *Dinero. Esta buen, si?"*

Chico casually waved them down as Larner slid the money over. "Here's your five up front. I'm guessing my competition should be coming through Tikal tomorrow, sometime around midday. They'll be driving a green Toyota 4x4. There will be four men and a woman."

The creature crouched on the heavy limb of a mahogany tree, deep in the Guatemalan jungle, licking the blood from its huge jaws, the remains of a young sloth draped across a branch next to it. Even though it was relatively safe, its huge, dark eyes were constantly alert. The jungle was not a kind place, and if he wandered beyond its natural borders, there were the two-legged creatures and their sticks that killed at a distance. His shoulder still ached occasionally from a wound inflicted by one of those sticks.

This jungle had been its home for over 20 years, ever since the animal found itself foundered and gasping on a shoreline at the end of a wrathful storm. Somehow, he had escaped the steel-barred lair in which he'd been held, only to be washed into a convulsing sea. Continually tossed from crest to crest, its strength had begun to ebb, and even the adrenaline of fear was surrendering to exhaustion, when suddenly he bumped into a floating wooden pallet. The animal grasped it with a single-minded tenacity that only fear can render.

A few hours later, when he regained his senses, he found himself on a stretch of dirty sand at the edge of a tropical labyrinth, much like where he came from. After he recovered, the creature began to move slowly inland, deeper and deeper into the jungle. It was young then, so uncertain. Those who had imprisoned him had run out of the food he liked, so they had fed him canned dog food on much of the sea journey, and he had come to appreciate the taste of meat equally as much as he hated those pale, two-legged animals. Over the years, there had been times when that combination of anger and hunger had suited him well.

CHAPTER EIGHT

Fill your life with experiences, not things. In the end, great stories are worth their weight in gold.

—B. Lightfoot

The sun had just crested a blue-green Caribbean sea as we loaded into our Toyota. I was the designated driver to begin with. Will sat up front with me. Santino and Talia sat behind us, and Benji in the back seat with Santino's hawk, Pixan. That fiery globe was just beginning to cast a golden warmth over eastern Guatemala, its tendrils reaching out and caressing the last of the Mayan ruins of Chichén Itzá, Tikal, Yaxhá, and Chetumal.

Just outside of town, we drove by a small but remarkable pyramid—a testament to the ingenuity of the Mayan culture—and as we did, Santino sighed quietly. "The tourists, with their cameras, sunscreen, and color brochures will soon be listening to the tour guides as they tell them of a proud people and their history," he said, to no one in particular. "The guides will tell them of the Mayans' extraordinary accomplishments in architecture, astronomy, medicine, and art, and their ultimate destruction by a race more advanced than them in only one aspect—war." Santino exhaled. "If we should remember one thing from all this, it is that 'the Huns' are always waiting at the gates of civilization."

"Amen," said Talia quietly.

Coming out of Belize City, we picked up Western Highway and headed southwest for about 60 miles, passing through La Democracia, Belmopan, Teakettle, and San Ignacio. We were beginning to relax a little by the time we reached Melchor de Mencos, the official border crossing from Belize into Guatemala. There was a small roadside guard shack on the Guatemalan side, which had the traditional candy-cane colored pole that rose up and down. The guard shack was built on the same side of the road as a small cantina/general store, just to the front of the border entrance.

As we approached, a guard stepped out from the cantina and entered the guard shack.

"Buenos dias," I said in my best Spanish, as we pulled up.

"*Buenos dias,*" replied the guard in the shack, cautiously peering into our vehicle. "Where are you going?"

"We are going to visit Tikal," I replied somewhat truthfully.

The guard glanced at us again. "Could I see your papers, please?"

Santino had forewarned us of this, so we all had our papers ready.

The fellow casually glanced through our passports and necessary documents, then returned them. The gate pole came up. "Please pull forward, to the side of the road, and turn off your vehicle," he said.

I wasn't sure why, but my stomach did a little flip-flop, knowing that we were now in Guatemala. I did as he suggested.

"Please exit your vehicle while we examine its contents," said the sentry.

I was beginning to like this less and less, but we did as he requested. All the really important things, like dynamite, pistols, and ammo, were seriously well hidden.

The fellow relaxed a little after we were out of the Toyota, saying that it would be only a few minutes, and we could wait inside the cantina if we liked. Will looked at me and our eyes spoke. *Sometimes things can disappear at border crossings...*

"I'll stay out here," said my partner. "I need to walk around a little." He looked at the sentry and said in very decent Spanish, "My butt hurts from those cheap Mexican seats." That won a brief smile.

Mexico produces a number of automobile parts. Guatemala doesn't have quite as strong a production economy, which leads to a degree of enmity.

There were two more guards in the cantina sitting at a table. We all found a table and pretended to be invisible.

A few minutes later, the fellow who was inspecting our car came in with Will and announced that we could leave, providing we paid the "new" border-crossing fee of 30 American dollars. I know a scam when I see one, and the looks on my friend's eyes said the same, but good old Will stepped in before we had a chance to screw the pooch.

"No problem, Officer," he said, reaching into his pocket and pulling out two 20s. "We want to stay within the law while visiting your country. You keep the difference."

There was an immediate and pronounced change in our custodian. He relaxed and took the money with a smile, saying he hoped we had a nice stay in his country as he escorted us to the door. He returned to a table inside. (It was too damned hot in that little wooden box outside and he could see the road from the windows.)

We were all piling into the car when Benji signed that he needed to use the restroom. There was a collective sigh somewhere between angst and impatience, but he signed that he would be right back. I don't know why, but I just decided I'd go in with him. It sure as hell wasn't that he needed protection, but occasionally the "not being able to speak" thing made life difficult for him. The other problem with Benji was his immediate appearance. With his small stature, curly hair, and pale-blue eyes, he looked like a guy who worked in a flower shop and was challenged by women and dark nights. The truth was, he was a wolverine who only ate people who gave him a hard time.

Benji stepped back inside the cantina and mimed the need to use the restroom. One of the guards made an offhanded nasty remark about him probably playing with himself on the potty. Benji, whose understanding of Spanish wasn't bad, glanced at him but let it slide. Another guard pointed to the back.

As Benji strolled down the hallway toward the back and closed the bathroom door, the big guy who made the nasty comment—heavy shoulders, legs like tree stumps—offered his friends an ugly smile, saying he bet the little *maricón* wouldn't mind "a visit" if he was encouraged a little. The other guards knew this wasn't a good idea, but Jario was known for being a masochistic bastard who occasionally "pressed" tourists when he thought he could get away with it. Most of his companions just tried to stay out of his way. They shrugged and found something to do. Jario grinned—nothing nice about it—and moved off toward the hallway and the restrooms.

I was hoping—*praying*—that the guy would get a grip and not do anything stupid, but like our old Rastaman buddy Rufus says, "Sometimes the magic works, and sometimes it don't." It was quiet in the direction of the bathrooms for a few moments, then there was a thunderous banging, and Jario started yelling—really howling, like something was badly wrong. And there was. Officer Jario came crashing from the bathroom, taking the door with him, his wrist bent at a very nasty angle, as was his nose. He stumbled down the hallway in a pain-filled crouch, the only good hand he had left clutching his groin. Benji stepped out behind him, not a scratch anywhere, and side-kicked him in the back, sending him flailing into the bar/store.

I had been standing by the door of the cantina, praying that we'd get out of there without a problem, when I heard the ruckus. I turned just as Jario tumbled out onto the floor still screeching. Another guard decided this was not good, and went at Benji with his baton. Bad move. He lost the baton and inherited a concussion from a spinning back kick. The baton skidded across the floor, stopping at my feet. The last guard was drawing his handgun. I could see the fear and the anger in his eyes. There was no question he was going to shoot my friend. Benji took a couple steps forward. He was just about to leap at him, his eyes filled with an almost calm viciousness, part and parcel of the violence he'd been trained for all his life, when Talia, who had just come back in, began screaming.

I was standing to the side, and slightly behind the guard. I did the only thing I could think of. I snatched up the baton lying on the floor and smacked the policeman on the back of the head. The fellow dropped like a sack of potatoes. I glanced at Talia and Benji. Simultaneously, we made a dash for the car. There would be no explaining this to the authorities. In just moments, we had completely botched this little vacation.

We stumbled out and jumped into the Land Cruiser. I jammed it into gear and we surged off. The gate pole was down and a guard was stumbling out of the cantina, pistol drawn. So, I headed in the direction the car was pointed, into Guatemala. In retrospect, I realized I should have turned around and smashed through the gate, back into Belize, but it was what it was. Belize or Guatemala, it hardly mattered. We were screwed.

"Just a simple, uncomplicated vacation," muttered Will from the back seat.

Chico Rogale learned about the border-crossing incident about an hour after it happened. He was certain the gringos were headed into the interior, on the run. *Just like in a John Wayne movie...* But there was a four-way crossing shortly after Melchor de Mencos, and no one knew which direction we had taken...except for the man Chico had posted there.

When his man told him, Chico pulled at a corner of his black mustache, thinking, *This is good. A job like this is best done in the jungle—no witnesses but the monkeys and the parrots.*

But now he had to get to them before the *Federales* did. “Twenty thousand dollars is a lot of money for a pretty chicken,” he muttered to himself. “And they got no cages with them...” He snapped his fingers at the two big men with him. “We got business,” he said. “Pack a bag.”

Earlier that same day, Doctor Larner and his associates, using false identities, had rented a plane—a single engine Cessna 172. His long-legged partner, Serina, the licensed pilot, would fly it. They were of the same mind as their competition. A view from the air might give them the insight they needed. Unfortunately, for them, they weren’t quite as perceptive, and the run along the River Chuj didn’t yield them any definite returns. Although, by sheer intuition, Larner picked up on the subtle change in topography where the cliffs lay hidden, and decided that area would be a good place to start. His reasoning wasn’t based on any solid information—it was strictly intuitive. There was something about that area, the way the river turned, that jarred something deep within him. It seemed like a dream he’d once experienced. There was a room cut out of the rock, with a large cat etched into the floor.... The dream was clouded and carried a feeling of intrigue. But he could never quite see past the fog around him.

When Larner and his people returned to the airport at Belize City, it was decided that they needed to make a trip into the interior, probably by helicopter, to the river they’d found. Larner would find a helicopter to rent. Serina would fly it. But it would take a day or so to gather the additional equipment they'd need. Hopefully, Chico Rogale would have eliminated some of the competition by that time.

While I was certain the Guatemalan authorities had been apprised of the border fiasco, this wasn't the U.S. of A. We were in the boonies of a country that was in the boonies. Fortunately, the police had guessed poorly, thinking that we had lied about going to Tikal, and turned south at the four-way, toward the town of El Naranjo. Besides, the truth was, a couple of *gringos* punching out a border guard was small change for this revolution-torn country. They generally had much bigger fish to fry.

It wasn't long after passing through Tikal that we reached Uaxactun, the last of civilization, if it could be called that. There was little more than a few slat-boarded shacks with corrugated tin roofs mixed among the fading ruins of a once-great civilization. At that point, the road went from gravel to an old logging trail with ruts that challenged our 4x4. In addition, there was a storm building in the west, and coming our way. Huge, ominous thunderheads had begun to spit jagged, yellow lightning, and sheets of rain accompanied the light show, darkening the horizon. The terrain was just starting to rise. We would have to go over a small battery of hills before dropping down into the gorges and lowlands that nurtured the Chuj River.

Chico Rogale had just arrived in Tikal with two of his best men. They were about two hours behind us. But the good news was, the storm coming in was a monster. Lightning strikes and near hurricane winds were shutting down communications everywhere. The authorities—what there was of them in that section of Guatemala—were stalemated. With the spider web of jungle and the old logging roads, they had no ability to set up an organized pursuit of us, even if they had been bright enough to figure out that we had come this way.

The wind was rising now, and fat pellets of rain were beginning to slap the windshield. We needed higher ground.

"We've got to stop somewhere and ride this out," said Will, reading my mind as he stared out the window.

Santino immediately agreed. He had seen what these quick, heavy storms could do.

Moving into the hills along our battered roadway, we forded a sizeable creek that was already showing signs of rising. I pulled off the road and up onto a high embankment that was somewhat protected by large trees. The storm was ripping at the treetops now, and even our heavy Toyota was giving slightly.

"Might as well make yourselves comfortable," I said. "I think we're going to be here for the night."

Unfortunately, the night was anything but comfortable. There was no way for any of us to stretch out, the Land Rover being constantly hammered by rain and literally shifted by the fierce winds. Lightning exploded so close I thought we'd been struck several times, and we could hear branches snapping like gunshots all around us.

Somewhere in the middle of it, after an enthusiastic burst of lightning, Will muttered, "Welcome to the Guatemalan outback, vacation paradise of Central America."

"This is one of the many reasons even the Guatemalans don't like Guatemala," huffed Santino.

By sunrise, we were all awake. I wasn't sure anyone had actually slept, but the initial storm had passed. Everything was hushed and still. Water dripped from the leaves of the huge rubber trees with a slow calypso rhythm, parrots shook the moisture from their feathers in an aggravated fashion, and wild turkeys began to call for their mates. Through the foliage above us, I caught sight of a lone osprey winging over the greenery, in search of breakfast. Benji was already up, struggling with an uncooperative breakfast fire. Santino opened Pixan's cage and freed her. She hopped out and tentatively looked around. Then, after a glance of appreciation at her companion, she threw out her wings and lifted away. I asked if he was sure she'd come back and Santino laughed.

"She will follow us from above and join us when she wants." He smiled. "She is my friend, not my pet."

Will and I got out and politely decided to take a walk, so Santino and Talia could organize themselves and find a place for morning activities.

It was a remarkable thing, this instant romance between these two. I couldn't remember ever seeing two people "meld" so quickly and completely. It was almost eerie. They liked the same things, and they used the same expressions. It wasn't one of these "blindly attached teen romances" where they couldn't keep their hands off one another. It was more a melding of souls. They were comfortable with each other from the moment they'd met, and Will and I were definitely eliminated from the competition at that same point.

Unfortunately, toward the west it looked like we were about to get one more volley from Mother Nature. Once more the clouds were darkening, and the tops of the trees were whispering fearfully. We chose to take a quick walk down by the creek we had passed over. But it was more like a river now, at least three feet higher than it was earlier, with numerous trees along the banks battered and down.

As we worked our way along the roiling water, I excused myself for a call of nature. Will turned and moved the other way, for the same purpose. I walked off about 20 feet and relieved myself, but as I was zipping up, I caught a movement along the muddy bank, on the opposite side, against the trunk of a recently felled tree. There was something under the trunk, pinned against the bank, with a strangely dark, silver coat. An animal of some sort. It was a big animal, with heavy brows and huge, dark eyes. It shifted when it saw me, its head barely above the water, and a deep growl issued from its large, fanged mouth.

"Son of a bitch," I hissed under my breath, as the hair on my arms stood up. I slowly started to turn, to call Will, when I realized he was behind me.

"Whoa shit," he whispered incredulously. "What in the freaking hell is that?"

It was human shaped, like a giant monkey or gorilla, but it was silver. I knew that there were African gorillas called silverbacks, but there were no gorillas in Central or South America. It huffed out another growl and tried to move, but I realized then that its shoulder was twisted into an unnatural position. It probably wasn't broken, but it lay in such a position as to allow the creature no leverage, leaving only its huge head and part of one shoulder above the surface. It was trapped, and the dark clouds were moving in again. Raindrops began to pelt the water.

The creature shook once more, trying desperately to dislodge itself, growling angrily as it did so. The trunk of the dead tree, which stretched from the bank out into the middle of the creek, shuddered, but didn't give.

"If we wait much longer, the water will rise over its head," I said.

"Wait for freaking what?" hissed Will. "If you're suggesting that we...whoa, man, I don't even know what that is. How do you know the son of a bitch won't eat us if we free it?"

I looked up at the darkening sky. "It's gonna die if we leave it here."

Will sighed angrily, his blond hair plastered to his head,

eyes filled with angst. "Jesus! Why do I let you get me into these things? Why?"

I shrugged. "Because if I didn't, your life would be boring, and, as Crazy Eddie would say, you would have no great barroom stories."

Will exhaled hard and shook his head, a somewhat bitter smile touching the edges of his mouth. "In the end, he who has the most stories wins…huh?"

I couldn't help but grin, as frightened as I was. "C'mon, let's go free the centaur and win immortality."

"You've been reading that freakin' Greek mythology again, haven't you?" my friend muttered.

As we moved into the center of the rising stream, the creature watched us intently, an almost steady growl issuing from its throat. Will positioned himself on one side of the trunk and I braced myself on the other. It was raining steadily now, and the creek had begun to writhe with mindless energy. The animal was forced to lift its head to breathe. Yet those dark, passionless eyes watched us intently.

"On three," I said. "One, two, three!"

We heaved, putting our backs into it, but the trunk barely moved.

"Again!" I yelled. "One, two, three!"

Once more we strained, and the creature, somehow realizing what we were doing, threw in what effort he could offer. The trunk gave, and the gorilla (if that's what it was), moved slightly, but not enough to free itself. While we stood there, debating on another plan, the storm arrived. Swirling wind whipped around us, rain beat down in torrents, and the current was now raging.

"God! I don't know what to do!" I cried.

In the background, I could hear Santino and Talia calling for us. But the water was almost up to the animal's mouth.

Suddenly, Will glanced at the shore and his eyes brightened. "Hold on, Tonto, we're not done!" he yelled, as he quickly sloshed toward the bank.

I saw it then—a hefty limb almost bereft of branches—and I knew instantly what Will had in mind.

We grabbed the limb and dragged it out into the water and over to the canted trunk, part of which was on the bank and part in the stream. With all our strength, Will and I lifted our branch and jammed it under the submerged trunk of the downed tree, the point burying itself in the gravel streambed. The rain was hammering us in sheets and the current was fierce now, almost lifting us off our feet. The creature issued a hoary, guttural roar as the water finally rose over its head. I could see its wide eyes just below the surface.

With every ounce of strength, my partner and I heaved, letting the angle of the branch under the trunk serve as a fulcrum. The trunk gave, lifting up slightly, and I could see the creature shift its weight with the very last of its breath.

"Again!" I screamed, and once more, Will and I gave it one last frantic effort.

At that moment the trunk lifted just enough—only inches, but it was enough. The drowning beast forced itself out from under the dead tree, and pulled itself up on the bank, coughing out water and inhaling huge gasps of air.

We quickly dropped the branch and moved back, the rain hammering us, lightning rippling across the sky above us in brilliant forks.

"Let's get the hell out of here!" Will yelled to me over the roar of the wind and the rain.

As we turned to wade out of the creek, we both looked back toward the partially submerged trunk. The animal was gone.

Just about that time, Santino and Talia came trudging through the jungle in waterproof ponchos. "What the hell happened to you two?" called Talia.

"Let's get back to the Rover," said Will. "Then you can call us crazy, or liars."

Surprisingly, our incident wasn't such a stretch for Santino, who had spent a lot of time in the jungle and had heard the stories about the "Silver Spider"—a creature that could move through the treetops like a spider. Talia just shook her head and asked if we'd been drinking our breakfast.

"We didn't get a real good look, because most of it was under the water and blocked by the tree trunk, but it looked like it was real close to a gorilla," I explained. "But the damned thing was all silver-gray."

"Nature is always producing mutations," said Santino cautiously. "There was an all-white gorilla that was captured in 1966 by natives in equatorial New Guinea, so that is possible." He paused and shook his head. "But a silver gorilla in Central America? While the scientist in me says this cannot be, this is strangely familiar to the reports from so many villagers in the interior of *La Araña de Plata*—the Silver Spider.'"

"Nobody knows everything," muttered Will. "Or life would be like chess without kings."

CHAPTER NINE

Finding treasure is a very cool thing. But searching for treasure is three-quarters of the cool.

—Roy Stevenson

While we prepared and ate a quick breakfast, we discussed our latest major problem. Given that we had assaulted the Guatemalan police and run a border crossing, we were now fugitives from the Guatemalan government (maybe even the Belize government as well). This created a number of problems, the major one being we could no longer leave these countries in a conventional fashion. Without question, our names were going to pop up on their "wanted" lists at every port of debarkation. Secondly, and certainly the most terrifying aspect of this whole thing, was a place called *Granja Penal de Pavón.* Santino explained that Guatemala's one and only prison was the most terrifying penal facility in Central America.

"*Pavón* was a nightmare from the very beginning," Santino said. "It was built in the 1970s, outside Guatemala City, but it soon became so overcrowded, with dozens of murderous gangs operating inside, that the guards themselves were becoming victims of the inmates daily. It became impossible to manage, so the authorities decided to try something altogether new in prison systems. They built a huge wall around the prison and controlled only the parameters, and let the prisoners run the interior on their own." He paused, his eyes displaying genuine fear. "It is virtually Hell on earth. And it is where we will end up, my friends, if we are caught."

"Well, that's enough for me," said Will. "We need to call Eddie and prepare for an extraction."

Benji, who had been somewhat reserved throughout the morning, signed to Talia.

"Benji and I agree," she said, "but that doesn't mean we can't stick to the plan. Call this Crazy Eddie friend of yours and give him the coordinates for the beach in front of the white limestone walls. There's no reason in the world for us not to have a look at that before we leave. Once we're in the air, they're not going to shoot us down. I don't think..."

"Famous last words," I said as I pulled out our maps.

At that moment, we heard a helicopter sweeping in the distance. We all turned to each other.

"Get the radio out," I said. "I'll climb that tree and string an antenna."

Ten minutes later, we were graced with the voice of Petie, Santino's cousin. After cordialities, I explained I wanted him to call Crazy Eddie on the phone and put the phone receiver to the ham radio microphone. This required a little juggling for talking back and forth, but a moment later we faintly heard Crazy Eddie's bleary voice.

"Dude, it's eight o'clock in the freakin' morning! My eye is glued closed!"

"Sorry to take you from your beauty sleep," I said. "But we've got problems."

Eddie offered a chortle. "Didn't Eddie tell you that you were gonna need him? Huh? Huh?"

"Yeah. Yeah, you did, and we do. Seems we got into a little trouble at a border crossing. One of our team sort of beat up several policemen."

Eddie grunted. "Whoa, bad scene, dude! Especially there! Those fuckers have no sense of humor."

I could hear Eddie strike a match and inhale as he lit his morning doobie.

"Okay, I'm gonna need a day to get ready," he said, holding his breath, then exhaling while speaking. "And I'm guessing that's close to an eight, maybe 10-hour run for me." He paused and took another hit. "You gonna need anything that makes loud noises? Any instruments of mayhem?"

I thought about that for a moment. "If we're real lucky, no, but why don't you just use your imagination. You should have some stuff lying around from our last gig."

"Okay dude, gimme some landmarks and coordinates…"

Afterward, Eddie hung up the phone and scratched his nose. He leaned over and picked up the half-empty beer on his nightstand, took a pensive sip, and gingerly swallowed. He grimaced, holding the beer up to the morning light, making sure nothing had crawled into it overnight, then shrugged and took another slug.

The culvert bridge just after Uaxactun had been washed out and Chico Rogale was forced to wait two hours while a bulldozer from Tikal repaired it. The lanky bandit, attired in blue jeans, boots, and a T-shirt, stomped around, fuming and cursing at the repair people. He took out his pistol and shot at one fellow who was taking a cigarette break, which encouraged the others to maintain a vigorous pace. His two men did their best to distance themselves from their volatile boss.

"When I find 'em, I'm gonna kill those sons a bitches twice, just for the inconvenience," Chico muttered angrily, spitting on the ground. "Thas' what John Wayne would do!"

The good news for Rogale was that he was part Indian, and he knew the roads in the outback well. He took a little-used, somewhat challenging road that cut an hour off his time.

Once we were underway, the storm began to dissipate. But the tempest had knocked down trees everywhere. We were constantly removing obstacles from the muddy, deteriorated track, but by midday, the ridges around us peaked and began to move downward. We had heard one helicopter after the weather had begun to break, but there had been no sign of one since.

"Toward midafternoon we should be there," said Santino from the back of the bouncing vehicle, his arm around his lady.

As we pushed forward, we passed through two small native villages—primitive outback people, the men clothed in loincloths or crude cotton pantelones and the women in crudely dyed cotton shifts, children at their breasts. At the second village, Santino spoke briefly with them, as he understood some of their dialect. Suddenly, Pixan appeared, winging her way through the jungle treetops, gliding down and alighting on Santino's shoulder. The natives were very impressed—lots of wide eyes. As we were leaving, the old chief blessed us, offering a protection, as *La Araña de Plata* had been sighted in the area recently.

As Santino translated, Will told the chief, "Yeah, we know. We're friends of his…"

"Hold on, Tonto," I said. "It was me who introduced you."

Will smiled and held up an index finger. "How many times do I have to tell you? Me, Lone Ranger. You, Tonto…"

The chief asked Santino what we were saying. Our friend sighed and translated.

The fellow looked at Santino, and pointed a thumb at us. *"Loco, si?"*

Santino nodded. *"Si, un poco."*

One of the elders of the tribe was squatting against the side of a hut, watching all this, smoking a cigarette—a real, commercial cigarette, not a home-rolled native thing. He got up and strolled over. The guy was stubby short, with a barrel chest and skinny legs. He was wearing, of all things, a ragged Jimmy Buffett shirt and a battered pair of cotton pantelones...and tennis shoes. When he reached us, he straightened up and offered a two-fingered hippie peace sign.

"You goin' to the walls on the river, huh?" he asked in relatively good English.

We all took a step back. The damned guy was speaking English with a Texas accent!

"What the hell..." whispered Will. "How could he know?"

"Hey, dat's why I'ne de assistant medicine man and you're not," he said.

I couldn't help but chuckle, even as startled as I was.

"You wanna guide?" he said. "I know a way. Cut off much time. You pay me $50 cash, American." He paused. "You can call me Anaka de Sante Dericho…or Blingo."

Blingo seemed a lot easier.

I stared at the Indian, amazed. "How is it that you speak English?"

He leaned forward and spit some tobacco juice on the ground. "I work on oil rig off coast of Mexico for a while. Owned by gringo company. When job was done, I go live in Corpus Christi for two years."

"And you came back here?" Will asked incredulously.

"It was a slow process. I had to taste da wind in a few places." The man offered a shrug, much like Santino. "I miss de jungle, where it's quiet and honest." He held up a finger. "Nothing tells lies in da jungle. Here is brutal honesty." He threw up his hands and did a little shuffle. "An' it's always so damn noisy in your country! People shouting, machines hammering, an' de music! Sounds like somebody stranglin' a duck, always so loud to crack your ears!" He spat another splash of tobacco juice at Will's feet and held up a finger. "Silence is the food that nourishes wisdom. Now, I get de job, or not?"

Will and I looked at the others.

Santino exhaled, uneasy. *"Amigos*, I must admit, I have barely been past this point. It would be comforting to have someone who actually knew…"

Talia glanced at her brother. Their eyes spoke for a moment. Benji signed and Talia translated. "Better to have someone who knows where they're going, eh?"

As we rolled out of the village with our new companion, Blingo took a seat in the rear of the vehicle with Benji. As Blingo settled in, he pulled a bottle of homemade hooch from his cotton shoulder bag and took a solid hit, then explained that he wasn't *exactly* the medicine man for the village. He was the *brother* of the medicine man, which gave him sort of a "second-seat" position by heritage. Will rolled his eyes, and Blingo saw it.

"Jus' cool your jets, gringo. It don' take much magic to get you to da white walls of da river." He paused for a moment. "What chu goin' dere for?"

"No offense, Shaman junior," said Will, "But that's above your pay scale. We just need you to get us there. Then you can go."

"Den you gonna grow wings and fly out?" said Blingo with a smile.

"Something like that."

Professor Larner and his two companions were impatiently waiting for a "heads-up" call from Chico Rogale (hopefully five heads, actually).

The professor had the helicopter on standby at the airport—a beefed-up, five-seat Bell 206B-L4 with a useful load of just over 1,000 pounds and plenty of range for what they needed. He was certain, after their first trip in by plane, that there was enough gravel beach to bring in a chopper. They had been gathering supplies and loading them when the storm hit, and that had set them back several hours, but they were loaded now. Assuming that his bandit accomplice would take care of his end, Larner told the FBO to be on call, at their service for the next two days. If Larner and his team found something, they would hopefully be able to bring it out in the five-place helicopter. Larner had secured a remote location just across the border into Belize, with a canvas-covered truck waiting for them. He had also paid for the services of a shrimp boat and its crew, docked at the harbor of Ladyville, above Belize City—the ticket home for anything they found.

At about that same time, a Colonel Enrico Stata was addressing a small contingency of personnel and pilots at the Guatemalan Base, *Aérea de Izabal,* just outside the city of Puerto Barrios on the east coast of Guatemala.

"It has been brought to my attention that recently we have had two groups of Americans come into the country—one by commercial airline and one via their private aircraft, landing initially at Belize International, then crossing the border at Melchor de Mencos," the colonel explained. "One of these groups managed to get weapons permits from the Belize Ministry of the Interior, which is strange to begin with, and I am looking into this, but more on that in a moment. Oddly enough, both of these constituencies have expressed interest in a specific location—Reserva De Biosfera Maya, along the Chuj River. Our man at the Belize International FBO has confirmed this." He held up a finger. "It becomes more interesting yet. An individual whom, for some time, we have suspected as a possible insurgent, is a member of one of these factions."

He paused and drew a breath. "This is what makes me curious. The group this person is with recently ran a border crossing from Belize into Guatemala. Their timing was good. The huge storm that came through and the ineptitude of the local police allowed them to escape any pursuit. But we have a general direction. In addition, a little investigation has shown that, of the group our suspected insurgent is traveling with, two are pilots, and they have somewhat nefarious records, with difficulties in numerous countries, including Mexico quite recently. The second group includes a college professor from Miami, who is suspected of numerous antiquities violations. One of his entourage is also a pilot." The colonel paused again. "As you can see, an interesting situation. I would like to maintain radar surveillance on activity coming in and out of the Chuj River Valley, and I would like a squad of soldiers and a truck on standby in Tikal." He brought up a finger again. "Just in case..."

We were leaving the hills that cradled the Chuj River. It wouldn't be long and we'd begin the hunt for the enigmatic gate to what was supposedly a hidden quarters within the mysterious limestone walls. Will had taken readings during our first flight over. All we needed was a little of that luck we'd been blessed with so many times before.

I was at the wheel as we bounced down the old logging road, but as we rounded a turn, we discovered a heavy log canted sideways near the center of the road. I might have been able to get around it, but it would be easier to move it. No use getting stuck in the mire of the recent storm when we were this close.

I stopped and turned off the ignition, staying in the vehicle. Will and Santino got out to move the log. Benji and Talia took our two pistols and moved apart, one at each end of the vehicle, watching.

As I handed my gun to Talia I asked, "Can you handle this okay?"

She looked at me and answered deadpan, "I'm the

daughter of an Israeli Special Forces colonel. What do you think?"

Blingo got out with us and leaned against the hood of the truck, smoking a cigarette. Then he walked around the log and blew some yellow (presumably magic) dust at it from a pouch at his side—supposedly to make it easier to move. Will just shook his head again.

Blingo looked at him. "Faith is the hawk that feels the warmth of sun in the darkness before dawn."

Then he bent down and slowly ran his hand along the log from one end to the other. He came back to the center and paused, then backed up and kicked it—hard, for a little guy. There was a distinct crack. The log was rotten in the middle! Santino laughed, then came over and gave it a solid kick with his jungle boots, and the log fractured into two much more negotiable pieces.

It was a small thing, but it boosted our morale. In truth, we were all starting to get a little giddy. We were damned near there. There was something in all of us that said this was it—this was going to happen.

Will and Santino began rolling the pieces of the broken log off the road. They just about had them all moved, and I was about to yell that it was enough, when a burst of gunfire erupted from the jungle. I watched Santino recoil from a round and drop to his knees, a red patch blossoming on his shirt under his ribs. At the same time, the windows on the passenger's side of our vehicle shattered from a shotgun burst. As I hunkered down in the seat, I saw Will dive behind the log he was working on.

I think the only thing that saved us was the quick reactions of Talia and Benji. Benji may not have looked like it, but he was every inch a soldier. He instantly zeroed in on the locations where the fire was coming from, and standing there, emptied the magazine on his 9mm in the direction of the shotgun. Talia opened up as well. A cry echoed from the jungle across the road, and the weapon there went silent.

As Benji was popping out the empty mag and snapping in another, Chico Rogale was hammering away with his six-gun, but there are times that efficiency can suffer from style. He banged out six rounds and had to reload. In the process, he watched one of his men take two rounds in the chest from the little guy with the curly hair. Moments later, as he finished reloading, he heard his other man across the road issue a shriek. The woman with the pistol had been firing in that direction. Now it was quiet over there. This wasn't looking so good—not the way he had planned it. Not like in the John Wayne movies. He backed off into the shadows and settled into a trot, back to where he'd hidden his 4x4.

Our new guide had virtually disappeared the moment the first shot was fired, slipping into the jungle like a lizard on crack. Will had been grazed on the ball of his right shoulder. Talia and her brother were okay, but Santino was seriously wounded. He'd taken a bullet in his right side, a through-and-through below the rib cage, and he was bleeding badly. Talia was at Santino's side immediately, her hands pressed tightly on his wound, blood seeping out between her fingers. Benji covered them, eyes working over the jungle. But it was quiet. It appeared whoever had attacked us was gone...or dead.

As it turned out, dead was more apt. Will and I did a quick reconnaissance and found two bodies—big guys, Guatemalans, upscale bandits from the looks of things. One had been hit twice in the chest (Benji's work); the other had taken a round in the shoulder, but that hadn't killed him. His neck had been broken. It was strange, but it appeared he might have stumbled over a log behind him when he was hit, but his neck was oddly twisted. I grabbed his shotgun and a handful of unused shells.

In moments, everyone was gathered around Santino, our

medical kit out, while Benji and I stood guard. Santino was conscious and sitting up, leaning against a tree, but in a lot of pain. Will gave him a shot of morphine from the medical kit, while Talia poured some antiseptic on the wounds and bandaged them, wrapping gauze around his waist to keep the bandage pads in place. Blingo had cautiously slipped out of the jungle and was standing to the side, muttering an incantation.

I knelt next to Santino. “How are you doin’, buddy?” I asked guardedly.

“I’ll be okay,” he gasped, looking at the blood on his hands. “The blood is not dark, so I think the bullet missed my liver.” He eased out another soft gasp as the morphine started to do its thing. “But I think no tennis for a week or so.”

At that moment there was a fluttering of wings and Pixan dropped in next to him, landing next to his leg. Santino smiled, a little groggy, but still inhaling harshly from the pain. “Ahh, Pixan, my little lady, you have come to check on me.”

The bird trilled and ruffled its feathers.

Talia quickly dressed Will’s wound. It was nothing more than a scratch, another story in his life. Like our old Jamaican buddy Rufus used to say, “Scars are nothing more than evidence of courage or stupidity, sometimes exercised at the same moment.”

I glanced around again nervously. We had a bad situation here. Any other time we would have returned to civilization to get Santino taken care of, but right now “civilization” wanted to arrest us. The only chance we had, for us and Santino, was to forge ahead and hope that Crazy Eddie showed up on time. Basically, we were placing our survival in the hands of somebody with the word “crazy” in front of his first name. Not great…

“I hate to break this up,” I said. “But we need to get

moving. Now. If these folks knew where we were, that means somebody else does. I'm gonna take a wild guess and bet that our buddy, Professor Larner, is mixed up in this somewhere."

"You've got my money," muttered Will, as he checked his magazine then snapped it into his pistol, glancing around. "He knows as much about this gig as we do, probably more."

As we moved out, Will was driving and I was riding shotgun (literally, now, with the dead bandit's weapon). Santino was lying on the middle seat, his head in Talia's lap, and Benji was in the back with Blingo, reloading our magazines. Pixan had disappeared into the treetops once again. Talia was using pressure and nerve techniques she had learned from her father, and Santino's bleeding had slowed greatly. It appeared he would survive, but he needed a doctor, soon.

CHAPTER TEN

Life's a poker game. Never be too anxious or too timid, and never be afraid to bluff.

—Billy Drescher

Larner was still at his motel in Belize City, impatiently waiting for a call from Rogale. His two accomplices were with him. The phone rang. It was bad news. In a routine inspection before flying over the jungle, the FBO mechanic found a damaged bearing on the tail rotor drive shaft of the helicopter. It looked like it would be down until the following morning.

Larner threw the phone against the wall.

Serina looked at her big Slav partner. He hadn't even flinched when the phone hit. Their eyes met, and for the first time, Larner felt a little out of control.

"So, we wait it out," he growled. "There's nothing else we can do."

"We don't even know if there's anything actually there," said Serina.

"No, we don't," Larner replied. "But are you willing to bet there's not, and just walk away? After all this?" He huffed angrily. "Go ahead, leave if you want. I'll pay you for your time. Then I'll send you a postcard from the Bahamas when it's all said and done!" He paused and composed himself. "I'm telling you. I know it's there. I know it is…I…" He started to tell them he had seen it in a dream, but he caught himself. These folks dealt in the here and now. That kind of statement wouldn't buoy his position.

"What about another helicopter?" asked Balac.

"Not a good idea," Serina said. "As much as I would

like to get this done, we don't need any more people knowing about us than necessary."

"Okay," said Larner, holding up his hands, palms out. "Okay. So we wait this out. Maybe that asshole Rogale will get his part done in the process. You're going to have to remember, I've read the dialogue on the parchment—where they talk about a room full of golden artifacts and incredibly valuable gems. History tells us that almost all the people in Chetumal died of the plague." He paused again. "I'm telling you, the stuff is still there..."

A little less than four hours after the ambush, bouncing along a barely discernable road at about 10 miles an hour, we found the River Chuj. The sun was setting, casting golden tendrils on the river as the water opened a fissure through the dense green jungle. Our coordinates showed that we were about a half mile above the curves in the river, where the limestone walls were. There was no point in pushing it, especially with Santino, who wasn't looking good, so we decided to set up camp. In the process, the sky began to darken. The jungle was quieting into shadows. The first of the evening bats swept out in jagged arcs across a mauve horizon, and the evening creatures began their calls. After we set up camp, I shimmied up a tree with our antenna wire and we called Petie in Belize. No word from Eddie. This whole thing was becoming a role of the dice.

As the last of the light was fading and the stars were emerging from the encroaching darkness, Benji put together a meager dinner and we prepared for the night, rolling out our sleeping bags and getting comfortable. Pixan had just found her way to us and sat peacefully on the limb of a gumbo limbo tree above Santino, her hooded eyes reaching out into the waning light of the jungle. Talia had cleaned and bandaged Santino's wounds again. The good news was, the bleeding had slowed considerably. No major arteries had been hit. He would live, but for now he would hurt. Talia gave him another light shot of morphine and they curled up on the far side of the fire, against the trunk of a large rubber tree, a blanket collecting them. The morphine was stroking our new friend and he began to speak softly to her. We pretended not to hear.

"I don't understand this thing with you," he whispered. "I don't understand. My religion tells me this is not possible. My priest would excommunicate me for thinking like this. But I can't help but know in my heart that this is not the first time with you. I know you from before, somewhere…" He drew a breath. "There are moments that I recall…the touch of your fingers on my skin, your voice, the way your mouth melds with mine. I just remember, and I have no way to explain it." He sighed. "I hope my God forgives me for such blasphemy."

Talia smiled and touched his lips with a finger. "My love, I don't think it matters so much what you believe, or who you claim as God. I think the High Spirit is a far more forgiving soul than we give Him credit for. What really matters is, does your belief work for you? Does it make you a better person? Are you kind and forgiving, and honest? It shouldn't have anything to do with threats of eternal damnation or promises of a couple dozen virgins." She caressed his cheek softly and smiled. "Faith is about the goodness that's born and lives inside you, and grows because you want it to—because you believe in the potential of a power and a compassion greater than your own." She paused. "I think our problem is, there are way too many people claiming to know the truth, and not near enough practicing it."

"Amen," muttered Will, as he rolled over in his sleeping bag, headed toward slumber.

"Aaahh," sighed Blingo, curling up in his blanket just a few feet into the flickering shadows. He stifled a yawn. "I like sleep. It's like death, without the commitment…"

Benji, who had just settled into his sleeping bag, suddenly sat up for a moment and signed to his sister.

She nodded to him. "Yes, I do, now that you mention it." Talia turned to the rest of us. "Do you smell something strange?"

And sure enough, now that she had said the words, I did—a heavy, musky smell that seemed to have passed through the camp on the evening breeze.

We had no idea that just a few feet into the dappled shadows of leaf and vine, a pair of large, dark eyes, sheltered under heavy brows, studied us. A moment later, the eyes faded into the darkness.

The following morning, soft trellises of sunlight eased through the thick foliage and brought us around. Parrots and monkeys chattered and called, and somewhere in the distance, a leopard coughed. Blingo, who had moved closer to the fire in the night, sat up and farted. It sounded like someone tearing a bed sheet.

"Jesus, Blink," moaned Will, waving his hands to ward off the odor. "Didn't those Texans teach you any manners?"

The little Indian grinned, with only a tad of contriteness. "Farts is just the ghosts of things we's eaten, trying to escape. We must set them free!"

After a quick breakfast, we contacted Petie, who tried to reach Eddie again, without luck. Now I was worried. Eddie was wrapped a little loose, but in the past, he'd always been spot-on when we needed him. Something had to have happened.

We packed as much necessary gear as we could carry, and started the last leg of the trek on foot. The actual road had ended, so the last half mile would take us through the jungle at the edge of the river. This was murder for Santino.

We took turns supporting him, and I had to admit my respect for him grew as he bit back the pain and forced himself onward. The truth was, there was only one escape for him now, or us. With the affair at the border station, there was no going back.

"Where the hell are you, Eddie?" I muttered. "Where the freaking hell are you?"

Unfortunately, Eddie had his own problems…

Cancun Airport Customs – Interrogation Room

"Listen, sir, I got no idea how those guns got in that compartment," said Eddie. "It's an old airplane, probably had four or five owners before me. You saw how well sealed the compartment was. How would I have known, dude?"

The ponderous Customs agent stood—dark, accusing eyes, a Pancho Villa mustache that wrapped around his fat chin, his body stretching the limits of a wrinkled blue uniform. He stared at the prisoner from behind his desk. Eddie was standing, attired in shiny handcuffs, a guard on each side of him.

"It hardly matters, *señor*, because you have no way to prove your defense. All I know for certain is, you have flown into a Mexican airport with weapons hidden on your plane." He sighed heavily, still staring at the American in front of him. "We have no choice but to hold you on charges of smuggling weapons into Mexico. Automatic weapons—a very serious charge."

Larner sat in his motel room smoking another of his endless cigarettes, his mouth locked in a scowl, the arrogance in his blue eyes suffering with uncertainty, when his newly installed phone rang. It was the manager of the FBO. The helicopter was repaired and ready. He clicked the cradle disconnect and called the others.

After two hours of brutal hiking along the dense river shoreline, Blingo led us to the limestone cliffs, which were fairly well disguised by their heavy growth. I noticed Santino had stopped and was staring at them, his eyes growing strange for a moment. He slowly eased out a breath as Talia came up and put her arm around him.

"Old ghosts, my friend?"

He did that shrug of his and winced from the wound in his side, placing his hand on it. "Perhaps…"

We had found a sandy bluff by the river on which to pitch camp, and unloaded our gear. I turned to Blingo. "Well, buddy, you lived up to your word, and got us to the cliffs." I took out $50 American and handed it to him. "I think we can take it from here. You've got the better part of the day to make it back to your village."

Blingo looked at me, then glanced around at the cliffs and the river. He came back to us. "You sure you don' want me to stay and help—with whatever it is you're doing? Dis damned jungle a pretty spooky place, *amigos*."

"No, I think we got it," I replied.

"I had a friend who told me dem same words—'I got it,'" Blingo replied with a bitter smile. "He was gonna pull a young howler monkey out of its lair. Now dey call him Lefty." He stared at us. "You know, everything happen for a reason. But sonetimes the reason is, you be stupid, and make bad decisions."

"We'll be okay, Tonto," said Will, moving up next to me.

Blingo shrugged. "Okay, I go." He held out his hands, palms up. "Whatta I care?" He reached into his pouch, threw some magic dust at us, and said goodbye. He moved off toward the edge of the jungle, turned and shot us the bird, and the next second he was gone.

As we watched Blingo disappear into the jungle, I admit, a pall fell over us. We were in the middle of a very dangerous place, on one of the wildest freaking goose chases we'd ever pursued—even for people who lived for wild goose chases.

"Son of a bitch!" Will muttered, breaking the moment. "We made it. We're here! Now, we've got a few hundred yards of growth-covered limestone in which to find a small entrance into an ancient king's man cave. No pucking froblem!"

Talia looked at me. "Is he always this…crazy confident?"

I grinned. "As long as he takes his meds."

"But first," said Will, "I gotta make a call to nature. It's been a long hike."

We were at the fringe of the jungle just before the gravel beach, and Will cautiously wandered into the brush. Moments later, a mere 50 feet into the dark-green labyrinth, Will was zipping up, greatly relieved, when he caught a whiff of the heavy, musky odor we had sensed at camp the night before. Slowly, cautiously, he began to scan the jungle around him. There was nothing out of place, but that sixth sense that had preserved him numerous times was on high alert. He shrugged, glancing around once more, and muttered to himself, "Getting jumpy in my old age. It's okay. It's okay…"

The smallest movement above him caught his attention.

There, crouched on the huge limb of a gumbo limbo tree, was the creature we had saved from drowning only days ago. "The Silver Spider" was squatting on its haunches, its slow, heavy breathing just audible, the creature's huge, dark eyes riveting him. Its thick, silver-gray fur glistened from a single ray of sunlight that had found its way through the trees, and the monster's mouth was open just enough to reveal a pair of massive fangs.

"Whoa shit!" whispered Will, taking a cautious step back.

Suddenly, the animal scuttled along the branch and down the trunk with a fluidness and speed that defied his size. It stopped then, staring at Will, only a few feet away—its big, intelligent-looking eyes neither violent nor friendly—and slowly backed away into the jungle. One moment it was there. The next, it was gone.

"Nice seeing you too," whispered Will shakily, glancing down at his crotch. "Damned good thing I just peed."

Will, of course, told us of his encounter, adding yet another page to this bizarre adventure, but we had no time for speculation. There was business at hand. We spent the next four grueling hours cutting away vines and plants along the limestone walls with our machetes, looking for the opening that led to an ancient fortune. When we reached the far side of the beach, where the jungle started in earnest again, we had found no opening.

While we worked, Larner and his people had loaded their gear, boarded their helicopter, and departed the airfield at Belize City.

"Okay, we're obviously missing something," said Will. "Either the topography has changed—which is certainly possible in a few hundred years—or the entrance was disguised in some fashion."

Talia shook her head. "I can't actually read the damned parchment. I'm only getting a word or two here and there. All I know for sure is, we're in the right place. And that comes as much from inside me as anything else."

While they were talking, I watched Santino's eyes subtly change as he studied the limestone wall. He got up and began to limp back the way we'd come, holding his side, his eyes focused on something just ahead. Not a hundred feet from us he stopped, looked back at us, and pointed at the wall. It was then that I noticed the anomaly.

Almost all the bushes and small trees that were growing vertically out from the wall started at one point, the roots having originally found a hole in which a seed/root could flourish. But there, in that one spot, was a fairly healthy kapok tree growing out then upward, toward the sun that fed it.

Santino drew a breath. "The kapok was the most sacred tree to the Mayans," he whispered in a somewhat disconnected voice. "As it was before, so it is now…"

Aside from Santino's strangeness, we'd missed two other important things: first, the base of the possible opening started about four feet off the ground. For the last few hours, we had been searching ground level. We had failed to take into consideration the height of the river. Four hundred years ago, the waters in Central America were more significant, and the river was higher. I was reminded of Tenochtitlan, the great Aztec city built on an island in Lake Texcoco, where there is little or no water now.

Secondly, and most importantly, while the tree began at the base of the cliff, the roots had burrowed up into the limestone in a most distinctive fashion—in the shape of a door. It wasn't perfectly square mind you (and it wasn't meant to be, for disguise was of the essence), but it looked as if someone might have chiseled a small opening into a comfortable entrance and later cut a rock to fit it. The roots had followed the remaining crevice for the sake of purchase, virtually showing an outline of what could have been an entrance. If it hadn't been for the roots of the revered kapok tree, we would have never noticed it.

I took my hand pick from my pack and began to scale the wall, cutting away at the roots, grabbing a tendril and crawling up, cutting away a piece at a time. In moments, Benji and Will had joined me. For the next 20 minutes we worked, holding on to adjacent shrubs and trees, and cutting and pulling the tenacious roots from the wall, until finally, the shape of a jagged entrance appeared.

Grasping a branch above me, I leaned in and kicked the door-shaped stone. Nothing. Again, with Will's assistance, we leaned in and pushed. Still nothing. We had driven ourselves to near exhaustion, certain, with Santino's encouragement, that we were in the right place, but it wasn't happening.

"Get back!" yelled Talia, standing behind us. "Move away!"

We all turned and found her holding the shotgun we had taken from our ambushers.

She pushed back her mane of dark-red hair with her free hand. "Get away!" she yelled again.

"My mother taught me to never argue with a woman holding a shotgun," muttered Will, as he scrambled down and away from the wall.

It seemed to be good logic. Benji and I followed.

As soon as we were clear, Talia aimed at the edges of the stone door and fired round after round, the stone exploding around the perimeter, rock shattering in fierce shrapnel. When she had emptied the weapon and nothing had changed, she didn't hesitate. She reloaded and fired again—another six rounds. We all stood there, ears ringing, smoke in the air, staring at her and the unforgiving rock.

"Son of a bitch," she hissed, her gray eyes alight with

anger and confusion. “Son of a bitch! I was just certain…”

Above us, Pixan circled and called.

I walked over to Talia and gently pushed the barrel of the shotgun down toward the ground. “You win some, you lose some,” I said. “Maybe this just isn’t the spot…”

About that time my partner walked over to the rock and stared at it. He swept his long blond hair back from his face with his fingers. “I woulda bet money,” he whispered, as he reached up and pushed on the rock, as if to convince himself of its invulnerability.

At that moment there was the sound of a distinct crack. Not loud, but heavy and portentous, and the door that had pretended to be a simple rock for the last 400 years guilelessly surrendered its secret with a moan, then a harsh crack, and tumbled heavily to one side in a cloud of ancient dust.

“Whoa shit!” exclaimed Will, stumbling back, staring at the dark opening in awe. “Floody bucking amazing!”

We stood there like statues, lost to the incredulousness of it all. There it was, the portal that, like a time machine, might well lead us to another era—a time of magnificent civilizations, of painted kings and queens in exotic feathered headdresses, of brilliant white cities, and sacrificial rites. And then there was the gold...

I stepped over to my friend and placed my hand on his shoulder. “Let’s go, Tonto.”

The others followed. We grabbed our flashlights and our courage, Talia pulled a camera out of her pack, and we crawled up into the entrance of another world.

Above us, Santino’s Pixan sailed in the invisible currents, watching.

We were immediately greeted by two skeletons that sat leaning against the rock walls, their white cotton breechcloths deteriorated into a gray transparency, their skin shrunken tight against brittle bones.

"The slaves, who drank their poison and performed a final last task for their king, closing the door…" said Santino almost reverently. He seemed removed, indifferent to his wound, yet apprehensive of what he might find—or perhaps afraid of what he might *not* find…

Talia and Benji, behind him, had grown quiet, their blue eyes shining in the glow of the flashlights.

Immediately, we began to see relief carvings on the walls as the narrow tunnel widened out into a comfortable, carefully cut passageway. This opened up into a large, comfortable living room with incredible colored murals on the walls depicting the multiple facets of Mayan life. On one side, carved mahogany chairs sat like silent statues around a beautifully engraved table. There were bowls carved of stone and wood, sitting on polished rock countertops that jutted from the walls with incredible perfection, marred only by the dust of time. Remarkable bas-reliefs of birds and animals above them leaped from carved stone. Above, near the top of the walls, we could see several ducts leading to the outside, providing fresh air, cut by slaves—torturous work, chipping small tunnels through the limestone with their hard, jadeite chisels. The vents had long since been clogged with earth, and the air was heavy and old, but it hardly mattered. We had just tumbled back centuries, into the life of a Mayan king. It was magnificent and humbling in the same moment.

Santino pointed to the small stone staircase that ended in a wide opening. "There," he whispered. "There…"

Slowly, we all gathered and ascended the few steps. Santino led, his mind whirling between present and past, his heart hammering, the wound in his side bleeding again, but forgotten. We stepped through the rounded entryway and there was a mutual gasp. It was a sight I'll not easily forget. The back of the small room was filled with some of the favorite treasures of a Mayan king—decaying bamboo baskets filled with golden trinkets, smaller wooden boxes flowing over with precious stones, and small golden statues of all the Mayan gods stood in a semicircle on a sculptured floor, watching over the God-King, Nachán Can. But the most startling, the most astonishing sight was that of Nachán Can himself, attired in a faded red cotton robe inlaid with gold, and a magnificent golden headdress of elongated quetzal feathers and embedded precious stones, seated in a modest throne of mahogany, also inlaid with gold.

The king's shriveled skin told of the centuries he'd sat with his treasure. His eyes were gone, just hollow, shrunken pits. In his lap, he cradled a small, golden image of *Ah-Puch,* the god of the underworld.

It wasn't a King Tut find. In truth, it was only a handful of very specific items, most likely held dear by Nachán Can himself, but it was a very valuable selection.

"He came back," whispered Santino. "One last time. To be with his treasure, and to add to it." He sighed, somewhere between disappointment and sadness. "His city was dying, and in the end, he had nothing left but his wealth..."

Like sleepwalkers (and truly it felt like a dream), we moved to the old king and his hoard. Santino, with Talia at his side, knelt and touched the remnants of Nachán Can's robe, his eyes distant and bewildered, softened by a memory he didn't understand. The rest of us, with a degree of reverence, began to examine the treasure of a Mayan monarch.

Will knelt and picked up a golden goblet with small emeralds embedded around the lip. "Mucking fagnificent," he whispered fervently.

I paused to run my finger across a circular Mayan calendar carved in mahogany—two feet across, a half-inch thick, and inlaid with gold. Benji had just discovered two reed boxes full of emeralds—some the size of quail's eggs—and here and there were small piles of necklaces and amulets, as if the king had held them, then discarded them indifferently. All the while Talia had begun snapping pictures.

"I hate to spoil the party, but I'm betting if we figured this out so has Larner," I muttered, looking around once more. "We need a plan…"

"Damned right there," said Will. "The question is, now, without Crazy Eddie, what do we do with it?"

"We'll help you with that," growled a familiar voice from behind us.

Startled, we all turned in unison. There stood our Professor Larner. A huge man with long blond hair stood on one side of him, and an attractive but cold-looking brunette on the other, all holding pistols.

"Speak of the devil…" mumbled Talia.

"We'd have been here earlier and all you would have found was an empty cave, but our damned helicopter had problems," said Larner. "We landed on the gravel beach, at the far end of the limestone cliffs. We'll have to move the bird a little closer, now that we have something to take home." He sighed. "You know, I had a damned premonition that this was the place. We just started walking along the foliage-disguised walls, and came to the entrance, with the big slab of rock lying to the side, saying, 'Here it is!'" Larner offered a sarcastic grin, his blue eyes smiling. "Can't thank you enough for all your help."

CHAPTER ELEVEN

It's not the bullet that kills you. It's the speed of the bullet…

—Robert Simpson

"What about us?" I said. "We found it."

"Ahhh…that is a bit of a problem," said Larner as he feigned a grimace. "However, he who has the guns makes the rules." He paused, ran a hand through his gray hair, and exhaled dramatically. "I think you're probably going to be disappointed." The professor pointed toward the pistols Will and I carried on our belts. "Take those out very carefully and lay them on the floor, now."

Unfortunately, Talia was so enthralled by the possibility of Nachán Can's treasure that she had left her empty shotgun by the entrance to the cave.

They had the drop on us. There was little choice. The alternative left someone—maybe several people (mostly us)—dealing with speeding bullets. Balac, the big Slav on the professor's left, moved in and snatched up our weapons while his dark-haired accomplice kept us covered with a nasty looking .380. Larner produced some nylon cord from the side of his backpack and pointed toward a barren corner.

"Tie them up," he said to his companions. Then he looked at us, his hard, blue eyes full of malice. "You do anything but breathe quietly and I'll kill you. Stay at ease and you might walk away from this."

"Yeah, when pig's fly," whispered Will.

After they tied our hands and feet, Larner and his people began examining the find. After a very preliminary inspection, the professor turned to Serina. "Go get the helicopter," he said. "Let's get this loaded."

Serina nodded wordlessly and was gone.

I watched the professor for a few moments as he began to move around the room. There was a look in his eyes that wasn't right...as if he was struggling with something. He saw me staring at him and instantly the look in his eyes faded.

Benton Larner was generally a "here-and-now" person, unattached to spiritual speculation. He was a man of little faith in the hereafter. But something was taking place that he couldn't fully grasp. He had always been drawn to early Central American history, but for the last week or two, since he had read the writings about the Mayan woman and the story of the ruler, Nachán Can, he had been having strange dreams. He was "seeing" glimpses of ancient Mayan life, as if he had been there—a white-walled city, a palace… He needed to keep a lid on this. He was a realist. But now, surrounded by this ancient history, he felt like a man standing on the shore of a great sea, and the tide of distant memory was washing over him. He shook his head to clear it, then glanced around to make sure no one else had noticed him. "Stay on top of this, Larner," he muttered angrily to himself.

There was one other issue the professor was dealing with. He was an astute character. Moreover, he was an unbridled larcenist who trusted no one. He didn't like the way the eyes on Balac and his friend, Serina, had touched occasionally when one of them held a particularly valuable piece. There seemed to be a communication taking place that excluded him.

Ten minutes later, the professor turned to the big guy and clapped his hands. "Okay, my friend, let's start getting this stuff out of here. Remember, we've got a 'useful load' problem with this bird, so take the most valuable items first."

Stacked up against the wall and bound like geese on the

way to the chopping block, we watched as our nemesis and his big friend began cleaning out the room. Now I could faintly hear a chopper landing. Larner immediately headed down the small stone stairway to the main room, then out the passageway. The big man with the blond hair manhandled a couple more of the incredible golden statues onto his shoulders, and moved out as well.

It had taken Serina about 20 minutes to hike back to the Bell helicopter, get it in the air, and land in front of the cavern's entrance. Balac was just bringing out the last of the small golden statues that had surrounded Nachán Can. Working in an uncharacteristically frantic fashion, Larner had managed the majority of the boxes of gems and many of the most valuable artifacts. Watching the Slav take another quick glance at Serina as she opened the cockpit door, Larner found himself reminded of an old bandit's saying, attributed to Pancho Villa: *"Integrity diminishes in proportion to the amount of gold on the burro."*

Balac set the statues down in the sand and stood, easing out a breath as the blades on the copter rotated to a stop.

"Oh well," said Larner as he pulled a gun from the small of his back and shot the man twice in the chest.

The large Slav's eyes registered the ultimate surprise as he took the shock of the rounds, and wavered like a tree sensing the breeze.

"Sorry, my big friend," said the professor. "But you're just not worth your weight in gold."

In desperate slow motion, Balac tried to reach the gun in his shoulder holster as he dropped to his knees, but nothing was working quite right.

Larner shot him again.

Serina threw the cockpit door open and was coming out in a rush, reaching for her pistol. The professor turned his weapon to her, holding out his other hand in supplication.

"Whoa! Whoa! Not to worry, my friend. You are an

integral part of this operation, and you will get your cut, which is now greater than it was a minute ago."

There was an uneasy pause and a shadow passed over her eyes.

"Truthfully," said Larner. "Which would you rather have—a giant, flat-faced Russian with a 12-word vocabulary, or another 250 pounds of gold, huh?"

Serina stared at him for a few moments, then glanced at Balac, face down in the gravel. Slowly she brought down her gun. "You'd best remember the part about the cut," she hissed.

From the cave, we heard the faint but distinctive crack of a firearm—twice, then once more.

"That can't be good," muttered Will.

Moments later, Larner and his lady partner were back. There was no sign of Balac. Wordlessly, they began snatching up the last of the valuable items, moving back and forth to the copter at a brisk pace.

As the floor was cleared of treasures, we began to see a fantastic mosaic that had been cut into the stone—a jungle scene of birds and small animals surrounding the face of a jaguar. Santino had grown weak and morose from the constant pain and exertion, and the loss of blood. He'd been running on the last of his adrenaline and his breathing had grown shallow. Not a good sign.

Finally, when everything of any real value had been taken, Larner came back to the treasure room. He was carrying our two sticks of dynamite, a blasting cap, and the 20 feet of slow-burning fuse from my pack. He saw the look on our faces.

"Yeah, we riffled your gear before coming in—for a little insight. Seems you had just the thing to make you and this little find disappear completely." He smiled. "You folks have been a huge help in the promotion of my finances and professional success. Can't thank you enough." He sighed dramatically. "But all good things must come to an end." He held up the dynamite. "This will close these rooms for eternity, and eliminate the possibility of anyone knowing I was ever here. Then I'll ride off into the sunset in my incredible flying machine." He grinned again. "Don't you just hate me?"

"You got that right," said Will.

It was useless to argue or plead. None of us even tried. The bitterness of failure and loss was like sawdust in our mouths.

Without any further ado, the somewhat twisted academician moved down the few stairs and placed the two sticks of dynamite at the tunnel entrance in the main room. He plugged in the blasting cap and attached the fuse to one stick, then turned and took a few steps up the stone stairs, so he could see us. While holding the end of the fuse in one hand and his cigarette lighter in the other, he said, "Well, all good things must come to an end." With a wicked smile, he lit the cord. "It's a slow-burning fuse. I figure you've got maybe five minutes for your lives to pass before your eyes while we hop into our helicopter, stay on the deck out of radar, and disappear with the wealth of a Mayan king." Larner dropped the dynamite cord, offered a casual salute, and disappeared down the passageway to the outside.

The room was silent for a few seconds, the only sound the hiss of the burning fuse.

Then Will spoke. "He's right, I hate the son of a bitch." He exhaled hard. "This is not at all how I pictured it. I figured something dramatic, or heroic—something Crazy Eddie and the Hole in the Coral Wall Gang would have talked about for years."

"I'm not ready to be so graceful about this," I gritted, as I started wiggling like an epileptic snake, trying to break away from the others. "If I can get to the fuse, maybe I can smother it or something..."

It was a shot—albeit a long one.

In the background, we could hear the helicopter lifting off.

Larner tightened his seatbelt and turned to his pilot. "Keep us on the treetops, Serina. I don't want radar picking us up on the way in. You know where we left the truck. From there, it's to the coast and the shrimp boat."

Santino edged closer to Talia, their faces almost touching. "I will find you again," he said. "I've loved you before and I will love you again. I don't understand it. But I know it."

Talia leaned over and kissed her lover gently. "I don't understand it either, but I'm graced with a love for you, and a knowledge that this is not the end." With an almost peaceful sigh, she whispered, "It's time for us to go now, heart of my heart. The gods are waiting..."

I fought with balance and direction for the next two, almost three minutes, wiggling and rolling madly, and managed to reach the stairs that led to the main room, where the fuse was burning brightly. There was no easy way to do the next part. I just took a breath and rolled down the steps—and promptly knocked myself out on the hard stone floor when I hit the bottom.

When I came around a moment later, the room had begun to fill with smoke from the fuse, and I could faintly hear Will yelling at me. But strangest of all, it felt like someone was throwing dirt on me. I spit out a mouthful and looked up.

There above me was a true apparition, and I was certain I'd been addled by the fall. There were two skinny legs sticking through the ceiling, wiggling and tossing centuries-old dirt everywhere. I realized that above me was one of the air vents that Nachán Can had installed to provide circulation, but someone was blocking it and yelling curses in English and Spanish. The apparition kicked and screamed again, and once more I was covered with dirt.

I glanced over at the fuse I hadn't managed to reach. There was little more than two feet left. In a minute or so, none of this would matter.

Suddenly, the dirt-clogged vent gave way in an avalanche of soil, rotten leaves, and roots, and the apparition came soaring down, limbs outstretched like one of those flying squirrels you see in *National Geographic*, screaming obscenities, and landing squarely on top of me.

I couldn't believe my eyes. It was our wild apprentice medicine man, Blingo. He was a little beat up, and covered with muck, but from the continual barrage of curses, I would say he was doing okay. He rolled off my chest and sat up next to me, brushing himself off, trying to get the dirt out of his hair and his eyes.

"Son a bitch! One minute I be walking along in da jungle peacefully at da top of da cliffs, trying to keep an eye on dat heelycopter and those other crazy people." He threw up his hands, tossing dirt everywhere. "Dey be shooting each other! Bang! Bang! And da next minute, I'ne doin' sonething like that crazy Alisee in Wonerland, fallin' through sone stinking worm's hole."

I couldn't believe it!

"Blingo! Blingo!" I yelled. "The dynamite! The fuse! Put it out!" I couldn't point, bound as I was. All I could do was move my head erratically, toward the fuse, which was now nothing more than a five-inch nub. We had maybe 30 seconds to go before everything disappeared in a roar.

Blingo looked at me like I was mad. "What fuse? What you all tied up for?"

"Behind you, you freaking idiot!" I screamed. "Put the freaking fuse out!"

The word "dynamite" got his attention. He told us he had worked on an oil rig earlier in his life, and they used dynamite occasionally. He turned around, spotted the sticks, and screamed, "Holy shit! You da most unpopular people Blingo ever meet!"

"Put out the damned fuse!" I yelled again, bouncing around madly in my frustration. Will and Talia were echoing my concerns as well.

Blingo finally got the message. With a shriek he vigorously stomped out the last few inches of burning fuse with the heel of his sandal.

"A floody bucking miracle," whispered Will from his vantage point on the treasure room floor. "A floody bucking miracle…"

In minutes, Blingo had us all untied.

There's nothing like a near-death experience to make you appreciate breathing.

Will stood and snatched up Blingo in a huge hug. "You wonderful, grubby little bastard! I'll never say another bad thing about you ever again!"

Blingo, his feet dangling off the floor, burbled out a moan from Will's enthusiastic embrace. "Let me go, *idiota!* Blingo gotta breathe!"

We all felt like we'd been given a new lease on life—all of us but Santino. The last 24 hours had been too much, and although he'd held up admirably, he was fading. He stood shakily with the help of Talia and Benji, and drew a breath. But it was then that I saw him straighten up slightly. He was staring at the relief carved into the stone floor, his eyes distant, yet animated.

"It is the right eye that holds the most value," he whispered. "It needs but a touch…"

"What was that about?" I asked, sensing from the faraway look on his face that something unique, or significant, was taking place.

Santino exhaled softly, and pointed at the jaguar carved in the floor. "The right eye," he said again, as he moved over and knelt by the relief. "He showed me," he whispered, his voice carrying the huskiness of emotion and recollection. Reaching out slowly, tentatively, he caressed the stone eye. Then he pressed it.

Nothing happened.

"We need to get him to a doctor, soon," whispered Will respectfully.

Santino looked up at my partner. "Ye of little faith," he muttered, as he turned back to the jaguar and pressed the eye once more.

Suddenly, there was a popping sound, as if a cog or a gearwheel had been thrown, and with a weary, grating sound, the square in the floor that held the jaguar relief dropped down a few inches and began to slide to the side, under the floor, revealing a small stone staircase.

"Holy freaking moly!" croaked Will.

I quickly grabbed a flashlight from my pack by the wall, came back, and as my friends gathered around, I shined it into the darkness. The first thing reflected by the light was gold—lots of gold. Slowly, with Talia and Benji assisting Santino, we descended the stone steps into the world and the wealth of an ancient Mayan king. Under the glow of our flashlights lay the most valuable artifacts of Nachán Can. What we had found above the floor had been an afterthought. This was the main act.

Blingo, gazing around like a kid in a candy shop, muttered, "I don' think I gotta be an assistant medicine man anymore."

"Probably not," I replied hoarsely, simply lost to the grandeur of wealth about us.

There was much of the same type of artifacts that Larner had stolen from us—personal effects like plates and goblets of gold, and baskets of precious stones. But here, in this cache, were also historical items that were simply priceless. Solid-gold Mayan calendars nearly four feet across, scrolls of gold leaf depicting the history of Chetumal and the Mayan Yucatan, and the golden armor of a Mayan king. Goblets and urns embedded with emeralds, and solid-gold chain link over a half-inch thick were piled in corners. Two-by-four-foot bas-reliefs of Mayan life were etched in solid-gold plaques, aside from numerous mahogany boxes filled with gold and silver necklaces. And finally, as with almost all cultures, there were ultra-thin golden scrolls of religion and history, written by the priests (and probably amended to the pleasure of the king). It was not just wealth in dollars, but an immense wealth in historical value.

Rolling out one of the scrolls and studying it for a moment, Talia paused and whispered, "Some things never change. Each civilization is a product of its priests and kings…"

When we had finally glutted our senses, we returned to the main floor. Santino studied the entrance for a moment, then reached down, touched a lever under the jaguar square, and it slid back into place.

"How did you know?" I whispered. "How could you possibly have known?"

Our friend's eyes were alight with a distant fire. "If I told you I simply remembered, would you believe me?"

CHAPTER TWELVE

Never mind the odds against you. If you doubled your effort, what would the odds do—send for reinforcements?
—Robert Brault

Cancun, Mexico

Crazy Eddie had spent the last 32 hours in a holding facility. It was so nasty, even the rats had packed up and left. He was being "softened." He understood. They wanted to know what he knew about the guns in his plane, but he also suspected that the ponderous Customs agent was playing another game as well. Eddie had been around the block once or twice. They hadn't allowed him a phone call, they hadn't shipped him out to a mainland prison, and they hadn't arraigned him yet. Maybe there was a horse in this pile of crap…

Guatemalan Airfield, Aérea de Izabal

Colonel Enrico Stata was sitting at his desk reviewing duty rosters when his second-in-command knocked, then entered. Major Latan stopped sharply and snapped a quick salute.

"Sir, as you know, the helicopter from the Belize International FBO entered the interior of Reserva de Biosfera Maya earlier this morning. Our latest radar surveillance indicates they landed on or near the banks of the Chuj River about an hour ago. Needless to say, that seems to be the direction the individuals who ran the border station were headed. A report from Uaxactun today said the same vehicle was seen headed into the jungle yesterday—toward the river."

The colonel tapped his pen on the desktop for a moment. "That's enough of a coincidence for me. Notify the Army outpost at Tikal and put one of our PC-7s on fully-armed standby."

Six years earlier, when the colonel had taken command, he had arranged for the Guatemalan Air Force to receive several PC-7 prop-driven fighter aircraft from Switzerland. They were similar to the famous American P-57s, equipped with wing machine guns and light rocket launchers, and had proven highly effective against the insurgency that had plagued the country on and off for the last 25 years.

"Well, we've found the treasure of a lifetime and we have absolutely no way to move it," said a frustrated Talia, as we sat outside the cave on the gravel beach. "And Santino needs a doctor—*now*."

"Damned right on both accounts," I agreed. "But unless we grow wings, I don't know what the hell to do. It'll be tough getting across the border into Belize by road. Most of Guatemala is looking for us, and we have only enough food and water for about two days—if we're lucky."

"Doesn't matter," said Will. "We're gonna have to take the chance and see if we can get back to the Land Rover. We stay here, it's gonna become a spooky version of 'Gilligan's Island.'" He glanced over at the body of Larner's partner—the big Slav—lying in the gravel about 75 yards away. "And we end up like that..."

I exhaled hard. "We'll make a stretcher for Santino, and take turns carrying him."

"And the treasure?" whispered Santino.

"It's been there for 400 years and nobody's bothered it," said Will. "We pull the door stone back in place and go. We've still got weapons."

Larner had left our pistols on the cave floor, and God knows why, but the shotgun was still lying in the gravel outside the cave entrance, right where Talia had left it. We also had two sticks of dynamite, with a very short fuse.

"Yeah, the weapons are a bit of luck," I added, "but first, let's try to reach Crazy Eddie one more time. We've got nothing to lose."

In less than five minutes, Blingo had scooted up a tree like a brown monkey, the antenna wire between his teeth, and I was tuning in the frequency. A moment later Petie came back.

"You still alive! I so happy! I no hear from you, and I think…"

"Petie, sorry to interrupt, but I gotta know—have you heard from our friend?"

There was a reluctant pause. "No, *mi amigo.* I am so sorry, but not a word…"

I thanked Petie for his help and signed off, then looked at my friends. "We're on our own. Something bad happened to our friend. I know it. But it doesn't matter now. There's nobody pointing to the Yellow Brick Road..."

An hour later, we had managed to manhandle the door stone into place, and cover the cracks with wet, powdered limestone. The entrance wasn't as perfectly disguised as before, but no one was looking for it now. After packing a few supplies, grabbing the weapons and the dynamite, and assembling an acceptable stretcher from a blanket and a couple of saplings, we started out. Benji led the way with Blingo. Will and I were carrying Santino, and Talia and brought up the rear.

We had managed most of the challenging trek through

the jungle along the river, heading back to the logging road, when we heard it—the rumble of trucks.

"Ohhh chit..." muttered Blingo. "Them's Army trucks. I know dat sound."

Will huffed out a brutal expletive. "Well, that puts the bloody fat in the fire. What do we do now?"

"We run the other way," I said. "Maybe, if we can make it back to the cave, we can hide there."

"I don't think we can outrun them with Santino," Will said hesitantly. "Somebody's gonna have to delay them."

That gave us pause, and we glanced around at each other.

Blingo held up his hands. "I'ne sorry. I no can do that. I got a family to think about."

Talia turned to him sympathetically. "I didn't know you had a family."

Blingo did a little shrug. "We'll, I don' 'xactly have one now, but I'ne thinkin' about it."

My partner drew a breath, and I knew what he was going to say.

"Give me the shotgun and I'll hold them," he said.

Will wasn't a soldier. Hell, he wasn't what I would call overly courageous a lot of the time. He'd rather run than fight. But today, he was offering himself, for us.

"No," I said, "I'll—"

But Benji interrupted me, signing furiously, and Talia translated.

She wasn't happy, but she hesitantly relayed his words. "My brother says, let him hold them. War is part of his life. Will won't have a chance, but with the shotgun and his pistol, Benji can delay them long enough for us to make the cave." She stopped and turned to her brother. There were tears in her eyes. She came from a nation of people for whom sacrifice had become second nature, but in the end, it made it no easier. She took his hand. "Benji, are you sure?

You don't have to do this. We could make it to the cave with just a little luck—"

Benji interrupted her with another wave of signs. Talia's shoulders slumped, her eyes lost their animation, and reluctantly, she nodded. She stepped in and passionately embraced her brother, caressing his face with her hand, tears filling her eyes, then she released him and turned to us. "My brother will hold them," she said. "We must go, now!"

Benji shook our hands stoically, accepting his fate, and signed briefly.

"God bless you too," said Will, interpreting.

With that, our friend turned and was gone. Will and I picked up the stretcher, and silently, we all moved out.

Not 10 minutes later, we heard the first report of weapons—the popping sound of Benji's pistol, then the rapid return fire of automatic weapons, then a blast from the shotgun. It continued intermittently for almost 10 minutes. When the firing stopped I heard Talia inhale sharply, then ease out a wretched breath. There were tears in her eyes. The sadness overwhelmed me, but there was nothing I could do or say. We had to move on.

We were nearing the edge of the jungle, but everyone was breathing in heaves, our legs like lead—especially Will and I, who were carrying Santino on the stretcher. We had to stop for just a moment, or exhaustion would overwhelm us and we'd lose what little edge we had.

"Just a moment to catch our breath" I gasped as we set the stretcher on the ground. "Just a moment…"

I was kneeling, Will next to me. Talia was sitting next to Santino, lines of tears staining her dark cheeks. She was holding one of her lover's hands while she wiped the sweat from his face with the other.

Suddenly, we heard a noise in the foliage behind us. We swung around in unison, and there stood a guy dressed like a cowboy—hat, boots, and an actual six-shooter, pointed at us. Although we hadn't known about him, it was easy enough to put the package together when he spoke.

"Ha! You think you gonna get away from Chico? I don' think so! You don' got one stinkin' bird. Not one! You never were gonna have one, huh? You damned sons of bitches cost Chico two soldiers and a day in dis sweaty jungle, but I'ne gonna make up for that." He shook his head angrily. "That damned gringo professor gonna pay me every peso he owes me! He wants heads, he gets heads." He saw the guns in our belts. "Drop de *pistolas*, *hombres*, slowly."

We had little choice. But as I was removing the gun from my belt, I noticed the heavy foliage behind the bandit waver, then slowly part. I couldn't believe my eyes. It was the giant gorilla creature Will and I had rescued from the river. His dark eyes were studying us, his mouth open slightly, displaying those monstrous fangs. The others saw it as well, but somehow managed to contain the surprise that would have normally overwhelmed them. Chico was too busy being a gangster cowboy to pick up on anything.

The report from Chico's pistol brought me around as the dirt next to me kicked up. "Get with da program, *gringo*," growled the bandit.

As I set my gun on the ground I noticed the foliage was still again, and the gorilla was gone. Long gone after the discharge of the weapon, I was certain.

It was obvious from his raving conversation that this guy had been hired by Larner to eliminate the competition. I had no idea what the part about birds meant, but none of this was good. We'd struggled so damned hard to find the treasure and stay alive, and now we were going to be shot and decapitated by some crazy Guatemalan gangster.

"Okay, I don' got no more time, and you don' got no more time, so let's get this done," said the bandit, backing up slightly and bringing up his six-gun. "One bullet for each of you, then I reload for whoever's still wigglin'."

As he aimed at me, I saw Will brace himself for a charge, but at that very moment, a huge, hairy hand reached out from the foliage, grabbed Chico around the neck, and lifted him off the ground. The monster silver gorilla stepped out of the brush, and the muscles on his arm that held the Guatemalan rippled. The bandit's eyes bulged in surprise and fear, and he gasped, his dangling legs squirming. He trembled, his face turning an ugly shade of purple as he wheezed helplessly. The gun dropped from his hand and he issued a final gurgling noise. The muscles on the creature's arm tightened once more, there was a distinct snap, and Chico Rogale was on his way to bandit Hell.

We were still kneeling, paralyzed by what we'd witnessed. It was like something out of a low-budget horror movie. The creature dropped Chico's limp body and just stood there, staring at us. It looked at me, then slowly turned to Will, and I swear to this day there was a single, startling moment when an understanding passed between us. A debt paid. I could see it in the creature's eyes. It was an experience that half the people in the world would deny, and the other half would give a week's pay to say they saw it happen—when man and animal actually shared a cerebral, maybe even moralistic moment.

Then the creature was gone.

"Did that really happen?" whispered Will, obviously shaken.

"Yeah, it happened," I said, pointing to our neck-snapped nemesis. "Ask Chico."

"Nobody gonna believe Blingo when he tell this story," muttered our Indian friend. He silently reached into his old cotton carry bag, pulled out his bottle of homemade hooch, and finished it in one, long gulp. "Nobody gonna believe me. Dey gonna say I'ne a filthy stinkin' liar." He shrugged.

"Which I am, sonetimes..."

As he dropped the bottle, the distant shouts of soldiers moving our way brought us back around. We looked at each other. Will and I picked up the improvised stretcher holding Santino, and we were on our way again.

Ten minutes later, my legs felt like hot lead and my breath was coming in gasps. I was putting one foot in front of the other in a barely organized stumble. Talia had kept pace with us, but she was breathing heavily. Blingo was the only one who didn't seem too fatigued—or maybe his fear drove him better than ours. Or maybe it was his magic hooch. Every once in a while he would stop to throw some of his yellow powder toward our pursuers and mumble a few words. It didn't look like it was working. The soldiers' voices were growing louder.

Finally, we turned the last bend in the river. The limestone walls and the cave were dead ahead. But we'd run out of places to hide.

At that moment, I heard it. The sound was distant, and for a second I thought it was my imagination. But I knew that sound. I knew that deep, purring rumble on those big, Pratt and Whitney air-cooled radials. I stopped, wanting to believe in the impossible. Will staggered to a halt in front of me. He had heard it too. He was looking ahead of us, downriver. Slowly, we eased Santino and his homemade stretcher to the ground, still gazing ahead.

I've always had a tendency to believe in the impossible. I love the novels with remarkable rescues and incredible heroes, because somewhere in my heart, I believed. I had known the "incredibly lucky"—the pilots who crashed airplanes, the sailors who fought the wildest seas, and the battlefield miracles—all who survived to raise a beer at the next smoky bar. Hell, I had been one of those people. And as if to prove me right, the gods themselves decided to throw me another bone. There, around the bend of the river, came Crazy Eddie in his magnificent Grumman Goose!

"Mucking fagnificent," whispered Will, his eyes glued to that incredible sight.

Talia moved up next to us and took Santino's hand as they stared ahead.

"Is that…?" whispered Santino from the stretcher.

"Ya mon," replied Will, hoarse with emotion. "That's the cavalry."

Eddie had seen us, and he wagged his wings to let us know. He dropped some flaps and pulled back on the power, and his wonderful old lady responded faithfully to his touch. He was no more than a hundred yards from us when the hull of the flying boat touched the water, tossing up a light spray on both sides of the bow, and in moments he was taxiing over toward the beach. But it wasn't "game over" yet. He had passed the Guatemalan troops moving toward us along the shoreline as he landed. They may not have been real quick studies, but they had this one figured, and within seconds they were firing at him as they double-timed along the trail toward us.

Eddie nosed the plane into the shallow water on the opposite bank from the soldiers. He shut down her engines, and as she glided gently toward the shore, he dashed back into the cabin, opened the hatch, and threw out an anchor he had ready. Will and I lifted Santino, drew his arms over our shoulders, and staggered into the water toward the aircraft, with Talia and Blingo behind us. In no time, we were at the hatch of the seaplane.

The soldiers were barely a couple hundred yards behind the plane. Bullets were slapping the water, whining as they ricocheted off the river, tearing holes in the light metal hull of the old bird.

As we reached the plane, Crazy Eddie read the situation and grabbed Santino first, dragging him into the cabin. Will and I quickly crawled in and together we lifted Talia aboard. Blingo scrambled in behind us like a monkey on crack. Fortunately, from our position on the river, and the location of the soldiers moving upriver toward us, the hull of the old Goose was protecting us, taking most of the rounds. The bullets slapping the hull sounded like popcorn popping. I found myself flinching like a smack addict. We could only hope that they continued to miss the vital parts—ours and the plane's.

"Is that everybody?" yelled Eddie from the cockpit.

I nodded while pulling up the anchor, and Eddie straightened up for takeoff. Will pulled the hatch closed as Eddie dropped 20 degrees of flaps and slammed the throttles to the firewall. The Goose surged ahead, gradually leaving the soldiers behind. Unfortunately, I realized that Pixan, Santino's hawk, was out there somewhere, but I couldn't do anything about that now.

We lifted off, then made a sweeping, sharp, 180-degree turn that took us back up the river on the far side of the soldiers, the way Eddie had come in, out of range of their weapons.

"Where the hell you been?" I yelled over the roar of the engines as Will and I got Santino to a seat.

Eddie spoke over his shoulder as he watched the river on his takeoff. "Long story, dude. But mostly I been sitting in a freakin' holding cell in Cancun, negotiating with a bastard Customs agent for my freedom." He huffed angrily. "Son of a bitch found one of my secret compartments with three M16s in it. It took us a while to come to an agreement. Thanks to a little foresight, I hid some cash in my bird as well. The problem was, if I told the freakin' agent where it was, the rube would have bogarted my stash, then burned me for smuggling guns anyway. You dig?"

He drew a breath and adjusted the throttles a little. "Finally, the rat-bastard allowed me a phone call. There was no use calling a freakin' Mexican lawyer. I'd still be sitting there. Hell, I'd have been there for years. So I used my call to contact a buddy of mine who lived in Cancun—a guy I knew back in the day…" He paused and drew a breath, adjusting the throttle a little. "I had him break into my Goose and get the money. Five grand. He did the gig for me. He met with the Customs agent and gave him the money. He also told him that I had 'friends'—not nice people—and now they knew his name. That did the trick. The next day I was out."

While Eddie was explaining his recent situation, he banked toward the river, crossing it as he headed toward the coast. Talia had scooted into the window seat next to Santino, doing her best to comfort him, just as Eddie banked. For just a moment, she glanced out the window at the river. Suddenly, her eyes went wide. She released Santino and swung around in a snap, staring at the water below.

"Benji!" she cried. "It's Benji! In the river!"

While Eddie instinctively drew back on the throttles to buy a little time, Will and I were out of our seats in a flash and over to her side of the cabin, staring out the portal behind her.

"Unfreakin' believable!" muttered Will. "It's him," he whispered. Then he yelled, "It's him! It's Benji! Like some freakin' miniature Sylvester Stallone!"

And sure enough, as if God Himself was there to prove my theory of extraordinary survival, there stood Benji knee-deep in the middle of the river, furiously waving his shotgun at us. He'd been wounded—his left shoulder was stained with blood—but he was still standing.

Will was already yelling at Eddie. "Get this damned plane down! Get it on the river, now!"

Eddie was an old hand at sudden changes and emergency flying. He didn't ask, he just kicked the big bird over into a nosebleed dive and brought her around perfectly. Inside of two minutes, we were aimed up the placid river, the hull slapping on the surface, our diminutive but incredible hero dead ahead. Eddie brought the plane past our friend, then swung around and drew back the throttles to a windmill, letting the current bring us right by him.

Benji scrambled over, splashing through the shallow water, and we dragged him through the hatch. Talia grabbed her brother and crushed him to her as they knelt on the cabin floor. It was obvious he'd taken a round high on his shoulder. He was bleeding, but not critically. Talia was sobbing with relief. Hell, I think we all had tears in our eyes as we gathered around to hug and clean up that damned little hero. It was touching and glorious at the same moment. We had survived the impossible—again!

Eddie glanced back at us for a moment and grinned. "Kryptonian, man! Freakin' rapturous!" he yelled with heady emotion. "That son of a bitch drinks for free at my bar forever!"

I felt Will's hand on my shoulder. "Nice job, Tonto," he said with a smile.

"How many times do I have to tell you," I replied with a grin. "You, Tonto…"

Once again, the amazing Crazy Eddie straightened out his bird in the middle of the river, pushed in the throttles, and drew us off the water like the sky magician he was.

We were headed home.

CHAPTER THIRTEEN

When was the last time you sat in a bar and listened to a guy telling a story about the risk he didn't take…
—Billy Ray

There was an impatient knock at Colonel Strata's door.

"Come in…"

"Sir, we have just received word from radar surveillance that an aircraft entered the Reserva de Biosfera Maya airspace about an hour ago, headed west into the interior on course to the same area as the helicopter that went in this morning. It dropped out of sight for a few moments, and now it's headed east, toward Belize and the coast."

"What about the helicopter?" asked Strata.

"We're not sure, sir. Surveillance picked up a couple of blips a while back, headed toward Belize, but they faded. While it may have stayed on the treetops going out, there's nothing to indicate for certain that it has left."

"Well, Major, someone just left, didn't they?"

"Indeed, sir."

"Call the airfield for me," said the colonel.

I found the Goose's medical kit. Talia gave Benji a shot for pain and began dressing his wound. It was a through-and-through on the ball of his shoulder. He had lost a lot of blood and would hurt like hell for a while, but he was going to survive.

Unfortunately, we had left Pixan in the jungle. With all the excitement and the gunfire, she had disappeared completely. When I told Santino how sorry I was, I could see he was upset, but he looked at me and said, "She is my friend, but she is a creature of the wild. I have never made her dependent on me for this very reason. She will be fine, until I return to find her."

Eddie's $5,000 had also bought him full tanks of fuel. With the additional long-range tank that had been installed by the original owner, and a top-off stop somewhere in Mexico, we might just make the Keys.

After we'd reached a cruising altitude, I moved up into the cockpit, eased back into the co-pilot's seat, and turned to our buddy, Eddie—his long, sun-bleached hair tied in a ponytail, that leather patch over his right eye, and his ever-present Margaritaville ball cap perched on his head. "Thanks, my friend. I know this hasn't been a picnic for you either."

Eddie nodded. "You got that right, bro."

"I'll make it worth your while," I said. "I promise. You have no idea of the ancient goodies we left behind. You can be part of that when we go back, if you want." I couldn't stop the sigh that escaped me. "This started out like such a nice, simple little gig, and in just a few days we've managed to become wanted by the authorities in a couple countries, find and lose two treasures, get chased by a sociopathic professor, ambushed by a psychotic Central American cowboy, and in the end, pursued by the Guatemalan military."

Eddie smiled as he adjusted the trim a little. "Funny how you dig yourself into a hole by the teaspoon," he said with that funky grin of his.

In a little over a half hour, we reached the coast. Most all of us were just enjoying the luxury of safety, lulled by the hum of the big radials. Even Blingo was silent—no farting, no quasi-sage comments about life. Santino and Talia were curled up together. Santino was hanging on, but he was way past needing a doctor. I had settled into the co-pilot's seat, and Will was in the seat behind the cockpit partition. The plan was to run offshore about 10 miles, then make a hard left to the north, toward Playa Del Carmen. Eddie knew of a small strip just outside the city where we would refuel, although we weren't looking forward to explaining the bullet holes in the plane. Eddie just chuckled and said $100 would buy blindness in almost any small FBO operator in Mexico.

We made it to the coast without incident, passing to the north of Belize City and heading out into the Gulf. We were just about to make our northern turn, toward Playa Del Carmen, when suddenly an older-looking, prop-driven fighter aircraft slid up on our starboard wingtip. Eddie's radio issued a burst of static and a voice broke through. It was heavily accented and there wasn't an ounce of friendliness in it.

"Grumman Goose November 55048. This is Pilatus TG77988 of the Guatemalan Air Force. You have departed Guatemala and Belize without prior ground or airspace authorization. We are requesting you make an immediate return to the Guatemalan airbase of Puerto Barrios."

Eddie looked at me. "Shit! Didn't see that coming. Most of the time these folks don't pay too much attention to departures. Could be they had an eyeball on you."

"Doesn't matter," I said. "We're not going back. We just had a major gunfight with the Guatemalan Army." I paused, glancing over at the fighter. It was almost exactly the same as the famous American P-57s, equipped with wing machine guns and light rocket launchers. "Can you delay them until we get out of Guatemalan airspace?"

"We're already out of their airspace," mumbled Eddie. "They don't care. You guys must have seriously screwed the pooch."

At this point, the others, with the exception of Santino and Talia, had gathered around us.

"Well, we did beat up a couple guards and run a border

crossing," said Will. "And I suspect Benji probably shot a few people."

"Don't tell me any more," barked Eddie. "I don't freakin' wanna hear it!"

The radio crackled again. "Grumman Goose November 55048, I repeat, return to the coast, now. Return to Guatemalan airspace. I am authorized to shoot you out of the air if you do not comply."

Eddie began intently studying the horizon. There was a large freighter a few miles out. We could just discern the outline of the huge ship. Eddie reached between the seats and found a cordless electric shaver. As he brought it up to his microphone, he muttered to us, "If we could make that big momma out there, this guy wouldn't risk shooting us...I don't think. Witnesses and all. You dig? Might make for an international incident." He shook his head angrily and wagged a finger at me. "And don't call Eddie no more. Eddie's new little bar is looking better and better." He put the shaver to the mike, turned it on, and in a high, distant voice said, "TG77988, this is Grumman Goose November 55048. We are experiencing electronics difficulties. I cannot read your transmission. Please repeat."

"This is your final warning," the PC-7 pilot replied. There was a darkness in his voice.

"Cannot make out your transmission," said Eddie, razor to the mike, as he gradually pushed the throttles to their max and began a descent at the freighter in the distance. "We want to comply, but we are not reading you clearly."

Without another word, the PC-7 ripped upwards and away.

"Maybe you wore him out with your idiot act," said Will.

Don't know," Eddie replied, still losing altitude, the freighter dead ahead, about a half mile out. "But I wouldn't bet on it."

At that moment, there was a monstrous hammering across the top of the Goose as a battery of .30 caliber rounds ripped through our aircraft.

"Whoa shit!" yelled Will, who was standing, hunched over, in the cockpit with us. He quickly glanced to the back of the plane. "We got serious holes back here!"

Thank God, no one was hit, but everyone was paying attention now. There was no question this guy wasn't planning on us going home. We'd barely had time to assess the damage when the PC-7 rolled over across the sky and dropped on us again. This time, the pilot came at us high, straight on, and slightly above, his machine guns sawing across the starboard wing. Immediately after his pass, the engine on that side started throwing out heavy, white smoke. It hadn't quit yet, but it was badly wounded.

Eddie had installed mirrors on both sides of the cockpit, as the World War II fighter/bomber pilots had done, to provide an image of who was coming at them from behind. It was a throwback to Eddie's smuggling days. It just made him feel…"comfortable," as he put it. I checked the mirror on my side and watched the PC-7 roll down and away from us, then begin a methodical, wide turn. He was going to come at us again from the rear and underneath. He wasn't in a hurry. He was enjoying this. It was obvious that he either hadn't noticed or considered the ramifications of the freighter in the distance.

When I saw him begin to roll into a slow bank, I was struck with a thought. It was desperate and probably useless, the odds miserable, but man, there was nothing left to lose. I turned to Will, who was behind me. "Buddy, find us that dynamite and what's left of the fuse. Should be in my pack."

"Oohh good," muttered Will. "We're being shot to pieces and now you want dynamite. You gonna blow us up?"

"Not if I can help it," I said. "Just find it for me, quick!"

With most private aircraft, you can't dump fuel easily, if at all. But I remembered Eddie's Goose had been owned by an old smuggler before Eddie got it. There were times when weight became an issue in the business of late night, burlap-wrapped packages. The long-range tank in the belly of the bird had been designed with a release valve that would spray fuel out the back and away from the plane. A lever between the cockpit seats activated this operation.

I leaned toward Eddie and shouted over the engines. "You can still dump the fuel in the long-range tank, right?"

"Ya mon," replied Eddie, working with the starboard engine throttle and pitch levers, trying to keep the old girl in the air and us from becoming a fireball. "You got a plan, dude?"

"Yeah, I think so," I muttered, checking my mirror again. The PC-7 was just completing its turn and coming back at us. "I want you to dump the fuel in that tank when I yell at you, okay?"

Eddie looked up at me. "You gonna do something crazy, aren't you?"

I put my hands up, not knowing what to say and not having time to say it. "Eddie—"

My old friend interrupted me, the fatal acceptance in his eyes countered just slightly by his enormous passion for the next barroom story. "It's okay, dude. Eddie likes crazy. Crazy is an old friend."

Will called to me from the cabin of the plane. He held up the dynamite, the tiny three inches of fuse still attached. One final glance at the port mirror told me we were running out of time. The Guatemalan fighter was closing in, coming up underneath us like a white shark on a sunbathing seal. I looked at Eddie, sitting in that old, weathered cockpit, facing the jaws of death with a smile on his face. "Unfreakinbelievable!" I muttered to myself. "Open the exit port on the fuel tank!" I yelled.

As Eddie threw the switch, I staggered back to Will and grabbed the dynamite. He held up a lighter just as a burst from the fighter hammered us again. I lit the cord as my lifelong friend threw open the hatch, the door slamming furiously against the fuselage from the force of the wind. We stood there for just a moment, the gale outside sucking at us like Dorothy's tornado, the sparkling fuse consuming the last inch to the powder as the wicked Guatemalan witch just below us closed in for the kill.

The pilot's machine guns chattered as the high-octane aviation fuel streamed from the rear of the old Goose in a hurricane of spray, covering his aircraft. I tossed the bundle of dynamite out the door without breaking eye contact with Will.

"Just a simple, uncomplicated vacation," my friend said with a smile.

Sometimes the gods are kind and they throw you a bone. The dynamite blew not a hundred feet behind the Goose, and just a couple hundred feet in front of the gasoline-soaked PC-7. A horrendous, fiery explosion consumed our nemesis in a searing ball that burned the paint off the tail feathers of Eddie's Goose.

In reality, it had been a crazy, dumb thing to do, because there was a 50-50 chance that the fire from the explosion would have chased the gas back to the tank on our plane. But once again, Crazy Eddie's remarkable intuition saved the day. He was watching his rearview mirrors the whole time. He had been through so many situations in his lifetime, there just wasn't much he didn't have a jump on. The instant he saw the explosion, he shut off his dump valve and threw the plane into a climb—because gas fumes sink. That probably saved our lives. For the moment…

We had one engine that had taken a hit from the PC-7's

machine guns. It was running, but it was smoking badly and needed to be shut down. From the holes we were seeing in the floor of the aircraft, it was a safe bet that the Goose's fuselage float system was shot to hell. It was no longer a flying boat. Hell, watching Eddie struggling with the controls, it was barely a flying airplane.

I stared at the huge cargo/container ship ahead, 20 degrees to our starboard, then shifted toward Eddie. "Will he stop for us if we ditch?"

Eddie shrugged. "It's a toss-up. Depends if he's behind or ahead in his schedule. If he misses us on the pass—and he probably will, because it takes about a mile for them to stop—he'll lose a couple hours turning around and coming back for us. Those sons of bitches make a sloth look like a racehorse."

Eddie glanced at his instrument panel, then out at the smoking engine. It was overheating and had started to miss.

"We're gonna have to get down pretty quick, one way or the other." He huffed out a bitter sigh. "My guess is, he'll kick out a life raft and call the closest FBO or military base." He looked back at us. "And that'll be Belize or Guatemala. He calls either one of those and we're gonna end up in prison."

I grabbed the binoculars from the console compartment and studied the name and registration on the bow of the ship. "Osprey Shipping, out of New Orleans," I said.

Eddie studied the ship again for a moment, while fiddling in his ashtray for a half-burned joint. He lit it and took a deep drag, exhaling slowly. "It's a container operation with only a few boxes up toward the bow and amidships. Dropped off everything at its last port and didn't pick up much. Nothing much on the rear deck. He's headed to his home port." He smiled. "I like New Orleans," he said. "Maybe we could hitch a ride. That way I don't lose my bird."

Will, crouched behind us, straightened up as much as possible. "You're talking about landing on that? There's not a whole lot of room for error and you become part of a sad story."

"It's that, or we dump in the water and gamble they stop," Eddie replied, adjusting the pitch of the prop on the wounded engine. "Good chance there we end up in a Guatemalan prison. One thing's for sure, that engine's dying, and I wanna be down before it quits."

Will reached over and snatched the joint from Eddie's fingers, took a deep drag, and looked around at everyone else. "Small rooms with bars make me nervous."

"No stinkin' prisons for this monkey," said Blingo. "I rather swim home."

The others sought a decision in each other's eyes, then nodded.

"Okay," Will squeaked as he exhaled. "Buckle up. It's New Orleans."

Eddie nodded and tuned his radio to the area marine emergency frequency, monitored by most seafaring ships. "Osprey Shipping, Osprey Shipping. This is Grumman Goose November 55048, off your port bow approximately one mile. This is an emergency. I repeat, this is an emergency! Come in, Osprey Shipping. Come in."

In moments, a Southern-accented voice came back. "This is Osprey Shipping. Read you loud and clear, Grumman Goose November 55048. We have a visual on you. How can we be of assistance?"

Moments later, the container ship's crew was clearing its stern and middle decks of obstacles in anticipation of our landing. All we needed now was a little more luck.

Eddie took his bird out a half mile and coaxed her up to 3,000 feet, to give him some gliding room if everything quit. His starboard engine was already coughing, and now he was having trouble getting full power out of the port engine. Could be a round from the PC-7 had damaged or pinched a fuel line. The Goose was like an old lady stumbling her way to the last vestiges of safety. Eddie put his bird on a glide path, gave her 10 degrees of flaps, and began gently coaxing her in. Then he turned to me, in the co-pilot's seat, and glanced at Will behind us, who was still standing.

"Well, she might just make—"

At that moment, the starboard engine suffered a convulsion. It coughed again, heavy gray smoke began bellowing from the exhaust ports, and it began to shudder. Eddie's dear old lady was on her way out. The big propellers on the engine began to slow, and he quickly feathered them, aligning the blades with the oncoming wind to avoid drag and loss of control. Then the engine stopped.

Eddie dropped another 10 degrees of flaps, and was practically standing on the left rudder now to compensate for the loss of control. He drew back the throttle on the dead engine's side and increased the power on the good one.

"Keep the pressure on that left rudder," he yelled at me, "while I try to convince this girl to keep flying."

Eddie was dropping the remaining flaps now, trying desperately to keep the Goose's nose up. The bow of the huge container ship was coming up at us fast. The captain had managed to get most of the rear upper deck cleared, but there was a small crane, about halfway through our impromptu landing field, that no one had gotten to. Whether or not we had enough room to get the starboard wing by that was a toss-up.

My clever, gutsy partner was buckling himself in behind me now. To my left, Eddie was checking airspeed and altitude, like the perfect pilot he was, holding tight to the vibrating control yoke, his one eye alive with excitement, the edges of his mouth curled into a slight smile—not a drop of fear anywhere. I glanced behind me. Talia had her arms wrapped protectively around Santino. What a find that woman was—tough as nails and as pretty as a prom queen. Benji, our small, inscrutable hero, was riding this out as he did everything else—in confident, courageous silence. Our little buddy Blingo was strapped in and staring straight ahead. Every few seconds he'd toss a little yellow magic dust into the air, then quickly grab the armrests again. I couldn't help but smile. The gods had given us a fine group of companions for our journey into Mordor.

We were 100 yards off the bow and about 200 feet above the empty container ship when the port engine started coughing and all control went to hell. To this day I'm not quite sure how Eddie managed to squeeze out those last few feet and get her wheels on the deck. He was popping the brakes now, trying to slow us down, using the last of our inertia and the ailerons to sidestep the crane. The metal beast stood there, intransigent and as immovable as the Colossus of Rhodes.

Eddie did his best, cursing vehemently under his breath, slamming the rudder, and instinctively turning the control yoke in a useless gesture, as pilots often do when caught in a ground emergency. It all did little good. The base of the crane caught the last six inches of our starboard wingtip, sending us into a spinning turn toward the edge of the deck. Beyond that, there was nothing but a 100-foot drop and lots of water.

At that point, hopeful silence gave way to serious concern. As the cabin filled with yells, the old plane lurched into a 180-degree spin toward the rail on the bulwarks. The port landing gear snapped, and that wing dropped onto the pontoon as we continued to skid toward the edge. There was nothing anyone could do. The ship's crew watched in stunned silence as the Goose ground sideways along the deck, its inertia driving it toward the gunwale. Its nose hit and snapped the chain guard at the rail of the ship, but the bulwarks held. We were still holding our breath when, somehow, the devil ran out of tricks and the old Goose shuddered and settled.

Crazy Eddie eased out a sigh. "Well, any landing you walk away from…" He dug into the ashtray, found another half-smoked joint, and lit it.

I couldn't help but smile. As the realization that we had actually survived caught hold, we were chuckling, then laughing out loud, slapping each other on the back and hugging.

The ship's crew quickly surrounded us with fire extinguishers, then had the hatch open and began pulling us out. The captain—a big, burly fellow with a shaved head and a dark, full beard—stood in front of us.

"I watched that little display up there with my binoculars," he said, pointing back to where we'd fought with the PC-7. "It just so happens I was a Navy pilot before I started sailing tubs like this." He took a breath and shook his head. "I don't know exactly how you pulled that off, but anyone who can take on a fighter plane with nothing more than an old Grumman floater, and beat them, can have a berth on my ship anytime."

I started to explain the situation about us and Guatemala, but the captain raised his hand, stopping me.

"I don't want to hear about it. In fact, I'm gonna pretend I don't know about it. I'm the only one who had binoculars on this affair, and you were almost too far out for me. As far as I'm concerned, you had engine problems and landed on my deck." He paused. Those heavy brows on that cragged face narrowed, and his eyes went hard. "You understand?"

We all looked at each other.

"Oh, yeah," said Eddie, holding up his hands, palms out. "We're very cool about this."

That evening, as Will and I stood on the stern of the tanker, watching the sun bury itself in the western horizon, it all came home. We had once again survived an impossible journey. Frodo Baggins had nothing on us.

We had managed to become wanted in possibly two Central American countries, had ourselves shot up, banged up, and battered by Guatemalan soldiers and backcountry bandits; we had found a treasure and lost a treasure, and found another. Somehow, we escaped an encounter with a killer jungle monster—not once, but twice—and finally, we had survived a battle with a Guatemalan fighter plane that had pretty much destroyed Eddie's Goose, and somehow we had made an impossible landing on a moving freighter.

While Crazy Eddie would argue that we were making some serious points on the barroom stories, we were coming home with nothing more than the clothes on our backs. But we were all still alive, and like a guy named Harry Crews once said, "Sometimes, survival is triumph enough…"

CHAPTER FOURTEEN

Live your life in such a fashion that death will tremble in its effort to take you, and your name will still be found on the lips of your friends long after you've soared into the heavens.

—Ned Patter

Three days later, we were sitting in Lafitte's Blacksmith Bar on Bourbon Street in New Orleans. Built between 1732 and 1772, it was heralded as the oldest structure used as a bar in America. It was originally said to have been a hangout for the famous Lafitte Brothers, used as a base for their smuggling operations in the late 1700s. Many a daring rogue had sat beneath that roof and planned his or her next escapade. Somehow, it seemed appropriate.

Santino had spent two days in the hospital, being cleaned up and stitched up and receiving blood transfusions. Benji was a guest of the local emergency room for a couple of hours, his shoulder wound being cleaned and sutured. Eddie's Goose had been lifted off the freighter by crane, partially dismantled, and taken to a hangar at a local airport. It was so badly damaged, there was some question about its ability to be salvaged. Eddie was not a happy guy, even though Will and I had agreed to pay for a replacement.

"Eddie liked that freakin' bird," he said, nursing a mid-morning Miller. "Now I got to physically and emotionally bond to another one." He huffed angrily. "That ain't easy, man. You got to find the soul of that metal creature. You got to run out the old *duppies*—"

I smiled at Eddie's use of the Jamaican word for *spirits*.

Eddie threw up his hands, spilling a portion of his beer on Talia. "And I gotta rebuild a new relationship with the heart of the machine. It's like cowboys and horses—you got to ride the horse till it gives up and belongs to you."

It seemed a bit much, but then Eddie's reputation spoke for itself. I'd never known anyone who could coax more out of an airplane than him.

The waitress appeared and we ordered another round of drinks.

Will finished the remainder of his whiskey sour, sat it down, and glanced around at us. "So, here's the question hanging in the air. What do we do about Larner? Who, just to refresh your memories, stole our treasure and tried to kill us. That is, assuming he managed to get back to the States with our loot."

"I'm betting he did," said Eddie. "Sonabitch is smart, and he's got connections."

Talia sighed. "I know what he did, but do you want to go back to war with him? Why don't we just let him go? Write it off. We've still got another treasure to retrieve."

I shook my head. "The son of a bitch tried to kill us—to bury us in a limestone tomb. I'm not willing to let him get away with it. Besides, he's going to discover that we survived. Hell, he's sure to find out. Then he'll have to silence us. His reputation would be at stake, not to mention the possible charges of international theft of antiquities and attempted murder." I paused. "Nope. It's him or us!"

Will, sitting to my left, nodded. "Bottom line, he's gonna come." He paused and glanced around the table. "You always have a choice in life. You can be the hero in the story, or you can be the victim."

Benji signed rapidly for a moment.

Talia exhaled hard. "My brother says, 'Damned right. Learn, grow, bleed for better reasons next time.'"

We sat at the bar for the next hour, trying to determine

Larner's weaknesses and how to approach him. At the end, I sat my drink down.

"He's going to sell the lion's share of this treasure. He has to, and he has to do it fairly quickly. I'm betting he's not sleeping much as it is, with all that treasure stashed close by. Somehow, we need to ferret out where he's got the stuff."

"There's one other big ace we have to play," said Will with a sly smile. "He doesn't know we're still alive."

"We need to keep it that way," said Talia. "I want to be the first to say, 'surprise, surprise!' Just before I shoot him."

We had guessed correctly, but what we didn't know was that Larner never had any intention of bringing the treasure into the U.S. Instead, his innocuous shrimp boat had carried its precious cargo around the tip of southern Florida and across the Gulf Stream into the Bahamas, to his vacation home on Eleuthera Island. Eleuthera was a crooked mélange of rolling sand beaches and colorful coral reefs, about 50 miles east of Nassau. The original inhabitants of the island were the Lucayans, an Arawakan-speaking Taino people. They were discovered by Europeans in the 1400s, and completely decimated through slavery and disease by the mid-1500s. It was always the same story, every time. It seemed to be the perfect damned place for Larner.

The professor had a mansion near the southern end of the island, at Tarpum Bay. That's where he, his shapely pilot friend, and their treasure, had ended up. It had been a long, miserable trip, during which neither he or Serina ever slept at the same time, but they had pulled it off.

Larner had played an ace before the shrimper left the dock. He told the captain, "I know you have a family. I know where you live. In seven days, if I don't arrive on

Eleuthera, my people will reduce your family and your home to ashes."

When they made it to Eleuthera, Larner had the captain follow the wide channel to the long set of docks in front of his home. That night he instructed the captain and the mate to help unload his precious cargo. Then Larner killed them both, dragged them into their shrimp boat, and had Serina follow him out to the reef in his Mako sport fisherman. When they got past the outer reef, he shot holes in the bottom of the shrimper. Fifteen minutes later, Mother Ocean had swallowed all the evidence. Professor Larner was not a man much bothered by ugly details.

Serina had helped Larner with the sinking of the boat, but there was a part of her that had begun to realize the ruthlessness that lived in the good professor. And when he killed Balac…

Three days later, after he'd had an opportunity to catalog and photograph his cache and determine what he simply had to keep for himself, Larner began, very subtly, to send out word to an ultra-select group of individuals around the Western Hemisphere. Then he went back to work at the University of Miami, as if nothing had ever happened. Just a little hiatus. It would take a few days for the big boys and girls in the antiquities profession to get back to him.

Almost a week after our remarkable ditching on the freighter, we landed in Key West via commercial airlines. Eddie headed back to his little rental on Ramrod Key, and we rented a cottage for Talia, Santino, and Benji. Will settled into his converted shrimper on Stock Island, and I returned to my home on Big Pine. Will and I drew lots to see who would get Blingo. I lost. We agreed to take a couple of days to relax and gather some information, then we'd deal with the professor. But we did need to know where he was. A quick call to the University of Miami told us he had just returned from his "sabbatical."

We decided to meet with an old friend of ours, Captain Shane O'Neal of the Florida Keys Drug Enforcement Agency. Will and I had become fairly good friends with the captain. He had married a lady friend of ours a year or so back, and a little after that, we had avenged an attack on him by a Jamaican drug lord. He didn't exactly owe us, but I knew he would do what he could.

Shane was tall, with Indian-black hair, green eyes, and the tight, hard muscles of a boxer. He had a deep voice and an easy laugh, but he could be as deadly as a leopard. He also shared our passion for the ocean, and our passion for an occasional evening on the town, although now that he was married, those were few and far between.

After a warm greeting and a little catching up, Captain O'Neal ushered us to seats in front of his desk. He leaned back in his chair and eased out a breath. "Okay, guys, what have you gotten yourselves into this time?"

When we gave him the *Reader's Digest* version of what we'd been through, he ran the fingers of one hand through his dark hair. "You don't do anything halfway, do you?" O'Neal sighed hard. "Okay, let me see if I've got this right. You ran a Guatemalan border crossing after injuring two guards—"

"Yes, but the fight wasn't our fault, and they didn't take our names," I said. "The border guard just looked at our passports and gave them back."

"Yeah, I'll admit that's a damned huge thing right there," replied Shane, "or you'd all be beyond screwed. Still, you killed the Guatemalan citizen/bandit guy."

"No," Will said. "It was actually the giant monkey that did that. We just watched."

Shane sighed again. "Nobody is going to believe any of this bullshit. You sure you weren't sampling the funky smoke there?"

"Nope," said Will, "but Blingo, the assistant medicine man that we picked up, did have a bag of magic dust."

Our friend ignored the last comment. "But you did get into a gunfight with the Guatemalan military, and apparently blew up one of their fighter planes?"

"Yeah," we replied in unison.

"But all of those people were trying to kill us," I added. "Including the Miami professor and his sociopathic sidekicks, who tied us up and left us in a cave with two sticks of dynamite and a short fuse."

Captain O'Neal held up his hands. "I don't want to hear any more. In fact, I never heard any of this conversation, you understand?" He looked at us incredulously. "You two ever considered writing a book? Under false names, of course."

"Here's what we need," I said, cutting to the chase. "I know this is an inconvenience, but we want to know more about this Professor Larner. We need addresses on him, telephone numbers, and we have to see if his name is coming up in any 'conversations' anywhere. I'm betting he's got to get rid of the lion's share of that treasure pretty damned quick."

"Yeah, *inconvenience* is a good term for this," muttered the captain. "But considering I have somewhat reliable witnesses who claim Larner tried to kill them, I can probably make that happen." He paused and drew a breath. "And I suppose you need this today, huh?"

"Yesterday," said Will, with that half-assed smile of his.

Will and I had a quick dinner at Two Friends Restaurant, then headed toward our respective homes. I called the gang to let them know what was happening.

As to our companions in crime, it looked like Santino was healing remarkably well. But then, he had a great nurse and real incentive to get all his body parts working efficiently. Eddie had already begun shopping for a new Goose—"A freakin' expensive one with all the bells and whistles"—and Benji was enjoying the beaches and the variety of vodka cocktails in Key West. Blingo was just chilling out at my place—ordering pizza, drinking beer, smoking cigarettes, and watching reruns of "Gilligan's Island" and "Gunsmoke." He liked "dem crazy people on dat island, and dat big guy with da big hat, dat's always chooting people he don' like."

The following afternoon, Captain O'Neal called me. He had some interesting news.

"Seems you two hit it dead on the head," he said. "We had our phone people in the South Florida area listen for info on treasure or gold, or auctions, and we put a quick tap on Dr. Larner's office and home in Miami. Our people picked up two floating conversations about a special auction—a very hush-hush thing, evidently—taking place in the Bahamas. The tap on Larner's home phone was even more entertaining. It was not so much what was said, but what wasn't said, and where the calls came from. One call was from New York and the other was from England. Each just a few words about a dinner party with a wonderful collection of items on the menu. The theme for the party was to be Mayan. It was to take place, as usual, at his home in the Bahamas, on Eleuthera Island."

"When?"

"You don't have much time," replied the captain. "This Thursday, two days from now." There was a pause. "I'm not supposed to be involved in something like this—especially when we have no credible evidence of wrongdoing."

"What was all the crap I told you?" I asked.

"Your word…no evidence. And if you come to me and officially tell your story, you could become liable for a number of misdemeanors and felonies in Guatemala."

There was another pause, then the captain spoke again. "I can tell you this. Larner has a place on Eleuthera Island, at Tarpum Bay, located at the southern end of that bone-shaped pile of sand, right on the water. I got this through a little question-and-answer with the police chief there. I'd worked with him before, on a couple of drug busts, and I think he's one of the good guys, but it's hard to tell over there. He may even be able to help you. The name's Cotter—James Cotter. I didn't give him shit. Just told him the Florida Census Bureau was verifying addresses of Americans who owned homes in the Bahamas."

Captain O'Neal sighed, signaling the end of our little conversation.

"All I can do is wish you luck on this one. I know this could get messy for you, but if my people are involved, you're gonna end up having to answer a lot of questions that will probably take you back to Guatemala." He shook his head. "All I can say is, good luck, you're on your own." The captain paused for a moment. "You guys are really something else. I don't know whether to be angry with you, or envious."

"Thanks, my friend," I said. "I'll send you a copy of the book."

Ten minutes later, I was headed over to Will's converted shrimper on Stock Island. We had called the others and they were meeting us there. Santino was doing well. He wasn't up to heavy lifting, but he wasn't going to be left behind on this gig. Blingo was still at my place, up on Big Pine. There was really no need to involve him in this. Besides, Blingo's philosophy was summed up in just a few words: "I got no monkey in dis fight. I already save you once. Jus' because you drink da crazy Kool-Aid don' mean I gotta."

Once we were all together in the shrimper's cabin, I explained what we'd learned.

"We've got to move really quick," said Talia. "Once he's dumped this stuff, it'll be gone forever."

There was no argument.

"We're going to have to get in and out of Eleuthera under the radar," I said. "Apparently Larner's home is on the water. The best way would be my Cessna 182 floatplane. It's got a beefed-up engine, an extended baggage compartment in the aft, and the long-range fuel package. If we refuel in Nassau on the way into Eleuthera, we can make it back without stopping anywhere." I paused. "But it still doesn't have the useful load to bring back much more than a few hundred pounds, when you include us and some gear."

"Screw the gear," said Will. "We take the bare essentials—candy bars and guns."

"Fortunately, with the exception of Santino, none of us are really heavy people," I added. "That'll help some."

"Okay," Talia said, looking around. "So we do it."

As a brilliant, late-afternoon sun warmed the sparking Keys waters, we taxied out into Pine Channel. I found my wind direction, ran through my takeoff procedure, and dropped 20 degrees of flaps. I took a quick glance at Will, in the co-pilot's seat, and waved to the others behind me. There was excitement in their eyes, but I could also see the fear.

Will changed it all in a second. "You can't do the same dumbass, boring shit for 70 years and call it a life," he muttered. "You gotta take a chance. You gotta challenge the gods occasionally." Then he faced me, and cried, "Onwards and upwards, Tonto! And if you have to, bury me butt-up, so the world can kiss my ass!"

Everyone was still laughing as we lifted off.

Captain O'Neal did us one final favor and provided an exact location of the professor's home. It was tucked into a cove on the southwestern end of the island, which provided us with easy access and exit. There were resorts in the immediate area, so floatplanes bringing in tourists weren't uncommon.

Eleuthera's proximity to Nassau made it a popular place for tourists and American expats. The long, bone-shaped island, like the majority of the Bahamas, was mostly populated by the descendants of plantation slaves. In the 1800s the English and American cotton growers had worked the uncooperative soil until it gave out, or until the Emancipation Proclamation, whichever came first, then packed up and left, leaving the slaves to fend for themselves. Most stayed, and many eventually interbred with the few whites that lived there. Out of that grew a nation of cocoa-colored people with a fair knowledge of growing things and living off the sea, and the Bahamas were born. Later, the tourist industry began to flourish, and the Bahamians discovered a much easier fish to catch.

In addition, by the early 1970s the Bahamas had become a smuggler's paradise. With its proximity to the U.S., the hundreds of discreet coves, and dozens of small landing strips everywhere, it was a runner's dream. That proved to be good and bad, depending on which side you were on, and whether or not you got caught. Business is business. People are people. Some things never change.

For the next three hours, we crossed the Florida Straits, passing over the northern end of Andros Island and slipping over the incredible blue waters of the Great Bahama Bank, before seeing the coast of New Providence and Nassau. I slipped into Nassau and refueled, then we headed due east for the last 50 miles. By this time, the edge of the sun was slipping over the horizon and darkness was drifting in, turning the brilliant blue waters to slate gray.

Onward and upward, as my friend said.

By the time we reached Eleuthera, the sun was buried in the horizon and the first of the evening stars were peeking through the darkening heavens. We set down a half mile from Larner's little castle and tossed out an anchor. Thinking ahead, Will had packed a small, inflatable raft and a couple of telescoping paddles. I stepped out on a float, set the tightly compressed rubber bundle in the water while holding its bow rope, pulled the CO_2 inflating cord, and presto! Instant transportation. It wasn't big enough to be comfortable, but it would get us to shore.

Larner's one-story island home wasn't hard to find. He had built a horseshoe marina in front of the house large enough for a small motel facility. Captain O'Neal had told us what to look for, and the bright half moon above aided as well. Ten minutes later, we were easing our raft through the mouth of the marina, paddling softly now, looking for sentries. There was nothing but shadows cast by the rising moon.

There were lights on in the house. Will tied off the raft at a piling and we all crawled out onto the wooden walkway that surrounded the small marina. Slowly, quietly, we began moving toward the house. As we reached the lawn, tropical foliage—coconut palms, royal poincianas, lignum vitaes, bananas, and the ever-present hibiscus—surrounded us and cast shadows across the grounds. It was beautiful and spooky at the same time.

We made it to the back doors without incident. Only a dim porch light cast a hazy glow. There was only one ceiling light lit inside, and there was no one to be seen. I glanced at my friends. Will had his pistol out, as did I. Santino and Talia were behind us. Benji, with his pistol, was bringing up the rear, his blue eyes wary, always moving.

I opened a door and we moved in, entering a covered porch that led into the kitchen. Still no one in sight.

"Could be they're out, robbing someone else," whispered Will.

I waved him to silence and we moved from the kitchen into a huge living room full of expensive rattan furniture, vases of flowers, and exotic ceiling fans turned lazily, their dimmed lights offering us some vantage. But there were still no people. I looked at my friends.

"Okay, they're not here. Let's take advantage of that."

We began to check bureaus and closets and bedrooms. All offered easy access except for one large door in the very rear of the house, which was padlocked.

"I want to know what's in there," said Talia.

Without even replying, Santino walked back to the outside porch and returned with a crowbar. "Saw this by the garage as we came in," he said as he forced the curved, forked end of the crowbar between the lock hinges and the door, and snapped it downward forcefully. It didn't take the lock from the hinges, but it took the hinges from the frame, and the door fell open. He reached around on the inside, found the light switch, and flipped it on.

We all involuntarily gasped. There was King Nachán Can's treasure, stacked neatly and apparently categorized—bamboo baskets filled with golden trinkets, smaller mahogany boxes flowing over with precious stones, large golden calendars, and those incredible golden statues of all the Mayan gods. Certain pieces, especially the two-foot golden replicas of the gods, had name tags attached to them. They were obviously promised.

"Son of a bitch," whispered Will, as we all stepped into the room, unable to resist the lure of touching it one more time.

Talia and Santino ran their hands over the golden gods, a distant smoke in their eyes again. Benji couldn't resist running his fingers through the emeralds. I saw Will rummaging through one of the baskets that contained jewelry and necklaces. He pulled out a particularly remarkable piece—a handcrafted golden chain with half-inch links attached to a three-inch-wide, quarter-inch-thick, solid-gold medallion that replicated the Mayan calendar. It was an absolutely striking piece of work, probably worn by Nachán Can himself. He smiled at me, then slipped the chain over his head for just a second. I was certain at that time, that piece belonged to him.

I found myself staring at a larger version of the calendar inlaid with jade and emeralds, which was leaning casually against the wall.

Suddenly, a heavy voice startled us from our reverie.

"You people are damned tenacious."

There, in the doorway, stood Professor Larner, a semi-automatic pistol in his hand. Just behind him and to his right stood his female partner, her pistol pointed our way. "All right," he huffed angrily, "put it all down and get the hell out here."

A moment later, we were all in the living room—Larner, in a casual dinner jacket and dark slacks, and his long-legged, tube-skirted partner, Serina, standing before us, brandishing their weapons.

"I'll give you credit, you're harder to kill than Haitian cockroaches," growled Larner. "But this time we'll make sure." He turned to Serina. "We'll take 'em out and shoot 'em with silencers. We'll go out to the reef later tonight."

I watched them closely, looking for an opening. I had nothing to lose. I glanced at Will and saw the same fatal determination in his eyes. I nodded, but just as I prepared to do my hari-kari charge, I saw Serina's gray eyes change. They suddenly lost their conviction. She sighed, turning to Larner.

"No, I'm not shooting anyone else for you," she said

quietly. Then she brought her weapon up and shot him in the chest.

Larner's eyes went wide and he stumbled back against the wall. The gun slipped from his hand and he slowly slid down to a sitting position, blood blossoming on the front of his white, Brooks Brothers shirt, confusion now taking the place of surprise.

Ignoring us, Serina walked over to Larner and knelt in front of him. "You've gotten way too comfortable with killing people," she said. "And I'll tell you something else. I liked that flat-faced Slav with the 12-word vocabulary. The one you killed for no other reason than to satisfy your greed." She paused. "I liked him a lot."

Then she shot Larner again, in the center of the forehead. That part was messy.

My friends and I stood there, somewhere between terror and awe, not knowing what to expect, breaths coming in small gasps.

Serina turned to us. "Here's what's going to happen. I'm going to let you walk out of here with what you can carry, but only one box of the emeralds," she said, nodding at the treasure in the bedroom. "That's the best deal you're gonna get."

"That's a good deal," said Will anxiously, hands up, palms out. "That's a real good deal."

Ignoring my partner, Salina continued. "I'm going to clean that up." She nodded at Larner's remains. "Then I'm gonna sit right here and wait for the customers to show up tomorrow evening. I've done this before with the good professor. I know the drill. The following day, after the auction, I'll be gone, and this place is going to suffer a gas leak."

Will shook his head incredulously and whispered, "The moral to this story is never piss off a woman with a gun."

A glimmer of a smile touched Serina's lips. "You got

that right," she whispered.

CHAPTER FIFTEEN

I'm not just a hunter of gleaming, ancient things. I'm a student of history, a seeker of experiences, and a teller of yarns. Half the "treasure" I find has no shine to it at all.

—William Snell

It took two trips to get our loot from the house to the airplane. Will chose one of the bamboo boxes of golden jewelry. Santino couldn't resist the two-foot, solid-gold goddess of love, Lady Xochiquetzal. Talia had chosen a solid-gold plate of the Mayan calendar, almost three feet wide. Benji took Nachán Can's gold-inlaid *macana* (battle sword) and his golden war helmet, and I took a box of emeralds, which I promised to share with my friends. It looked like things were working out. Maybe not quite the way we had planned, but we weren't dead and buried on the reef either.

On the first trip back to the plane, I took Santino and Talia, who had chosen heavy objects that challenged our useful load limitations. (I was extremely thankful for the calm evening, or much of this might well have been impossible.) At my request, Santino found the toolbox and started taking out the middle seats. It would make for an uncomfortable ride home, but like I told him, "You can have seats or you can have gold." I left them at the Cessna and went back for Benji, Will, and our mutual treasures.

As soon as we reached the house, we loaded our rewards into the raft, then helped Serina get Larner's body into the open sport fisherman at the dock. She would complete his "disappearance" later that evening.

Overall, it was a pretty acceptable deal. We had some ancient loot, and we were still alive. We still had a second, even more amazing cache under the floor of the Guatemalan jungle cave. And, we were all obviously anxious to get away from the woman who shot people she didn't like.

In less than an hour, we were back at the plane, which was bobbing serenely on the moonlit water. Santino had removed the seats and dumped them, Will tied off the raft to a float strut on the plane, Benji crawled in, and we loaded the last couple of items.

Will and I were about to slip aboard and release the life raft, when out of the darkness roared a large police boat. At a glance, it looked like about a 23-foot Mako with big, twin Mercury outboards. It laid a hull in the water with a dramatic stop as it pulled up next to us under our port wing, solidly rocking our plane. There were no sirens or flashing lights, as there would have been if they were expecting to find illegal drug activity, and I noticed there was only one officer in the boat. The fellow expertly tossed a two-pronged gaff hook over our port wing strut and tied the line off on his port rail cleat. The large, fairly heavy Bahamian officer stared at us for a moment with calculating, dark eyes, then smiled.

"You know, I was just betting dat dey might be some ginned-up soul wandering 'round on deese waters tonight, so I decide I take a little look, and here's what I find." He paused, and the smile faded. "You know, I get a call from da DEA yesterday. Da man was askin' about big conchey-joe who live on Tarpum Bay." He pointed toward the lights of Tarpum Bay in the distance. "So I do some checkin'. Dat conchey-joe been busy lately—lots of comin's and goin's at night." He tilted his head a little and scratched his chin, the moon lighting his dark face. "So I say to myself, maybe I just sit out here for a night and see what I see." He glanced around at the gold and jewels on the aircraft's floor and smiled again. Suddenly, before any of us could react, he pulled his pistol from the holster at his hip. "Now, I don' have time for chit chat, so dis is what you gonna do. You gonna put all dem goodies in my boat an' den I'm gonna go-way. You be good conchey-joes and maybe you get to go-way too."

Will, standing next to me in the rubber raft, got instantly indignant. "Screw you and the horse you rode in on," he snarled. "We earned this the hard way, and you're not—"

The big Bahamian just pointed his gun at my friend and shot him in the chest. Will was thrown backwards from the impact of the round, his eyes wide with surprise. He clutched his chest with one hand, stumbled over the rubber gunnel of the raft, and collapsed into the water. I was instantly at the gunnel reaching out for him, but as I grabbed his shirt, he gasped, "It's okay, man. Just let me go…"

"You're not going anywhere," I cried. "Just hang on!"

He stared at me with a strange light in his eyes and wheezed, "It's not as bad as it looks…" Then he slipped away from me and disappeared under the surface of the dark water.

I was already climbing over the gunnel on the raft, headed in after him, when a second shot rang out, and the officer shouted, "Stop now! Or I shoot da woman!"

I don't remember being so torn in my life. My friend had just been shot point-blank in the chest and swallowed by the ocean. But if I moved to save him—if saving him was even possible at this point—our nemesis would kill Talia. It was the hardest decision of my life. I looked at the bubbles breaking the surface where my friend had disappeared, and slowly fell back into the raft, trembling with anger, tears running down my cheeks.

"Sorry, mon," said Officer Cotter. "But I work too damn hard for too damn long and have nothin' but a pauper's pension to show for it." He eased out a breath.

"Sometimes you jus' gotta make hard choices, you know, mon?"

I didn't ever remember *wanting* to kill someone before. But I *wanted* to kill that man at that moment. God, I wanted to.

We were all stunned by what had just happened, and Cotter took advantage of it. He moved to his starboard gunnel and pulled the boat nearly up against the plane, the rubber raft acting as a buffer. "Get them damned things over to me, now!" he shouted, standing against the rail, still brandishing his weapon. "You gin this up, I shoot somebody else!"

We glanced at each other, realizing the futility of resisting. None of it mattered anymore with the loss of Will. Santino had pulled Talia behind him when the action had begun. Now he simply reached down and picked up the mahogany box of priceless jewelry. Still standing in the life raft, I pushed on the wing strut and moved it aside, so the Mako could be pulled in a little closer. Santino started to hand the box to Cotter, across the two feet of water between the plane and the boat's rail. Suddenly, I caught sight of Benji in the cabin, tensing for a leap. But just as the officer tucked his pistol in his belt and stretched his heavy frame over the gunnel, reaching for the box, the water beneath him erupted. Will came surging up like an alligator in a bad "B" movie. My buddy grabbed one of Cotter's outstretched hands and dragged him overboard, into the dark water.

I couldn't believe what I was seeing. It was surreal! I had watched my friend take a 9mm round to the chest. I had seen his eyes as he disappeared into the darkness of the sea. As Will dragged the struggling man under the surface, I found myself grabbing a breath and jumping in behind them. It was murky-dark, and I was working mostly by feel, but I found Cotter's wiry hair, grabbed a handful, and pushed him down deeper. Officer Cotter was a big man, and his girth and inability to swim immediately became an issue. Will and I held him down until he went limp, then we dragged him to the surface, and pulled him around to the stern of his boat, making sure he was still breathing. As much as I wanted to, it wasn't a good idea to kill a policeman in any country.

Will pulled himself aboard the Mako, moved to the bow, and grabbed the anchor rope. He released the asymmetric spring clasp Cotter had used to hold the line to the anchor, and scrambled back to me with the line, then slipped back into the water. Even though we were in a life-and-death situation, and time was an issue, I couldn't resist. I needed to know.

"How?" I asked, as we held on to the stern, supporting the unconscious policeman between us while the boat rolled in the light sea. "How in God's name did you survive being shot point-blank in the chest?"

Will grinned slightly and grimaced from the pain as he pulled up his T-shirt. There, hanging around his neck, was the incredible golden chain and the three-inch-wide Mayan medallion that had caught his eye at Larner's home—with a bullet buried in its center. "It hurts like hell," he said. "But it's better than being dead."

I couldn't help but stare with incredulousness. "Floody...bucking...amazing..." I whispered. "Absolutely unbelievable!"

"Sometimes the gods, they throw you a bone," he said. "Now, let's get this bastard tied up and get out of here!"

In moments, we had the anchor line wrapped around Cotter and knotted off. He was hanging off the stern, tied to the outboard motor's lower unit. It wasn't a great job, but he was too big to drag into the boat, and we needed to be gone.

Not five minutes later, two things were taking place.

We were floating away from the police boat while I was doing a quick run-up on the plane, and Officer Cotter, who had regained consciousness, was already working on his bindings.

Before we could actually get underway, Cotter had managed to cut his ropes with a pocketknife and drag himself over the stern. Will, who was witnessing this, muttered bitterly, "We should have held him under the water another minute."

But at this point, it was academic. I had the prop turning and was bringing the Cessna around into the wind. Cotter had started his engine, and was pulling a rifle from the box seat in front of the console.

Before I could swing into the wind, Cotter was firing at us. A back window on the Cessna shattered and Talia screamed. She wasn't hit, but a piece of glass had sliced her cheek. Will was reaching down under his seat, where I kept a 9mm taped. Three rounds smacked our starboard float. That could be bad news if the bullets hit at the waterline. It wouldn't take long, and water would be pouring into the compartment, or compartments in the float, and that could create enough drag to prevent takeoff.

I slammed the throttle to the wall while dropping 20 degrees of flaps, and we surged forward. I was trying to get her up on step (that part of the float that allows less drag and permits takeoff), and we were picking up speed, but Cotter and his Mako were racing up behind us, the policeman still firing that semi-automatic carbine over the top of his console windshield. I felt the plane take two or three rounds in the tail section, and suddenly I couldn't get the elevators to work. The control yoke would only pull back halfway. One of those rounds had damaged or jammed a cable or a hydraulic rod. It didn't matter which. Now we were really screwed. No elevators, no lift. No lift, no flight. In desperation, I held the throttle to the wall while

I pushed and pulled on the yoke, trying to get the tail feathers to work. In the meantime, the Mako was gaining. It had literally become a race, and I wasn't sure at all that we could outrun him, especially with a breached float that appeared to be taking on water. Thank God it was a flat, calm night.

Cotter wasn't sure why the damned plane hadn't lifted off, but he was so focused he didn't care. It was to his benefit, regardless.

With everything that was taking place, neither Cotter nor us had noticed that we had entered the Exuma Sound shipping lanes. Just to the south of us, a freighter from the Dominican Republic was headed for Nassau, using Exuma Sound as a shortcut. The captain had been at the wheel for the better part of 10 hours. The sliver of a moon had slid behind a large battery of cumulus clouds moving in from the west, and the dark, seemingly endless sea had seduced his senses. He'd had a tough day. His second-in-command had fallen down a stairway and broken his arm, and the damned radar was on the blink. They would try to get it repaired in Nassau. He checked his compass, then slipped out of his seat to get a cup of coffee in the officer's galley, below the wheelhouse.

We weren't gaining or losing much on Cotter and his police boat, but the fat in this fire was the starboard float. The rounds Cotter had fired had apparently passed entirely through the thin aluminum skin just below the waterline. The float was taking on water and we were beginning to feel the drag on that side.

Behind me, Santino forced open his door just enough to get a look at the float. He shook his head. "I think we got problems," he yelled. "I think there's more of that float under water than should be."

In the meantime, I had been sliding the control column

in and out, in a desperate effort to work the jam out of the tail feathers, but there was still no lift to be had, and Cotter was gaining.

In desperation, I threw the plane up onto the good float, using a combination of ailerons and rudder, keeping us headed offshore, in hopes that maybe the water in the wounded float would drain out and we could gain some speed, while still trying to break the jam in my elevators. It was truly some "rodeo flying," this "one float in the air and one in the water" thing, and I remember thinking it would make a great barroom story if I lived to tell it.

The huge Dominican freighter was closing in from the black wall of weather to the south. Its dark shape had been lost to storm clouds, Stygian waters, and the deepening night.

For a moment, the dark clouds pulled apart and a touch of moon shone through. I glanced up and suddenly, there it was—a giant behemoth on a dead, 90-degree intersection with us, not 200 yards ahead and to our left!

Will picked up on it about the same time. He knew intrinsically that it was a roll of the dice. Actually, the odds were against us getting past that huge bow, and if we stopped, the giant wave of water cut by the heavy ship would swamp us. Then there was Cotter, and he was still closing.

Another battery of rifle rounds hammered the aircraft and the front passenger's window shattered.

"Whoa shit!" yelled Will, more angry than frightened. "Son of a bitch," he muttered, as he turned to me. "You gotta get this sucker in the air, or we're gonna become a memory!"

In sheer desperation, I jammed the controls in and out viciously, and for no other reason than the gods had probably become bored, the jam in the elevators finally broke loose. I instantly slapped the high float down onto the water so we didn't flip, then instinctively pushed in the throttle, but it was already maxed out. The freighter was almost on us—so close that I had to look up to read the name on the bow. I drew back on the controls, double-checked my flaps, and almost cried out with relief as the plane lifted off the water.

I still have no idea how we managed to survive. I banked up and away to the starboard side, buying us as much time as possible before we hit the freighter's bow. To this day, Will claims he heard the bow rail on the big ship scrape the bottom of the port float. All I do know is, a moment later we were flying, climbing up into the dark heavens, everyone crying out with relief, shouting, and cheering.

Will turned to me with that crazy grin of his. "Kryptonian, man! Freaking rapturous!"

Officer James Cotter of the Bahamian Marine Patrol was equally as much of a gambler. He saw the freighter at the last moment, and he knew he should stop—that he should cut the power and cut his losses, but he had seen "that damn treasure." He just couldn't go home and sit in his little stucco house, listen to his wife complain, and watch that damned little television for the rest of his life. He slammed the throttles forward so hard, he snapped one of the plastic throttle knobs. He was gonna have those conchey-joes and their gold, or he was gonna die trying!

At the last moment, he witnessed the plane in front of him finally break free of the water and lift off in a curving ascent, just missing the freighter's bow. He screamed in anger and defiance, his hand still trying to force more from the maxed-out throttles as the freighter's bow loomed over him. But it was too late to turn back or stop. He was committed to try to beat the freighter. He was going to make it by the bow of that damned ship!

Unfortunately, that didn't work out so well for him. The huge steel bow caught his Mako squarely amidships, pretty much cleaving his fragile fiberglass craft in half. The last thing Officer James Cotter remembered was the sensation of flying, before he struck the heavy steel hull.

The captain of the freighter was in the galley when he felt a jounce from the outer hull. He paused and listened for a moment, but there was nothing more. He went back to adding cream to his coffee, listening as the big ship returned to the steady vibration he knew so well. Moments later, he was back in the wheelhouse with his cup of coffee, settling into his chair. He sighed and took a sip.

Thank God, our trip home was uneventful. My long-range tanks managed to make the distance with little more than a few gallons to spare. The following morning, we slipped onto the blue-green waters of Pine Channel just as a new sun broke over a pale-blue horizon. I quickly motored into my canal (given the holes in the one float), and up onto my boat ramp. As we wearily stumbled from the plane, I couldn't remember being more pleased to touch the earth of that sandy string of islands.

The following day *The Nassau Guardian* ran a piece on a missing marine police officer. A search was underway. But within a few days, the information on the incident dried up, and nothing was ever found. There were suspicions that the American DEA may have leaned on the newspaper to let it go.

It took us a couple of days just to recover from the trauma of it all, aside from the fact that we feared we might, at anytime, get a knock on the door from Guatemalan or Bahamian authorities. Finally, when that didn't happen, we began to relax. Then it became a matter of converting some of our Mayan wealth into dollars. Crazy

Eddie found a very wealthy man in Miami who wasn't interested in asking many questions. Problem solved.

Eddie had also found a Grumman Goose in New Port Richey that pushed all his buttons. Will and I gave him the cash. Another problem solved. We gave Blingo a small bank account for his assistance in our little caper. He bought a motor scooter and found an apartment on Stock Island. Crazy Eddie had settled into his bar again. He had a handful of new stories to tell.

Santino finally healed from his wounds. He had also contacted a friend at the Belize Department of the Interior, and it appeared that no one had connected him with the group that had recently caused so much trouble in Guatemala. Apparently, the fact that the guard at the Belize/Guatemalan border had copied no information saved him, and everyone else. Santino had contacted his boss and requested a three-month leave of absence, but he would have to return to Belize soon to deal with personal matters—apartment, car, banking, and to see if he could locate his beautiful hawk. He felt certain Pixan would return to the hunting areas that she knew best, near his home in Melchor de Mencos. He and Talia found a home they liked on Sugarloaf Key, with a studio apartment for Benji, if he decided to stay, and were in the process of negotiating a deal. But both Benji and Talia would have to return to Israel, and explain their plans to their parents.

Will and I had kept one item apiece from the treasure. I chose a golden goblet stamped with Nachán Can's seal, its rim garnished with small emeralds. Will, without question, had opted for the heavy golden medallion with a 9mm bullet buried in its center. Rarely does one get to possess an object that represents both their mortality and fortuity. The rest of our profits went into special accounts at our bank in Key West.

The night before Talia, Benji, and Santino were to

leave, we all got together for dinner and drinks on the docks at Schooner Wharf. It was a gorgeous evening. The western sky was smeared in purples and reds, a soft breeze flavored by the sea caressed us, and the seabirds provided nature's orchestra in the background. The alcohol lifted our spirits, the conversation was entertaining, and dinner was wonderful. Afterward, we all sat back and a soft silence fell over us.

"We were remarkably lucky," said Talia quietly.

"That's an understatement," I replied. "If I had to do it again, I probably wouldn't. I got serious scars from this affair."

"Scars are beautiful things, man," said Eddie. "They're the physical statements of challenges you overcame. They remind you of the places where the fabric of your character was forged—and when you rose to the occasion."

"Damn, Eddie, that's beautiful," I said, raising my glass. "To scars," I cheered. "And the adventures that come with them!"

And we all saluted with our drinks.

Will straightened up in his chair. "And don't forget, my friends, the adventure isn't entirely over. We've got a remarkable treasure waiting for us back in that little Guatemalan cave."

"And with it comes another story to tell," said Talia.

I grinned. "When it's all said and done, the person with the most stories wins..."

"Right you are, Tonto," replied Will.

I eased out a breath, trying to resist a small smile. "How many times do I have to tell you? Me, the Lone Ranger. You..."

I hope you have enjoyed this novel. If you would like to be added to my mailing list (to stay apprised of new novels, and to receive bimonthly updates and my newspaper columns), email me at: reisig@ipa.net

—Michael Reisig

And…be sure to read the rest of
Michael Reisig's best-selling

ROAD TO KEY WEST SERIES

THE ROAD TO KEY WEST

The Road to Key West is an adventurous, humorous sojourn that cavorts its way through the 1970s Caribbean, from Key West and the Bahamas to Cuba and Central America—a Caribbean brew of part-time pirates, heartless larcenists, wild women, Voodoo bokors, drug smugglers, and a wacky Jamaican soothsayer.

Kindle Book only $2.99

To Preview or Purchase this book on amazon.com, use this link: http://www.amazon.com/dp/B004RPMYF8

BACK ON THE ROAD TO KEY WEST
The Golden Scepter—Book II

An ancient map and a lost pirate treasure, a larcenous Bahamian scoundrel with his gang of cutthroats, a wild and crazy journey into South America in search of a magical antediluvian device, and perilous, hilarious encounters with outlandish villains and zany friends will keep you locked to your seat and giggling maniacally.

Kindle Book only $2.99

To Preview or Purchase this book on amazon.com, use this link: http://www.amazon.com/dp/B00FC9D94I

ALONG THE ROAD TO KEY WEST
The Truthmaker—Book III

Fast-paced humor and adventure with wacky pilots, quirky con men, mad villains, bold women, and a gadget to die for. Florida Keys adventurers Kansas Stamps and Will Bell find their lives turned upside down when they discover a truth device hidden in the temple of an ancient civilization. Enthralled by the virtue (and entertainment value) of personally dispensing truth and justice with this unique tool, they take it all a step too far and discover that everyone wants what they have—from the government to the Vatican.

Kindle Book only $2.99

To Preview or Purchase this book on amazon.com, use this link: http://www.amazon.com/dp/B00G5B3HEY

SOMEWHERE ON THE ROAD TO KEY WEST
The Emerald Cave—Book IV

The captivating diary of an amateur archaeologist sends our intrepid explorers on a journey into the heart of the Panamanian jungle in search of *La cueva de Esmeralda* (the Emerald Cave), and a lost Spanish treasure. But local brigand Tu Phat Shong and his gang of cutthroats are searching for the same treasure. If that wasn't enough, one of the Caribbean's nastiest drug lords has a score to settle with our reluctant heroes. (Something to do with an ancient golden medallion they "borrowed.")

DOWN THE ROAD TO KEY WEST
Pancho Villa's Gold— Book V

If you're looking for clever fun with zany characters, a blossoming romance, and electric high adventure, this one's for you! Reisig's newest offering is guaranteed to keep you locked to your seat and slapping at the pages, while burbling up a giggle or two.

In the fifth book of this series, our reluctant Caribbean heroes find themselves competing for the affections of a beautiful antiquities dealer and searching for the lost treasure of Mexico's most renowned desperado.

Kindle Book only $2.99

To Preview or Purchase this book on amazon.com, use this link: http://www.amazon.com/dp/B01EPI6XY4

Also, be sure to read...

CARIBBEAN GOLD
THE TREASURE OF TORTUGA

In 1668, Englishman Trevor Holte and the audacious freebooter Clevin Greymore sail from the Port of London for the West Indies. They set out in search of adventure and wealth, but the challenges they encounter are beyond their wildest dreams—the brutal Spanish, ruthless buccaneers, a pirate king, the lure of Havana, and the women, as fierce in their desires as Caribbean storms.

And then, there was the gold—wealth beyond imagination. But some treasures outlive the men who bury them…

CARIBBEAN GOLD
THE TREASURE OF TIME

In the spring of 1980, three adventurers set out from Key West in search of a lost treasure on the Isle of Tortuga, off the coast of Haiti. Equipped with an ancient parchment and a handful of clues, they embark on a journey that carries them back across time, challenging their courage and their imaginations, presenting them with remarkable allies and pitting them against an amalgam of unrelenting enemies. In the process, they uncover far more than a treasure. They discover the power of friendship and faith, the unflagging capacity of spirit, and come to realize that some things are forever…

Kindle Book only $2.99

To Preview or Purchase this book on amazon.com, use this link: http://www.amazon.com/dp/B00S8SR0WW

And...

CARIBBEAN GOLD THE TREASURE OF MARGARITA

The Treasure of Margarita spans three centuries of high adventure. Beginning in 1692, in the pirate stronghold of Port Royal, it carries the reader across the Southern Hemisphere in a collage of rip-roaring escapades. Then it soars forward five generations, into modern-day intrigue and romance in Key West and the Caribbean.

A staggering fortune of Spanish black pearls and a 300-year-old letter with a handful of clues set the course that Travis Christian and William Cody embark upon. But it's not an easy sail. Seasoned with remarkable women and bizarre villains (including a Barbadian treasure-hunting gangster, a duo of persistent South Florida scoundrels, and last but not least, the Russian mob), the adventure ricochets from one precarious situation to the next.

Kindle Book only $2.99

To Preview or Purchase this book on amazon.com, use this link: http://www.amazon.com/dp/B00X1E2X2K